NIGHT TERRORS
& OTHER TALES

NIGHT TERRORS
& OTHER TALES

By

Lisa Morton

Omnium Gatherum
Los Angeles

First Edition

In memory of a man who taught a lot of us how to write short fiction: Dennis Etchison

Contents

MONSTERS

Tested

As Ben fought the wheel of the spinning Lexus, his chest pinned beneath the inflated airbag, his wife screaming from the passenger seat, everything was slowed down and magnified. He could see every tree picked out in the gliding headlights, he was deafened by the shriek of the tires on the rough asphalt, he felt a sharp snap as an axle was sheared beneath him, and one thought kept repeating in his head: *Please God don't let me be crushed please God don't let there be blood please—*

And then the car was still, and it was over.

In that first second, as the flow of time returned to its normal speed, Ben looked down at himself. The airbag had already deflated, and he was covered with a residue of white dust. His neck hurt and he couldn't seem to stop shaking, but he was whole. He started to call out, *Angie*, then turned his head (a small eruption of pain) to look at his wife.

There was blood on her neck from where a pine branch had smashed through the windshield, and her eyes weren't open.

"Angie! Angela! Honey—!"

She didn't answer. She didn't even move.

Ben tried to reach for her and got tangled in his harness. He was struggling to release it when the sound came: An agonized bellow, a moan too deep and savage for any animal he knew.

He froze until the sound finished, then looked around frantically. The car had come to rest in a ditch by the side of the road, just below the shoulder. They were at a slight angle, tilted towards the car's right side, and he could only see part of the roadway and the relentless rain forest. The sound had come from his left, behind the car. Whatever had made that noise was just a short distance behind them.

His mind raced back to the seconds before the crash: he'd been maneuvering the Lexus along the winding mountain road, driving through a patch of dense growth, the only travelers on this back country two-lane blacktop. And then something had appeared before the headlights, revealed as the road hairpinned. It had been huge—at least seven feet tall—and black, and fixed him with two startled eyes.

The car hit it. Ben had tried to swerve aside, but he'd felt the sickening crunch and the steering wheel had wrenched itself from his grip.

The impact had caused the Lexus to spin at least twice; Ben thought they'd jumped a log on the right and that had sheared one, maybe both, axles in two. The thing that had been hit had probably been thrown, badly injured. It should have been killed.

But another shriek, this one closer, assured Ben it was still very much alive, and filled with the mindless fury of a wounded beast.

Ben's first instinct was to start the car and get the hell out of there. Without thinking he tried the keys, but turning the ignition produced only a dry clicking sound. The windshield was smashed in front of Angie, but the tempered safety glass had held on the driver's side, although it had spiderwebbed across Ben's field of vision. He could see smoke pouring from the front end of the Lexus, even while the headlights were still functioning.

He thought of his cell phone next and grabbed at his jacket pocket. There it was. He withdrew it, held it up—and saw that it wasn't receiving a signal. He moved it around, saw its glowing face flicker uncertainly. If he got out of the car, walked around, maybe he could find a signal—

The thing outside screeched again.

Ben locked the doors.

What was it out there? Ben tried to picture it in his mind's eye, the flash he'd had of it in the roadway. It had been on two feet, walking upright. Oh Christ, it hadn't been a man, had it? A hiker, maybe? No, it had been covered with what looked like black fur, and had been too tall. A bear? That must have been it. He tried to recall facts about the wildlife of the Pacific Northwest. They were only two hours outside of Seattle. Were there really bears here?

Of course he'd heard the other stories, the ones about the things that were neither bear nor human—but those were ridiculous, fairy tales manufactured by crackpots and conmen. Ben's world was a well-ordered one that didn't allow for such absurdities. He was a critical thinker, a strategist. He had an MBA, for Christ's sake. He believed only in what could be proven—

A shadow crossed through the headlights.

Ben craned his neck, trying to find a spot of uncracked glass to peer through, but he saw only steam and trees. He thought he heard a scrabbling off to his left, but it was dark there and he couldn't make out anything. Whatever it was, it had come from where he'd hit it, maybe ten yards back, and had circled around to the front of the car.

He needed a weapon.

There was nothing in the car he could use. In the truck was a solid, pig-iron crowbar; outside were sturdy branches and rocks.

In here, though, was his only chance for shelter.

He tried the cell phone again—nothing—then turned to his wife.

"Angie...can you hear me? Angie!"

Still unconscious. He tried to feel for a pulse in her neck, but it was sticky with warm blood. He pulled his fingers away quickly, dove under the shattered windshield for the glove compartment and the tissues Angie always kept there. He tore the pack open with trembling fingers and wiped the blood off. He saw he'd left a smear on the glove compartment, and he started to daub at it until he realized how ridiculous it was. His wife was bleeding to death (maybe already dead), and he was worried about staining the glove compartment. He turned to her and tried to clean her neck, but the blood was still issuing from some wound and the entire pack of tissue was sopping in seconds. Nevertheless, he kept the soggy bundle pressed to her neck tightly, not even sure if that's where the wound was.

As he did, he tried to force his breathing (when did it become so rapid?) to slow, his mind to focus. He thought about where they were: on a little-used back road that wound through the Washington state rain forest to the rustic French restaurant where they'd dined. The one Angie had read a rave review of in a national food magazine, and had wanted to go to, even though it was a two-hour drive. The meal had been spectacular, although neither Ben nor Angie had been in much of a mood to appreciate it. They'd started fighting before they'd even been seated. Ben had brought up the idea of the sailing vacation again, the one that involved just the two of them renting a boat alone on the high seas for two weeks, and Angie had exploded. A vacation, she'd reasoned, was something you did to relax, not put yourself in life-or-death situations. Why couldn't they just enjoy two weeks in a Caribbean beach resort? Was he going through some mid-life crisis ten years too early, or did he just feel some inexplicable need to prove his masculinity?

The fight at the restaurant had escalated and ended badly. Ben thought Angie was too unwilling to take risks. Angie thought Ben had been playing too many power games lately, that he'd brought them home from the office after the last motivational retreat.

Now Angie might be dying by the side of this roadway at least an hour from help, and it would be partly his fault. He felt her blood and knew he loved her and couldn't imagine life without her and wished to hell he could tell her that right now.

He had to get her out of this. It had been several minutes now since he'd last heard anything outside. If he could just find a signal, or pick up a good solid club...maybe he'd get lucky (he thought he deserved to, god knows) and flag down a passing car. They couldn't be the only traffic out here.

He unlocked his door, then opened it slightly and listened. Nothing. He opened it wider. It creaked and stopped, only a few inches ajar. The frame must have been bent out of shape and he'd have to work to get out, plus he was at a disadvantageous angle. It would make noise.

But he had to risk it.

He flashed on his grandfather, the family's one authentic war hero, who'd earned two purple hearts in World War II; he'd been a big, blustering man who'd liked to recount his exploits on the islands of the Pacific, of charging into battle and eating lunch on the bodies of "dead Japs." He knew his grandfather would have already had the door open and been out of the car; in his mind he saw his grandfather thumping his chest while his grandmother sat in a corner, smiling blankly and never saying a word. His grandfather had told Ben he'd never be a "real man" until he saw combat, and just before he'd died a few years ago he'd given Ben a copy of a book about "the greatest generation," namely those like himself who'd fought in WW2. Ben had dutifully read the book, and had to admit he was envious: up until now Ben's life had been lived in classrooms and offices, without any chance at glory or raw experience. The closest he'd ever come to danger had been when his grandfather had taken him skiing at 14 and he'd broken a leg on his first quarter-mile run while the old man had laughed. Ben wanted to know what it was like to be really tested, not in a corporate boardroom, but a real life-or-death struggle. He'd desperately wanted to find that human, inner strength he thought he might possess, that sense of honor, of personal faith.

But this wasn't how it was supposed to be. This was a situation where he had no control. No gun. No map. No general. All he had was something that he didn't believe existed.

But he had to accept that it *did* exist. And his wife—

She was his honor here, now.

He took a deep breath and held it as he listened again, then dug in his feet against the car's center divider and shoved. The door creaked loudly, but gave only another few inches. Trying not to grunt, he hefted again. There was a loud (too loud!) metallic snap, and the door sprang open.

He held it in place and strained to hear. Waiting. Every muscle tensed, frozen.

Nothing.

He clambered out of the car. It was difficult, and he stumbled once, then caught his balance and looked around. He could see farther onto the roadway now, his sight no longer obscured by shattered glass.

In the red glow of the taillights, he saw the black skid marks his expensive car had left on the pavement. He saw parts of the car—a tire, a mirror—scattered across the road, but there was nothing else.

He whipped open the phone and held it up. It flashed intermittently. He moved it around, but still no luck.

He bent to a crouch and tried to creep up the slight incline to the road. Pebbles skidded out from under him, creating a tiny trickle of sound that seemed deafening. He stopped again, then cautiously stepped onto the road, looking in every direction. Nothing but asphalt and dark forest. It was overcast tonight, so he didn't even have starlight to see by.

He tore his gaze away from the surroundings—and saw the signal lock in. He had it! His cautions were all forgotten as he punched in 911 and listened to the call going through, praying for a strong connection—

The 911 operator came onto the line. He choked getting

the first word out, and then the rest came too fast, a furious string of strangled whispers. He told them he'd had an accident, that his wife was badly hurt. He'd just started to describe their location—

– and something scrabbled in the woods near the car.

He whirled, forgetting the call. He was only dimly aware of the operator urging him to respond. Another sound, closer to the car now.

Something was in the trees, moving towards the car. Towards Angie.

Any help that was coming would be too late.

He shoved the phone back in a pocket while looking around for something, anything, that could be wielded as a weapon. He saw the heavy branch that had smashed the windshield and had been torn from a tree, four feet of rough pine, now lying on the dirt shoulder. He ran to it and picked it up, wincing as the bark grated on the tender skin of his palms (*"Oh, poor little hothouse flower!"* he heard his grandfather snarl out), but its weight gave him a small measure of reassurance. He could defend with this. Or kill.

He walked closer to the line of evergreens, eyes wide to penetrate the dark curtain—

The thing, whatever it was, shrieked, louder than before, in pain and fury. In challenge.

Ben suddenly felt cold. He wondered if his antagonist (for such was how he thought of the thing, now) could smell his fear.

A tree three feet beyond the car's passenger door—beyond Angie—shuddered.

Ben instinctively hefted the branch and stepped forward, adrenaline flooding him at the thought of *it* near his wife. He took one step, another, forward. Suddenly he was in front of her door, protecting, ready to swing—

—and he saw it.

Or at least part of it. Red eyes, a yard above his own. There was a smell, too, a rich, tangy odor redolent of animal musk, and Ben knew the scent of fear wasn't his. And the eyes—whether from blood, the reflection of the car's light, or their own internal fire, he couldn't tell. They were wide, moist. Looking at him.

Ben raised the branch and screamed, a primal sound ripped from somewhere deep within him. The thing in the woods blinked in fright and staggered back, then vanished. Ben kept screaming, screaming a war cry that finally left him hoarse and out of breath and exhausted.

When he stopped, he saw that *it* was gone.

He dropped to the ground, as if the line holding him in place had been cut. It was over. His enemy...the thing... had fled back into the forest, injured, to licks its wounds. Somehow he knew it wouldn't come back.

He'd been tested and had passed.

After a blank moment he used the branch to lever himself off the ground—his legs had suddenly gone weak—and staggered back to the car. He headed around to the driver's side, dropped the branch and was lowering himself into the padded seat when he heard a moan.

From his wife.

"Angie—!" He threw himself into the car and reached for her; her eyes were blinking, she called his name.

"Ben...what...?"

"It's okay, honey, don't talk. They're coming—help's on the way—"

Then he was holding her and tears were streaming down his face, mixing with the cold sweat he'd worn moments ago, and he wanted to tell her, tell her what he'd done for her, and he started to...

...and stopped.

Because he'd heard his own words and suddenly knew with horrifying clarity that no one would believe him. What he'd seen—what he'd fought—wasn't human or animal. It was something that shouldn't exist, that both science and common sense said could not exist... but Ben knew now that it did. He might be the only one who had seen it, faced it, and lived. Even Angie hadn't. When they asked, he'd tell them it had been a bear.

But he'd know, and he'd live the rest of his life with that knowing, that the world was not what he'd always believed, that there was no honor in combat and nightmares were real. Monsters lived, and they smelled like fear. He'd met the enemy, and the enemy wasn't us. And if his grandfather had been here, the old man would have convinced himself of the lie, would have told himself that it had only been a bear, that he'd faced it down and won, thinking already of the valorous tales he'd tell while his grandmother had bled her life out in the car. He would never have fought the real battle, and suddenly Ben saw that the bravado and machismo was just self-deceit and stupidity, and he knew that he hated his grandfather, hated him as much as he loved his wife, and he knew at last that he was better than the old man, because what had happened tonight was something he would spend the rest of his life remembering and fearing and trying to understand.

By the time the ambulance and police car arrived fifteen minutes later, Ben was dazed and weak. An EMT told him he was in shock, but he knew the truth:

That here, tonight, by the side of this road in the woods near Seattle, he'd been tested at last, and could only hope that the best parts of him had survived.

Poppi's Monster

Poppi had hurt her bad this time, worse than usual. She'd known it would be bad as soon as he'd walked in the door. It was after ten p.m., he was late and her babysitter Heather from down the street had left at seven.

She was sprawled in front of the blaring TV, working on an old cartoon movie coloring book she'd bought last year with lunch money she had secretly saved. She hadn't seen the movie, of course, but she liked to look at the bright printed scenes on the cover and the line drawings inside and pretend that she had. With her box of 64 crayons, she could make the movie within the drawings look the way it did in her imagination. She liked the pictures in her head because they were all hers. Poppi couldn't touch them.

When he'd come in, he was muttering under his breath. He immediately crossed to the television set and lowered the volume to an inaudible level.

"Christ almighty, Stacey, you always have to blast the goddamn TV? Last thing I need is some complaint from the neighbors."

As he turned, his foot kicked the box of crayons, and they flew in a multihued arc across the room. "Aw, what is this...?"

Poppi picked up the coloring book, glanced at it once, and then shook it in her face. "Stacey, how many times do I have to tell you, you're too old for this nonsense. You're ten years old, too old to play with this little-kid bullshit."

Stacey heard her crayons crack under his shoes. Vermilion, Burnt Sienna, Cornflower Blue, three broken colors she'd never use again.

She knew Poppi was right, though: ten-year-olds weren't supposed to play with coloring books, or Fisher-Price Farm Sets, or stuffed animals. The other kids in her class at school streamed favorite bands. They could win video games and dress like stars. Not Stacey. She knew they thought she was weird or stupid; one teacher had used the word "remedial." That had been when Poppi had taped a funnel into her mouth and force fed her a bad-tasting vitamin mash he said would make her smarter.

Tonight, though, she knew it wouldn't be that. He was already halfway out of his clothes, the heavy genuine-leather belt tugging loose from the loops in his expensive slacks. She didn't understand what he was saying, something about a boy in the office today who had screamed and bitten him. He showed her a tiny red mark on one finger. Stacey didn't understand; the marks he left on her once or twice a month were a lot worse than that.

He told her to go into her room and lay on her stomach on her bed. She didn't fight or try to escape; she knew that would just make it worse. She went into her room and grabbed Baloo her stuffed bear. If she held onto Baloo very tightly, it helped a little bit. Not much, but a little bit.

Poppi had his belt off and held in both hands when he lumbered in. He reached up under her little skirt, flipped it up and tugged her tights and panties down. She didn't realize she was biting Baloo's ear. The leather whistled, and she tried not to cry out or jerk; sometimes that just made it worse. All she could do was let the tears squirt out silently and hope Poppi was tired tonight.

❂ ❂ ❂

When it was over, he took her by the wrist and put her in the closet. She heard the latch he'd installed click into place, then he left the room and she was alone at last.

What Poppi didn't know was that she liked being in the closet. Her friends were there, Babar the Elephant and Pluto in his fuzzy orange fur. The tablet computer her Auntie Gina had given her last year was there. She even kept pillows and an old blanket in there; when she pushed her shoes aside, it was really pretty comfortable. Or would have been if it hadn't hurt so much to just lay.

She snuggled her animals close to her and turned on the tablet. She went to a video site and chose whatever was at the top of the screen; she didn't really care what it was. The tinny voices and moving pictures lulled her, made her feel a little less lonely.

After a while she dozed off. When she awoke, she was hot all over, her bottom an excruciating fire. She tried to find a comfortable position and ended up on her side with her face only inches from the screen. There was a man on it, he was talking in front of some curtains, he had on a funny suit and a funnier accent. Then the man finished talking and words came on, but Stacey wasn't a very good reader. She didn't care what they said anyway. There were eyes spinning behind the words...

Stacey was sick, she knew what a fever was and that she had one. She remembered when Mommi had been alive, the way she'd lay a hand on Stacey's forehead when she was sick, and could tell just by that how sick Stacey was. She remembered one time when she'd had a very bad flu with a very high fever, Mommi had gone into the bathtub with her and held her in the cool water, rocking her until the temperature had gone down...

Stacey awoke from the dream of her mother and found herself face to face with the dream on the TV There was a man who looked like her Poppi, a man with dark hair and sunken eyes and thin lips. The man and his friend, who was bent all crooked and walked with a little cane, were cutting somebody down from a wooden bar. The man who looked like Poppi said the body was broken and useless.

Stacey couldn't really sleep, but her eyes would close until the pain forced them open again. The next time she saw the man, he was wearing the same kind of white coat

Poppi wore at his work. He was showing the man with the funny accent how he had sewn a hand onto an arm it wasn't born onto. Somehow Stacey understood that the man who looked like Poppi had built this other man—monster, they called it—from all kinds of different parts. The monster was scary-looking, but it was afraid of being burned, of being whipped, of being chained up, of getting a shot. Stacey understood all those things.

She even understood when a little girl—who wasn't much younger than she—used flowers to ask the monster to throw her into a lake.

Stacey did fall asleep after that, relieved to know she wasn't alone.

◐ ◐ ◐

Poppi let her out in the morning, of course. She went to school dressed as always in heavy sweaters, skirt and tights, although it was nearly 80 degrees. She thought of the lovely blue swimming pool in their next-door neighbor's backyard and knew she'd never be able to use it. If Stacey's mode of dress was ever questioned, there was a standard response: her father was a pediatrician and said she suffered from a neurological disorder.

That covered a lot of the questions. Why Stacey often fell asleep in class, why she sometimes seemed to ache too much to participate in recess, why she had trouble concentrating or relating or remembering. There was also, of course, the story of how Stacey's mother had died of cancer six years ago, and her father had raised her alone since.

In fact, many felt sorry for Stacey's father, that a young pediatrician with such obvious concern for children should be left alone to care for such a dull-witted and sickly girl.

◐ ◐ ◐

That night Poppi got home early enough to send the sitter off and fix dinner for them. He made Stacey a ghastly-smelling soup and told her to eat it while it was hot.

She could see the steam curling off it, but she picked up a spoon and ladled some of the stuff in. It burned her tongue and the roof of her mouth, but Poppi insisted it was good for her. He made her eat it all while it was still steaming.

After that she did the dishes, then went to her room, where she laid on the bed snuggling Baloo. Her mind drifted through images from the movie that had played last night on her TV She floated with them, forgetting the burning in her mouth for a while.

Poppi is dressed in his white coat, but his office is bigger, darker, made of rocks. There's lots of equipment she doesn't understand lining the walls, some of it spitting sparks like 4th of July fireworks. Poppi is hunched over a worktable, his back to her, his hands moving rhythmically. The viewpoint moves around him until Stacey can see plainly what he's doing.

There's a figure on the table before him, a human figure but one that's unfinished, lacking. It has arms but no hands, legs but no feet, head but no face. Stacey sees a needle and thread in Poppi's fingers and realizes he's sewing, like Mommi used to when Stacey tore buttons off or ripped holes in her pants.

Stacey gets close enough to see what he's sewing. He's working on the mouth, which gapes like a blank black hole. There's a lump of dead gray flesh in his left hand, one end dark with stitches, while his right moves up and down, up and down.

He's sewing a tongue in.

The monster is begun.

◑ ◑ ◑

The next day Stacey's own tongue is badly blistered. Poppi has treated the welts on her backside and they feel better, but the tongue causes her to be even more closemouthed than usual. Finally Miss Washington, of all people, who works in the cafeteria, sees the tongue and asks her what happened.

Stacey doesn't want to answer, but the image of Poppi with needle and thread rears up before her vision. Unable to stop, she blurts it out.

"Poppi made me eat something hot."

Miss Washington, who has never spoken to Stacey before, knows only her face, not her name, asks who Poppi is.

"My daddy," Stacey says thickly.

Miss Washington, who runs the cash register, hesitates a long while. Then she says softly to Stacey, "Next time you say no, you hear?"

Stacey hurriedly gives Miss Washington her money and flees. She can't even taste the lunch, can only feel.

☢ ☢ ☢

A week later, Poppi comes home with a bitter smell of beer clinging to him. Stacey is writing a letter to an imaginary penpal, carefully penning the words and laboring over the spelling; the letter is about Poppi. Poppi finds it, reads the first sentence, and tells Stacey if she likes those words so much she can eat them. Poppi tears the page into strips and forces them into Stacey's mouth, holding it closed until she has no choice but to swallow. She is made to consume the entire page that way, then sent to bed with no other dinner.

☢ ☢ ☢

That night Stacey sees Poppi at work again. His creation is more fully formed; there are the beginnings of features on the face now. Poppi has cut it up the middle, and he's lowering in something that looks like a shimmery blue gray balloon full of jelly, with tubes dangling from either end. As she watches, he connects the tubes to those already within the monster, and then begins to sew it shut.

The thing has guts now.

❂ ❂ ❂

Stacey is in the middle of fourth period the next day when she vomits. She's sent home immediately; the other students are dismissed on an extra recess while the janitor cleans the mess up. He's dipping his mop back in the bucket when something catches his eye, and he leans over. There in the bile is a half-chewed scrap of paper with the crayoned words "then Poppi made" plainly visible.

He considers informing the teacher, then shrugs and goes about his work.

❂ ❂ ❂

Nearly a month passes without major incident. Stacey is beginning to think Poppi may have given up his monster when he comes home early actually crying. It would have been Mommi's birthday today, and Poppi stares at a framed picture of her while he drinks from a bottle of sour liquor. He's talking but to no one at all, about how he could have saved Mommi from the cancer if he'd been a real doctor instead of a pediatrician. When he sees Stacey looking at him he lunges at her; she unthinkingly puts out her hands to ward him off. Poppi takes her small hands in his and rubs them roughly along his unshaven jaw while he sobs. Finally he releases Stacey, lost in his grief. She flees to her room. Although there's no physical pain this time, the remembrance of Poppi's skin under her fingertips is as bad in its own way.

❂ ❂ ❂

She watches as Poppi attaches the hands. She sees he's been hard at work; the figure looks almost human now, beneath the bandages. She knows it'll be over soon.

The monster is almost done.

❂ ❂ ❂

They're working on an art project at school the following afternoon when Stacey's teacher, Mr. Torres, notices that Stacey is not applying her brush to paper but to her own arms. He takes Stacey into the back to talk to her about the strange red marks she has meticulously painted on each wrist. Stacey tells him that's how Poppi makes sure the hands will stay on. Mr. Torres looks around to make sure the other students are occupied before taking Stacey outside where he sits with her on the steps.

"Stacey," he asks carefully, "does Poppi ever do things to hurt you?"

Stacey, who has never been asked this question before and so doesn't know how to answer, just shrugs.

"Would it be all right if we let the school nurse look you over, Stacey?"

Again, Stacey shrugs. Mr. Torres gives her a hall pass and sends her to the nurse, but Stacey never makes it. She gets halfway there, and then is seized by an inexplicable panic. Her heart groans in her throat; she feels like she's going to wet her panties. She runs for home as fast as she can and buries herself in her closet, clutching Baloo and Babar and Pluto to her tightly.

❍ ❍ ❍

Stacey's own birthday is two weeks later. Poppi buys her a new "11th-birthday celebration" dress and takes her out to a fancy restaurant, where Poppi has so much to drink even the waiter in his little short jacket and bowtie questions him. Poppi brushes the polite enquiry off with a wave of his credit card; when he giggles as the man walks off, Stacey actually joins him. Poppi even gives her a little drink of his wine—"now that she's getting to be such a big girl"—and Stacey feels a surge of affection for Poppi, forgetting the monster for the moment.

On the ride home, Poppi stops by a liquor store and tells Stacey she can have anything she wants from the ice-cream case. She takes a pineapple Push-Up, Poppi gets himself a bottle, and they laugh all the way home about the messy yellow sherbet oozing out of the paper tube.

In the house, Poppi takes a long gulp from his bottle, then sees how Stacey has stained her chin and part of the new dress with sherbet. She expects him to become angry, she tenses in anticipation...instead he smiles sweetly and takes her into the kitchen. He wets a paper towel, gently wipes off her chin and then starts on the dress. The dress is beautiful crushed velvet, though, and he tells Stacey he doesn't want to ruin it, so she'd better take it off. He helps her, right there in the kitchen; she crosses her arms to cover her cold chest.

Poppi asks her what she's trying to hide—hasn't he seen her before? She wants to giggle, wants to think this is another birthday game, but the look in Poppi's eyes tells her this is something else. He pulls her arms away from her chest and begins to stroke her there. Stacey tries to pull away, and Poppi does become angry now. He asks her if she loves her Poppi. She doesn't answer.

He asks her again...only now he's pushing her down over the table, and Stacey smells his hot breath curling around her ear.

❂ ❂ ❂

Electricity is coursing through the monster now, a primal force brought by Poppi. The equipment shrieks and flashes, the monster under the bandages jerks and spasms... then the storm is over and the table is lowered.

A beat, a silent hesitation...and fingers begin to unflex slowly and curl out, the great chest begins to heave, gulping in the first new breaths of air. Poppi undoes the restraining straps and steps back to survey his work proudly.

It lives.

❂ ❂ ❂

Poppi has staggered off to his room to fall into a drunken slumber, leaving the misshapen wreck that was his daughter on the kitchen floor. She lays there until almost dawn, too terrified and pained to move. She can taste blood in her mouth, feel it running hot between her legs; one eye is swollen nearly shut and something aches in her chest.

When she begins to drag herself out of the kitchen, it's not to her room but out the back door. She nearly rolls down the three small steps to the grass lawn; then continues to pull herself towards the gap in the fence between her yard and the neighbor's. The sun is up now, but Stacey doesn't feel its heat, not when she has so much of her own.

She crawls through the space between the wooden planks, ignoring a splinter that digs into her arm. She can see the great blue expanse just ahead of her now, the calm waters inviting her. At last she's on the tile rimming the pool. She lets herself collapse there, her goal reached. Only her hand still moves, grasping at a nearby rose bush. The thorns tear her fingers, but she comes away with petals to scatter on the water, like tiny boats.

❂ ❂ ❂

She hears the giant footsteps, and knows he's coming, coming at last. He will see the petals and know what she's asking; because they understand each other's pain, he will help.

She sees a shadow on the other side of the fence, and her heart skips a beat. The shadow pauses before the gap, continues on around to the side-by-side gates. The gate in her backyard opens, the gate in this yard opens...

And the monster is there.

Stacey smiles in welcome and throws another rose petal. The monster staggers forward; Stacey sees he's returning her smile. He kneels by her; as Stacey looks into his death-glazed eyes, she sees only kindness. He reaches for her, and she feels herself cradled in those giant's hands.

Then the water is covering her, a soothing blanket, like when Mommi rocked her in that tub so long ago...

And through the clear water she looks up and sees Poppi.

She opens her mouth in shock; water rushes in. She lets it fill her and is surprised there's no pain or fear. Just floating, a delicious blue floating where no one can touch her and she's finally safe.

The gentle monster is waiting for her on the other side.

Blood for the American People

Tom leaned back against the closed front door and stared at all the blood. He sighed once and began mentally cleaning the apartment.

The couch had taken the worst of it. Fortunately it was cheap and typical; he could replace it in hours.

Likewise, the carpeting—standard issue low pile, light beige. Unfortunately, he'd have to redo the entire living room. He hoped it hadn't completely soaked through to the padding.

The walls.

Tom groaned, used a gloved hand to lock the front door behind him, and carefully crossed the room. As he stepped around the coffee table (which, to a cursory glance, looked untouched), he noticed a crimson-splotched hand just behind the sofa. He walked another yard, and saw that the hand had been severed from the rest of the body, which was apparently also behind the couch; a leg was flung into a far corner of the room, having just missed the window treatments.

Jesus fucking Christ.

In his career as a highly discreet "cleaner," Tom had dealt with a number of messy disposals—a man who'd been stabbed roughly 50 times, a woman beaten by a team of three professionals—but he'd never seen blood splattered at this magnitude before. He leaned over the couch and saw entrails three feet away from the main trunk of the body; and there, on the tasteful wallpaper—were those claw marks?

What the fuck did the killer use? A goddamn tiger?

Tom glanced at the pale, dead face, and saw the features frozen in a grand-finale expression of terror and agony. Just after he'd accepted the job and had been given the address, Tom ran a check and found out the apartment was rented to a Morgan Dempsey, a minor-league employee of the State Department. Mr. Dempsey was so far down the food chain he didn't even have a memorable title, but apparently he'd pissed somebody off.

Bad.

Tom tore his gaze away from Dempsey's wide eyes and focused again on the task at hand. He realized this job would require more than just new furniture and fresh paint; the crime scene was severe enough that he couldn't possibly remove all the evidence in a day. He'd dispose of the body, get the furniture and carpeting and wallpaper in place, then—since he'd been assured by the client that he had an unlimited expense account—he'd grease a few palms.

And, most importantly, he wouldn't ask any questions.

❾ ❾ ❾

The man on the other side of the desk gave Tom an envelope of cash and a smile. "Your fee and your expenses."

As Tom pocketed the envelope, the flabby, middle-aged man with the ugly comb-over chuckled once. "I don't know how you do it. I hear the D.C. forensics team hit the apartment this morning, and came away with nothing."

Tom let his relief course silently; outwardly, he nodded, apparently confident, sure of his own skills.

The client, Mr. Dickson, squinted. "My contacts said you were good. I trust it would be acceptable to hire you again in the future...if necessary, I mean?"

"Of course."

"Do you have any idea what we do here, Mr. Lightenour?"

Tom glanced around the walls. The Founding Fathers Foundation was housed in a converted residence, one of those old, thin two-story houses squeezed into parts of Washington like celery sticks in rancid dip. Dickson's office had once been a den, probably; it was spacious, with expensive pastel wallpaper and genuine antiques for furnishings.

Tom hoped he'd never have to clean it. Just the chair he was sitting on was probably irreplaceable.

He shrugged in answer to Dickson's question. "All I know is that you're one of those high-powered think tanks."

Of course he knew a bit more than that.

He always investigated a client before he accepted a new job. The Founding Fathers Foundation was a conservative think tank, with a mission statement that read like a Cliffs Notes version of the Pledge of Allegiance. Funded by private and corporate sponsors, it boasted an annual budget of nearly $50 million, and its dozen officers and trustees had their fingers in nearly every slice of the policy pie. The Foundation supported supply-side economics, the Monroe Doctrine, a strong national defense, and traditional American values...which *it* defined, regardless of how traditional they really were. Tom figured the fine folks who made up FFF had probably been involved with everything from the invasion of Iraq to the death of the public health care option. Tom's own politics—on the rare occasions when he thought about them—leaned considerably to the left of the FFF's, but he had to respect their strength. And, of course, their money.

Suddenly a low female voice sounded behind Tom. "Oh, sorry, Dix, didn't know you had company..."

Dickson waved a hand. "Quite all right, Anita—we're almost done here."

Tom rose, turned—and stopped just short of gaping.

The woman who stood in the office doorway wasn't Hollywood beautiful, but her shoulder-length, thick, light brown hair, half-lidded smile, and hip-cocked pose all smacked Tom like a bolt of erotic lightning straight to the crotch. He froze as he felt himself harden, hoping she hadn't noticed.

No woman had ever had such an effect on him.

She shifted slightly, the filmy material of her bright red dress hissing slightly as it slid over her thighs, and Tom felt another arc of pure sex. "Oh...you must be Mr. Lightenour," she said, letting his name slip from her tongue like drops of hard liquor.

Tom swallowed, unsure of how to answer—or that he even could answer—when Dickson rose from behind the desk. "Mr. Lightenour was just leaving—"

"I was hoping we might discuss some other business," she said.

Dickson and the woman stared at each other for a moment, eyes narrowed, nostrils flared. Then Dickson twitched and backed down, rustling papers as he looked away. "Fine."

The woman gestured out of the office, and Tom followed as she led him down a short hallway to another room at the rear of the house.

He worked to recall her from the FFF website, and remembered her on the page listing the Foundation's Board: she was Anita Curran, a Rhodes Scholar and CEO of at least one major corporation before joining FFF. In the accompanying photo she'd looked attractive, but more like a well-groomed middle-aged executive, not the most desirable woman Tom had ever met.

She paused before an office door that had her name on it. Tom entered; then she stepped around him, silently closing blinds, turning locks, and flipping off light switches before launching herself at him.

The miniscule part of Tom's mind not currently connected directly to his cock told him to resist, to take his money and run, to never accept another job from the Founding Fathers Foundation...but that part was quickly silenced by tongue and taste and hair and nails and the musky hot scent of her.

It was over in minutes, leaving them both sweaty and panting. As Tom re-buttoned his shirt, he glanced at her and saw her eyes flash in the dim light, and for a moment he had the unsettling sensation that he'd just fucked an animal in heat.

But when she told him she'd call him later, he didn't say no.

◉ ◉ ◉

She did call two nights later. This time they met at an expensive hotel where the desk clerks welcomed her by name and had a room key waiting.

It began as quickly as it had in her office, but lasted longer this time and took place in a king-sized bed. When they finally pulled apart, Tom was too drained to do more than just stare at the ceiling.

Anita rose, used the phone to order room service, and then lit a cigarette and stood naked before the fifth-floor window, looking down at the lights of Washington.

"You smoke," he said, watching her.

"Is that a compliment or an observation?" She didn't turn, only took another drag.

"It just surprises me."

Tom could hear amusement in her voice. "You only live once, right?"

"You don't seem like a conservative scholar."

Now she did turn to look at him, and he felt a chill ripple up from the small of his back. "What do you know about the Founding Fathers Foundation?" she asked.

"No more than what's on the website."

She nodded, then turned back to the view and the cigarette. The lights seemed to fascinate her, and he saw the hand without the cigarette spread on the cool glass as if she could reach through and take the city. She didn't say anything else.

❊ ❊ ❊

Two weeks later, she gave him an address and told him to meet her there at 7 p.m.

They'd rendezvoused a total of six times, but each meeting had consisted entirely of sex (*really amazing fucking sex*, Tom reminded himself) in a random hotel or her office. They never left the room, didn't enjoy a night out on the town, didn't talk much before or after. She certainly had never invited him home.

But when Tom pulled up before the tasteful two-story house in Georgetown, he knew it was hers. Somehow that realization made him more anxious, not less.

He parked, walked to the front door, rang the bell. Moments later he stood in Anita's large, elegant living room, hearing cloth tear as she raked her nails down his back and ran her tongue along his jaw.

She abruptly pulled away from him, spinning to the window. Tom ignored his throbbing crotch and tried to follow her glance, but saw only the night sky over the affluent cityscape.

"It's time," she announced, and took his hand, leading him out of the room.

They went through the kitchen, around the island with its copper pans and chrome fixtures, to a basement door. She opened it, turned on lights, and led him downstairs. The basement looked typical—boxes, old furniture, gardening tools—except for a solid metal door wedged into one wall. Anita opened it to reveal a small, sterile room within: One wall held a bank of video monitors, there were racks of canned goods and supplies, and a cot against the third wall.

"I'll be damned," Tom said, taking it all in, "a panic room. I've never seen one in person before."

Anita reached around him to close the door, and then stepped away from him. "I want you to watch me, Tom."

He grinned. "Is that all?"

Her response was nearly a physical slap. "Goddamnit, *watch me.*"

Silent, chastened, he nodded.

She reached back to a shelf and brought forth a vial of pills; twisting the lid off, she poured about ten into her palm. She threw the pills into her mouth and washed them down with a long pull from a bottle of water.

"Anita, what the hell...?"

"*Just watch.*"

Next she removed her clothing, which she carefully folded and placed on a shelf. By the time she finished, Tom could see the drugs working on her—her eyes were losing focus, her limbs moving as if she were underwater.

She lowered herself to the cot, stretched out there, and promptly lost consciousness.

Jesus...what is this, a suicide attempt? Christ, Anita...

Tom was debating whether to call 911 when she quivered.

At first he thought she must certainly be convulsing from the medication; but then he saw that somehow her bare skin seemed to be darkening. He bent closer to her, breath held, and saw that it wasn't that the flesh was changing color, but that it was growing hair.

Tom backed up so quickly that he rattled the shelving unit behind him. He stared in disbelief as she changed:

Limbs lengthened and bent. Features changed shape and color. Thick gray-brown fur covered her. The spine curved. A tail sprouted.

In less than thirty seconds, Tom stood over a large wolf that was twitching slightly in a sedative-induced sleep. She growled softly, Tom saw canines that were nearly as long and thick as his little finger, and he knew exactly who/what had killed the young man in the State Department.

He turned and stumbled out the door, slamming it behind him, double-checking it even when he heard the catch of the heavy interior latch.

But he didn't leave. He paced for a few seconds, until

his heart slowed, and then he found a cracking old leather armchair and fell into it.

Jesus, I've been fucking a wolf, he thought, and allowed himself a time for hysterical laughter. Then, when that had passed, he thought about what to do.

And decided simply to wait.

◕ ◕ ◕

He dozed off for a while, but jerked awake when he heard the door opening. Adrenaline flooded his system and brought him to his feet, but before he could run, the door was pushed back, and he saw her.

Fully human again. Partly clothed. Looking dulled, as if she was still slightly wrapped in the sedative's embrace.

"I need coffee," she announced before heading up the stairs, leaving him to follow. He saw morning light streaming in through the kitchen windows and realized the night had passed.

He sat at the dinette silently while she went about the absurdly normal motions of making coffee. Finally, she brought two steaming mugs to the table, sat down across from him, took a sip, and eyed him contemplatively.

"You stayed."

He nodded, his throat dry, his stomach in rebellion at the thought of coffee, which he swallowed anyway.

"I was bitten four years ago..."

Tom remembered the website. "When you joined FFF."

"Yes. It's kind of...let's say, a condition of being part of the Foundation—"

"Wait—do you mean that all of you in the FFF are...?"

"Of course. I was turned by Dickson."

Tom tried to imagine the pudgy, balding bureaucrat as a sophisticated predator, and was surprised to find that he could.

"The wolf," Anita said, drawing his attention back to her, "it changes you even when the moon's not full. Makes you faster, smarter—"

"More vicious." Images of shredded limbs and flung-about organs in the young man's apartment made Tom push the coffee aside.

"Yes," she said, and Tom wondered if her teeth weren't still longer, more pointed than they should have been. "We are more aggressive. But that's good for our work."

"For planning wars and police actions, you mean."

She laughed, then stroked his hand and Tom had to stifle an urge to pull away. "God, Tom, you sound so liberal."

"So what did he do? That kid in the State Department."

She sighed and looked away. "He had the bad luck of walking in on a cabinet head in a...well, compromising position."

"And that cabinet head is yours?"

She didn't answer, just turned that glistening smile back on him.

"So," he said, doing his best to hold her gaze, "what about me? How can you let me just walk away knowing what I know?"

Anita rose languorously from her chair, padded around the table, and draped herself over Tom until she could whisper into his ear.

"Darling, every wolf needs its dog."

❍ ❍ ❍

She was right, of course. She was always right.

If Tom tried to tell anyone—cops, media, iReporters, another think tank—he wouldn't be believed, but he would be dead, because the wolves of the Founding Fathers Foundation had his scent now and would hunt him down.

So he served them. He cleaned up when they tore apart an influential talk show host's assistant who was regularly blowing the blowhard. He disposed of a blood-soaked car when they attacked a street hustler who'd sold drugs to an evangelical leader.

And he had a great deal more mind-numbing sex with Anita, the kind of sex that left him chafed and sore.

Normally Tom would have done anything for that kind of sex, but his bouts with her also left him scared out of his wits. Even though she had told him she would only change on full moon nights, he knew she could strip the skin from his bones any time she wished.

The street hustler had been killed during a new moon.

But they also paid Tom well. It was amazing what money and sex had done to silence his conscience. He sometimes found himself embroiled in late-night arguments with himself, reasoning that he might as well be on the winner's side; or that he could take their money until he was wealthy enough to turn on them.

Or he could beg them to turn him.

Whenever the full moon came again, and he locked himself away in his apartment, imagining Anita roaming the streets, her smooth ash-colored fur protecting her from sight and cold, her attuned senses leading her to the prey, the remorseless kill...he wished he was with her.

Nearly a year after his first job for FFF, he awoke the morning after a full moon to receive his latest assignment. He was sent to a house in a New Jersey suburb, where he found the mutilated remains of a woman—and a baby girl. She still wore the shreds of a pink jumper and booties.

For the first time in his professional life, Tom vomited upon viewing the scene, then immediately cursed himself for creating a major evidence stew; one more thing to clean up. He forced himself not to wonder what anyone could have done to deserve this, or what anyone could be to commit this. He focused solely on the practicalities, and he walked through the actions like a stone man, a robot.

A dog.

When the job was finished, he returned to FFF and found Dickson waiting with the pay. "I trust everything went well...?"

Tom didn't answer. He took the money, left Dickson, walked down the hall to Anita's office and threw the door open.

She was on her cell and looked up in irritation. "I'll have to call you back," she said, watching Tom as he closed her door and then paced before her large, neat desk.

"Tom, what—"

"Bite me."

She blinked in surprise and then laughed.

"I saw what you—or one of you—did last night, to that woman and the baby. And I almost couldn't handle it."

Anita leaned back in her chair, eyes narrowing. "That's unfortunate, but—"

"So turn me. Make me like you."

She gawked for a moment, her mouth actually hanging open. Then she said, with some amusement, "You can't be serious."

"Why not?"

"Because," Anita said, rising from her chair, causing Tom's stomach to constrict in dread as she walked around the desk to him, "you will *never* be one of us."

She started to reach for him, but Tom leapt away. "I would be if you turned me."

Her amusement vanished, replaced with a fury that made her eyes glitter; flop sweat broke out on Tom's brow as she advanced. "What do you think I was before, Tom? Some weak-kneed left-winger with a useless fucking degree in Liberal Arts and a collection of 'Hillary for President' buttons? Some halfwit jabbering of equality and socialism? Some naïve *dog* who stupidly dares to dream that it can be a wolf?!"

She backed him into a corner, pushed her face up to his. "If you want to know the truth, even the sex has started to get boring. I'd like your dick better if it was attached to a backbone." Anita's nose wrinkled in disgust, and Tom knew she'd smelled his fear. She turned away, didn't bother to look back as she added, "Get out. FFF is finished with you, and so am I."

He left while he could.

❂ ❂ ❂

Tom had a month.

Somehow he knew she wouldn't risk attacking him while in human shape. He wasn't some spaced-out junkie too doped to put up a fight; no, he knew she'd wait to let the wolf take him.

If he ran, she'd find him. There was nowhere he could hide, no one he could talk to.

He only had one chance: fight back.

FFF's offices had its own security, and he knew he wouldn't be able to get near her while she was human. That was fine; he wasn't sure he could kill her while she still looked like Anita, and while he still wanted her.

Tom searched the internet, found instructional videos on how to cast bullets, and bought the molds, ladles, and other equipment online. It took him a few tries to get it right. Tom didn't like guns—he'd never had to use one in his work—but he did own a Smith & Wesson 327 that held eight rounds, so he made eight bullets. He went into the woods and fired one as a test, to be sure it wouldn't shatter or melt. He was satisfied with the results. He had seven bullets left.

He thought it would be enough for her.

❍ ❍ ❍

The night of the full moon arrived.

Tom had been his usual careful self as he'd arranged (under a false name) to rent the isolated cabin. He couldn't afford to have his D.C. neighbors hearing gunshots, or wolf howls. Or seeing him lug a body out to his car.

He knew she'd find him anyway.

It was past midnight as he sat in the cabin's main room, the gun cradled in his lap, a fire blazing in the old-fashioned hearth behind him. The moon had risen several hours ago, and outside he saw pines and scrub bathed in light the color of her fur.

Finally, he heard the small scratch at the door.

Tom stood, holding the gun firmly in both hands,

pointing it at the room's single large window. He knew she wouldn't get in through the door, but could easily leap past the glass, enduring only a few small cuts. He hoped to take her down in mid-leap, but would fire the rest of the rounds into her, just to be sure.

The hair on Tom's arms stood on edge as he heard her howl...

...and then came the answering howls of other wolves. Of course she hadn't come alone. She'd brought the entire FFF board with her. Their kind always hunted in packs.

Tom's knees gave way, and he sagged into the chair, cursing himself for his arrogance. He'd really believed he'd meant enough to her that she'd want to deal with him alone. Of course they'd tracked his online activity, knew how much silver he'd bought, and had calculated how many bullets he had. She had maneuvered one of the others to take out the window first. Maybe she even had human assistants out there, preparing to open the door, let them in to tear apart their dog in bites that would kill him, not change him.

She'd been right all along. He could never be like them.

Tom raised the gun to his own head as the first wolf crashed through the window.

Joe and Abel in the Field of Rest

It was still dark when Joe suddenly sat up in bed, chest hitching, calling out, "Da?"

As he sat in the pre-dawn gloom, breath slowing, he focused on the house, on the bed, on himself, and remembered:

Da was gone. He'd died a year ago; his ashes now rested in the urn above the fireplace.

Before Joe could stop to really wonder what had awakened him, he heard it: a thud on the front door of the house, followed by another, and another. Something was outside, knocking against the steel-reinforced door with rhythmic determination.

For a moment, absurdly, Joe felt an urge to cry. Of course Da was long gone, replaced by the constant threat of *them*. Of course Joe was completely alone, in a house without electricity and only an inch of metal between him and something that thought of him as nothing but meat.

Joe briefly considered waiting until dawn; he thought the door would hold. But without a clock, he had no way of knowing how far off sunrise was, and there was still a small, nagging doubt tugging him away from sleep. So he slid from his cooling sheets, lit a propane lantern, made his way down the hallway and past the living room to the front door. Once there, he picked up the loaded rifle he always kept waiting.

He paused, listening, but heard no indication that there was more than a single one of them out there. This should be an easy in-and-out, then—he'd let the thing in, and then take it out.

Joe placed the lantern on the side entry table, checked the gun (even though he'd checked it just before bed, as he did every night), and stepped back slightly from the door. He set his feet apart and reached forward, cautiously, carefully, knowing this would depend on timing. He finally took a deep breath, darted a hand forward and turned the lock and the doorknob, then leapt back, whipping up the rifle.

Almost immediately the door crashed in and a dead thing was grappling with Joe, too close to shoot, its flaking fingers reaching for him, jaw slack and venting a hungry howl. Joe tried to back away but hit a wall; he swung the rifle until the barrel was facing down and used it to hold his aggressor back. He gave a push and the gaping nightmare staggered back. Joe raised the rifle as a club, and it went off as the stock hit the dead man's head. He felt powder burn his leg, but he had no time to see if he'd been shot; instead he swung again, then changed his hold on the gun and drove the rifle's stock butt-first into the other's forehead. He felt bone crack beneath the blow, and all sound ceased. One more ramming and Joe stepped back as his attacker dropped, truly dead at last.

Joe smacked the gun into its head three more times to be sure.

Then he remembered the open door, swung the rifle around and grabbed the lantern. He saw one other figure outside and waited until it came closer; a single efficient shot and it went down. He looked at the corpse beneath him, kicked the stiff body out the door, then closed and barred it again.

Safe once more, Joe walked into the kitchen, intending to grab rags and water to clean, but instead he dropped into one of the old peeling chairs and let the gun fall from nerveless fingers.

"Da..." he whispered before slumping into the chair, too tired to do anymore.

○ ○ ○

In the morning, Joe ate his usual sparse breakfast of canned fruit, goat's milk and nuts, and then he opened the door carefully. He'd gotten started later than usual today, having decided to wait until the sun was completely up so he could spot any more of them.

Walkers.

When they'd first appeared six months ago, he hadn't known what to call them; he was a simple man and had no vocabulary to apply to reanimated corpses that sought to consume the living. He'd watched the first few days of the plague on the television, before the shows had stopped and power had followed. Joe and his father had been largely self-sufficient for years, selling crops from their little farm for the few necessities they didn't already have; after Da died, Joe had continued on the same way, growing corn and potatoes and walnuts, until the world had died, too.

Newly acquired by its own kind.

It had taken an accident to tell Joe how to stop them; one of the things had been bludgeoned by a heavy, swinging pulley in the barn, and it was the first one Joe had seen really die. After that he'd learned how to deal with them easily, with a single shot from his old rifle. He'd barricaded his house first; then, after losing all of his pigs and most of his goats, he'd fortified the barn to protect the remaining livestock. Joe had never been a reader, but a few cautious trips to the nearest library—empty now, forgotten, silent—had taught him how to put up stronger fencing, set up a hothouse, and cast his own bullets. Soon he'd fortified the entire farm, with a chain link boundary lifted from the nearest large hardware store and an extra supply of guns and ammo.

For the most part, he lived the way he'd always lived:

tending crops and livestock until the sun set, eating a simple final meal before collapsing into bed, sleeping eight hours, and rising to start again.

Except now he was alone.

When Da had been alive, they had never spoken much, two taciturn men who spent their energies on work; but there had been *two* of them. It had been enough. Two was all Joe could remember; his mother had died when he was only four, and he no longer had any memory of her. Somehow, though, he thought she'd been worn out by this life, wrung out early and left to die a husk.

At least she hadn't come back.

Joe had never put much thought into the mechanics of why some came back and some didn't. He occasionally arose in the morning and saw a walker raking its dry fingers over his fence and had some moment of dull shock when he realized he'd once known the fingers' owner.

Jenny from the convenience store...the pastor I used to see in the market...

After Joe got past the moment of surprise, he shot them in the head. And then he took their bodies to the Field of Rest.

That was what he called it, at least. In reality it was a pit he'd dug with the backhoe in the half-acre at the far northwest corner of the farm where nothing would grow; the land was stony and barren, not even good for grazing. One day Joe had used precious gallons of fuel (although he'd never regretted it) to dig the twenty-foot deep pit, three-dozen yards in diameter. From then on, he'd thrown the dead walkers into the pit, waiting until the bottom was lined with enough to shovel in a layer of dirt.

The Field of Rest was only ten feet deep now.

A quick scan of his fence today showed Joe where they'd broken through last night; they'd pushed in a section near the Field of Rest. He shot another walker near the perimeter (*I used to see her at the feed store, didn't I?*), then set to work repairing and strengthening the fence.

It was afternoon by the time he was done. Joe went back to the house to eat his small lunch (*almost out of the jerky*), then released the three remaining goats from the barn and retrieved a wheelbarrow. He loaded up last night's two dead walkers and made his way out to the Field. It was a warm day late in May, and he was sweating by the time he reached the edge of the pit.

He set down the wheelbarrow, preparing to dump its contents, when he heard something scrabbling. Moaning.

A walker. In the pit.

Joe carefully leaned over the edge and saw it. Moving, at the bottom, scrabbling at the dirt wall just below him.

It was trapped, and he paused to examine it. He thought he knew it—young man, no more than 27 or 28, friendly, stout, bearded face (the beard now hung in tattered clumps from a decaying jaw), used to drive a truck, stopped at the pub every once in a while...

Strange name like something from the Bible— Abraham? No...Abel. That was it. Abel.

Joe realized this one must have entered with the rest last night and staggered into the pit. He saw that one leg indeed bent strangely, forcing the thing to support most of its dead weight on the remaining limb. It stared up at Joe and moaned softly, desperately clawing at the dirt walls in a futile attempt to climb.

Joe looked down at it thoughtfully. He'd left his rifle back in the house. He'd have to go back and get it. He'd have to aim carefully, since the shot would be a high angle from overhead and he didn't want to waste a bullet he couldn't retrieve.

"Abel..." Joe muttered.

The thing in the pit stopped mewling for a moment. It looked up at Joe, curiously...

...and in that moment, regardless of what would come after, Joe knew he wouldn't be putting a bullet into Abel's brain.

He dumped the dead walkers into the pit, watched idly

as Abel turned away long enough to investigate. When Abel realized the bodies were dead and decayed, he turned his attention back to Joe, renewing his efforts to reach something warm and vital.

The sun was limning the western horizon when Joe finally remembered the rest of his chores and left the Field—and Abel—behind.

۞ ۞ ۞

Joe visited Abel every day for the next three weeks.

He didn't put much thought into what compelled him to look on the thing in the pit, whether it was curiosity or boredom or something else he wouldn't name. He just knew he found some value in sitting by the edge, looking down, eventually talking to the walker.

It began as idle thoughts, about the weather, or the food, or the crops. But before long Joe was unleashing entire monologues on his captive companion. He talked about his life, about how well he and Da had worked together, how they hadn't needed anyone else, how they'd taught themselves to do important and necessary things. Once or twice Joe started to talk about watching the cancer take Da, how it'd eaten him away until he'd been little more than taut skin over bones when he'd died, how he'd obeyed Da's wishes and had him cremated.

How he was glad now that he had.

Meanwhile, Abel grew weaker and weaker, down there on the dirt floor, until his bad leg would support him no longer and he slid to a sitting position on the floor, tattered fingertips still drawing runnels around him. He stared up at Joe, mirroring Joe's own hunger, and Joe felt a compassion he'd felt only once in his life, when as a child he'd rescued a lamb from an irrigation ditch.

When Joe shot more walkers outside the fence, he carted them to a far corner of the Field of Rest, unwilling to hurl them down atop Abel.

One morning he awoke to find one of the three remaining goats had died during the night. Whether from old age or sickness Joe didn't know, and he didn't think about it as he methodically butchered the goat, placing some of the meat in his homemade smoker to preserve, and carving a portion for his dinner that night. He'd eat well for a change.

After he'd cooked the goat steak, he walked to the Field of Rest, steaming plate in one hand and a bucket in the other. When he reached the edge, he set both down and peered through dusk's gloom.

"Good evening, Abel. We're eating together tonight."

With that he emptied the bucket—which contained the parts of the goat he couldn't eat—into the pit and then sat down with his own plate.

Abel uttered a dry moan as he crept across the floor to clutch at the remains. Joe watched, enjoying his own repast, as Abel shoveled the pieces into his mouth. When Joe had gnawed his meat down to the bone, so had Abel, and they both finished, Joe sated and Abel renewed. Apparently the meal had given the walker fresh strength, because he stood again, limping on his shattered limb to the wall underneath Joe; but this time he simply stood and looked up, a small sound escaping from his decayed mouth.

"You're welcome, Abel," Joe said, looking down into the pit and smiling.

❂ ❂ ❂

A week after that, the weather turned hot and Joe sweated as he worked among his crops. Even though he had a hat and plenty of water, he could feel a few exposed parts burning beneath the cruel sun.

He heard a motor.

He froze, thinking perhaps it was merely an insect drone, but no—there it was, nearing. He spun and looked past the fence where the road ran, and sure enough, he spotted the glint of metal approaching.

Numb, Joe stood where he was and watched a huge,

black, boxy vehicle drive up. Someone had welded chicken wire over the windows, including the front, and Joe could see that some of the glass in the rear had been shattered.

The car's brakes suddenly squealed, and it skidded to a stop just on the other side of the fence, perhaps a hundred feet from Joe. After a beat the driver's door was thrown back, and a tall, skinny young man leapt out. He took two, three steps toward Joe and stopped, peering.

They stared at each other for what seemed like hours, uncomprehending, each the first living human being the other had seen in weeks. Finally the driver broke the silence by calling out to Joe:

"Are you human?"

Joe blinked in surprise, tried to clear his throat, but it was suddenly too dry for words. He simply nodded.

"Do you have any spare food?"

Again, a silent nod. The driver's body relaxed, and he gripped the car door to steady himself. Joe waved to his left and finally found his voice: "Gate's that way."

The young man nodded, grinned at Joe, and then happily climbed back into his car. Joe began to trudge toward the gate, simply astonished.

Behind him, in the Field of Rest, Abel groaned.

❂ ❂ ❂

His name was Harrison, Harrison Melcher, but everyone called him Sonny. He was 23 years old and had worked as a print model until everything had fallen apart. He'd been driving ever since, looking for survivors, food, anything, but fuel was getting harder to find and he knew he'd have to stop soon. He hadn't eaten in two days.

He said all this around mouthfuls of Joe's pickled vegetables and two baked potatoes and a small portion of goat jerky. Joe listened and just nodded or shook his head when asked questions, like whether he lived alone (a nod) and if he knew of other survivors (a shake) and if it was safe here (another nod).

By the time Sonny had finished eating, the sun was setting, and he asked Joe if he could stay the night. He could stay in his car, which he'd been doing every night for the last month; he wouldn't impose.

In the end Joe offered him Da's room, despite the dust that had built up since Da had passed on. Sonny was nonetheless grateful and fell asleep almost instantly.

Joe stayed up most of the night, his routine interrupted, his mind struggling to process the surprising flood of thoughts and emotions that swept through him. He sat at the kitchen table, sipping a cup of mulberry leaf tea and listening to the sound of Sonny's snoring. Da had snored, too, although it'd been louder than Sonny's. Probably because Sonny was younger.

Joe didn't really know. In fact, he suddenly became aware of just how little he knew about anyone else. So he listened carefully as Sonny talked more about himself the next day: about how he'd left home at 18, lived on the streets for 2 years before someone asked him to model, had just been starting to make some real money when all the shit hit. He talked about his lover Willum, who'd been attacked in front of Sonny's eyes one day; he talked about how he'd seen one camp of survivors behind barbed wire, but had moved on when he'd heard screaming from within. He talked about how he'd run out of food and ammunition at almost the same time, and how every store he'd stopped at in the last week had been stripped bare.

Joe listened to it all and tried to process a life so different from his. He'd never had a job other than farming, enough money for a vacation, or a lover. Sonny was almost like some mythical creature to him, something he could barely relate to as his own species.

Then Sonny asked if he could stay.

"I really don't know where else to go," he said, and Joe was uncomfortable as he saw tears stream down Sonny's cheeks. "The cities are dead, the countryside's dead, there's no more gas or food...I could stay here with you. I can make myself useful. Teach me anything. I can learn to farm, we can grow twice as much together, right?"

He'd reached out then and touched Joe's hand.

Joe had stared in mute disbelief. No one but Da had ever touched him before. It was a light touch, and quickly withdrawn, but it left Joe stunned, unable to reply or even move.

Sonny must have sensed Joe's discomfort, because he abruptly wiped his eyes and stood, turning away. "Sorry, man...I know it's a lot to ask...hey, if it's okay, I'm just going for a walk."

Sonny walked out of the kitchen, and Joe continued to sit, still looking down at his hand.

Could Sonny stay here? Could he become a part of Joe's life? Joe knew he couldn't replace Da, but perhaps he could help, they could work the farm together, and with Abel they could—

Joe stopped, realizing that he hadn't factored in Abel yet.

Joe's pondering was interrupted by the sound of running feet and panting. He looked up as Sonny burst into the kitchen, sweating, eyes wide. "Hey, man, you got one of *them* outside—one of the dead things—in some kind of pit out there—" Sonny waved an indiscriminate hand wildly in the air, indicating every direction at once.

Joe didn't say anything.

Sonny took an anxious step forward. "I don't have any ammo left, we've gotta shoot that thing—" His eyes darted around Joe's house before they fixed on something:

The rifle. By the front door, where Joe always left it, loaded.

Sonny grabbed the rifle and ran from the house.

Joe was instantly on his feet, running after Sonny and the gun. Sonny was younger and in good shape, and he easily outdistanced Joe as they both raced for the Field of Rest. Sonny reached the edge of the hole easily 200 feet in front of Joe, and Joe could only watch, running in slow-motion dread, as Sonny pulled back the rifle's bolt, lifted the gun to his eye, and aimed down.

An incoherent shout from Joe startled Sonny into lowering the gun, and he watched in perplexity as Joe reached him, gasping for air. "What—?!"

Joe put a hand on the barrel. "You can't shoot Abel."

Sonny gazed at him in disbelief for a moment, and then burst into laughter. "He's fucking dead, don't you get that?! If you don't put a bullet in his head, he'll eventually dig his way out of there and turn you into a meal—"

Joe didn't answer, except to give a solid tug on the rifle, but Sonny didn't relinquish his grip.

"You're crazy."

Joe yanked harder on the gun, but this time Sonny stepped back and pulled the gun firmly away. "No way, man. No way am I giving you this gun."

In the pit, Abel looked up and cried out.

That was all Joe needed. He lunged for Sonny, barreling into him like a runaway bull. The action surprised Sonny, and although he was bigger than Joe, he went down. They both fell to the rocky earth, grappling for the gun, hands pushing, feet kicking, the uneven surface jabbing them both as they rolled one way, then another. At one point the gun went off, and Joe couldn't tell if one of them had been hit. He drove his fingers into Sonny's eye sockets, and the other man screamed, involuntarily releasing his hold on both gun and Joe. Joe took advantage of the moment to scrabble back, finding the gun, raising it and cocking it as Sonny sat up, screaming, blood gushing down his face.

Joe pulled the trigger.

❍ ❍ ❍

It was twilight before Joe finished, but he felt a surprising warmth flood through him, a serenity he thought he'd never known.

His full stomach protested slightly against the strange contents, but Joe had been surprised to find the taste reasonably pleasant. Below him, Abel still gnawed on an arm bone, dark blood smearing his ravaged face.

"You were right, Abel. It's good."

Abel finished eating and suddenly stopped to stare at the grisly bones he now held. Joe watched, peering through the gathering darkness, thinking that something had happened to Abel, something awakened in him Joe hadn't seen before. Abel jabbed the pointed end of the bones into the earth and created a sizable furrow as he pulled the bone towards him.

He looked up at Joe, and Joe thought he saw Abel smile.

Abel hauled himself to his unsteady feet and ambled to the side of the pit just below Joe. Joe bent over to watch as Abel, reinvigorated by his meal, determinedly jammed arm bones into the dirt, causing a sizable clod to fall. He did it again and again, and within a few moments several feet of the wall above him had crumbled. At this rate, Joe knew it wouldn't be long until Abel would create enough of a pathway to crawl up, that soon he'd be out of the Field of Rest and back to the world's surface.

Joe saw the rifle by his side, and for a second an image flashed in his head, an image of fighting Sonny for the gun, of the gun going off and Sonny falling back, dead. Murdered.

Joe's reverie was interrupted by the sound of more of the soil falling away below him. He looked up into the clear evening sky, and thought about how pleasant it would be to pass the warm night here, in the open, under the forgiving stars.

He lay back to wait.

Sparks Fly Upward

My breath is corrupt, my days are extinct, the graves are ready for me.
Job 17:1

Blessed and holy is he that hath part in the first resurrection...
Revelations 20:6

June 16

Tomorrow marks one year ago that the Colony was begun here, and I think just about everyone is busy preparing for a big celebration. We just had our first real harvest two weeks ago, so there'll be plenty of good things to eat, and as for drink—well, the product of George's still is a little extreme for most tastes, so Tom and a few of the boys made a foray outside yesterday for some real liquor.

Of course I was worried when Tom told me he was going (and not even for something really vital, just booze), but he said it wasn't so bad. The road was almost totally clear for the first five miles after they left the safety of the Colony, and even most of Philipsville, the pint-sized town where they raided a liquor store, was deserted. Tom said he shot one in the liquor store cellar when he went down there to check on the good wines; it was an old woman, probably the one-time shopkeeper's wife locked away. Unfortunately, she'd clawed most of the good bottles off to smash on the floor. Tom took what was left, and an unopened case of burgundy he found untouched in a corner. There are 131 adults in the Colony, so he figured he'd have a bottle for every two on Anniversary Day.

It's been two weeks since any of the deadheads have been spotted near the Colony walls; Pedro Quintero, our top marksman, picked that one off with one shot straight through the head from the east tower. It would be easy to fool ourselves into thinking the situation is finally mending...easy and dangerous, because it's not. The lack of deadheads seen around here lately proves only one thing: that Doc Freeman was right in picking this location, away from the cities and highways.

Of course Doc Freeman was right; he's right about everything. He said we should go this far north because the south would only keep getting hotter, and sure enough it's been in the 80s here for over a week now. I don't want to think what it is down in L.A. now—probably 120, and that's in the shade.

Tomorrow will be a tribute to Doc Freeman as much as an anniversary celebration. If it hadn't been for him...well, I suppose Tom and little Jessie and I would be wandering around out there with the rest of them right now, dead for a year but still hungry. Always hungry.

It's funny, but before all the shit came down, Doc Freeman was just an eccentric old college professor teaching agricultural sciences and preaching survival. Tom always believed Freeman had been thinking about cutting out anyway, even before the whole zombie thing, because of the rising temperatures. He told his students that agriculture in most parts of the U.S. was already a thing of the past, and it would all be moving up to Canada soon.

When the deadheads came (Doc Freeman argued, as did a lot of other environmentalists, that they were caused by climate change, too), it was the most natural thing in the world, I guess, for him to assemble a band of followers and head north. He'd chosen the site for the Colony, set up policy and government, designed the layout of fields, houses and fences, and even assigned each of us a job, according to what we were best at. It had all been scary at first, of course—especially with 3-year-old Jessie—but we all kind of fell into place. I even discovered I was a talented horticulturist—Doc says the best after him—and in some ways this new life is better than the old one.

Of course there are a lot of things we all miss: ice cream, uncallused hands, TV Del still scans the shortwave radio, hoping he'll pick something up on it. In a year, he has only once, and that transmission ended with the sound of gunshots.

So we accept our place in the world...and the fact that it may be the last place. Tomorrow we do more than accept it, we celebrate it.

I wish I knew exactly how to feel.

June 17

Well, the big day has come and gone.

Tom is beside me, snoring in a blissful alcoholic oblivion. Tomorrow he'll be in the fields again, so he's earned this.

Jessie is in her room next door, exhausted from all the games she played and sweets she ate. Tom actually let me use a precious hour of battery charge to record her today.

And yet I wasn't the only one crying when Doc Freeman got up and made his speech about how his projections show that if we continue at our present excellent rate, we'll be able to expand the colony in three years. Expand it carefully, he added. Meaning that in three years there'll be probably forty or fifty couples—like Tom and I—begging for the precious right to increase our family.

I know Doc is right, that we must remember the lessons of the old world and not outgrow our capacity to produce, to sustain that new growth...but somehow it seems wrong to deny new life when we're surrounded by so much death.

Especially when the new life is in me.

June 24

I've missed two now, so I felt certain enough to go see Dale Oldfield. He examined me as best he could (he's an excellent G.P., but his equipment is still limited), and he concluded I'd guessed right.

I am pregnant.

Between the two of us we figured it at about six weeks along. Dale thanked me for not trying to hide it, then told me he would have to report it to Doc Freeman. I asked only that Tom and I be allowed to be there when he did. He agreed, and we decided on tomorrow afternoon.

I went home and told Tom. At first he was thrilled...and then he remembered where we were.

I told Tom we'd be seeing Doc Freeman tomorrow about it; he became obsessed with the idea that he'd somehow convince Doc to let us have the baby.

I couldn't stand to hear him torture himself that way, so I read stories to Jessie and held her until we both fell asleep in her narrow child-sized bed.

June 25

We saw Doc Freeman today. Dale Oldfield confirmed the situation, and then gracefully excused himself, saying he'd be in his little shack-cum-office when we needed him.

Doc Freeman poured all three of us a shot of his private stock of Jim Beam; then he began the apologies. Tom tried to argue him out of it, saying a birth would be good for morale, and we could certainly handle just one more in the Colony...but Doc told him quietly that, unlike many of the young couples, we already had a child and couldn't expect special treatment. Tom finally gave in, admitting Doc was right—and I'd never loved him more than I did then, seeing his pain and regret.

He went with me to tell Dale we'd be needing his services next week, and Dale just nodded, his head hung low, not meeting our eyes.

Afterwards, in our own bungalow, Tom and I argued for hours. We both got crazy, talking about leaving the Colony, building our own little fortress somewhere, even overthrowing Doc Freeman...but I think we both knew it was all fantasy. Doc Freeman had been right again: we did have Jessie, and maybe in a few more years the time would be right for another child.

But not now.

July 2

Tomorrow is the day set for us to do it.

God, I wish there was another way. Unfortunately, even after performing a D&C three times in the last year, Dale still has never had the clinic's equipment moved to the Colony. It's ironic that we can send out an expedition for booze, but not one for medical equipment. Doc Freeman says that's because the equipment is a lot bigger than the booze, and the Colony's only truck has been down basically since we got here.

So tomorrow Tom, Dale and I will make the 18-mile drive to Silver Creek, the nearest town big enough to have had a family planning clinic. Dale, who has keys to the clinic, assures me the only dangerous part will be getting from the car to the doors of the clinic. They can't get inside, he tells me, so we'll be safe—until we have to leave again, that is.

Funny...when he's telling me about danger, he only talks about deadheads.

He never mentions the abortion.

July 3

I didn't sleep much last night. Tom held me but even he dozed off for a while. It's morning as I write this, and I hear Jessie starting to awaken. After I get her up, I'll try to tell her mommy and daddy have to leave for a while, and nice

Mrs. Oldfield will watch her. She'll cry, but hopefully not because she understands what's really going on.

∞

It's later now. Jessie's taken care of, and Dale's got the jeep ready to go. Tom and I check our supplies again: an automatic .38 with full magazine, an Uzi with extra clips, a hunting rifle with scope and plenty of ammo, three machetes and the little wooden box. Dale's also got his shotgun and a Walther PPK that he says makes him feel like James Bond. Everyone teases him about it, telling him things like the difference is that Bond's villains were all alive to begin with. Dale always glowers and shuts up.

It's time to go.

We climbed into the jeep. Tom asked why I was bringing you (diary) along, and I told him it was my security blanket and rabbit's foot. He shut up and Dale gunned the engine. We had to stop three times on the way out to exchange hugs and good luck wishes with people who ran up from the fields when we went by.

We're about 15 miles out now, and it's been the way Tom said—quiet. After the gates swung open, and we pulled onto the dusty road, it must've been ten minutes before we saw the first deadhead. It was lumbering slowly across a sere field, still fifty yards from the road as we whipped by.

A few miles later there was a small pack of three in the road, but they were spaced wide apart. Dale drove around two of them; they clawed in vain at the jeep, but we were doing 60 and they just scraped their fingers. The third one was harder to drive around—there were car wrecks on either side of the road—so Dale just whomped into him. He flew over the welded cage at the front of the jeep and landed somewhere off to the side of the road. We barely felt it.

We'd just reached the outskirts of Silver Creek when Dale slowed down and cleared his throat. Then he said, Listen, Sarah, there's something you ought to know about the clinic. He asked me if I'd talked to any of the others he'd already escorted out here.

Of course I had, but they had only assured me of Dale's skilled, painless technique, and that they'd be there if I needed to talk. None of them had said much about the clinic itself.

I said this to Dale, and he asked me something strange.

He asked if I was religious.

Tom and I looked at each other, then Tom asked Dale what he was getting at.

Dale stammered through something about how the deadheads tend to go back to places that were important to them, like their homes or shopping malls or schools.

We nodded—everyone knew that—and Dale asked if we'd ever heard of Operation SoulSave.

I swear I literally tasted something bad in my mouth. How could I forget? The fundamentalists who used to stand around outside abortion clinics and shout insults and threats at people who went in. I was with a friend once—a very young friend—when it happened to her.

Then I realized what he was saying. I couldn't believe it. I tried to ask him, but my words just tripped all over each other. He nodded and told us.

They're still here.

❂ ❂ ❂

Most of Silver Creek was empty. We saw some of them inside dusty old storefronts, gazing at us stupidly as we drove by, but they probably hadn't fed in well over a year and were pretty sluggish. Either that, or they'd just been that way in life: staring slack-jawed as it passed them by.

That wasn't the case, however, with the group before the clinic.

There must have been 20 of them, massed solidly before the locked doors. As we drove towards them, I saw their clothes, once prim and starched, now stained will all those fluids they'd long ago feared or detested. One still held up a sign (I realized a few seconds later he had taped it to his wrist as he died) which read OPERATION SOULSAVE—SAVE A SOUL FOR CHRIST! Several sported the obligatory ABORTION IS MURDER T-shirts, now tattered and discolored.

Their leader was the Priest. I remembered him from before, when he'd been on all the news programs, spouting his vicious rhetoric while his flock chanted behind him. Of course, he looked different now: somebody had snacked on his trapezius, so his Roman Collar was covered in dried gore and hung askew, and his head (he was also missing a considerable patch of scalp on that same side) canted strangely at an odd angle.

I saw Dale eyeing them and muttering something under his breath. I asked him what it was so I could write it down: "Yet man is born unto trouble, as the sparks fly upward." He said it was from the Bible. I was surprised; I didn't know Dale read the Bible.

Tom responded with a quote from one of the more contemporary prophets: "I used to be disgusted, now I try to be amused." Then he asked Dale what we were going to do. Dale, who was practiced in this, said he'd drive around the building once, which would draw most of them away from the front long enough for us to get in. They wouldn't bother the jeep when we weren't in it.

Dale headed for the next corner. Tom pulled the .38 and held it, and I remembered.

I was thinking about the time I had to go to a different clinic with my friend Julie. It was before I started you, diary; in fact, I started you about the time Julie disappeared with most of the rest of the world. So I've never written any of this down before.

Julie had gotten pregnant from her boyfriend Sean, who split when she told him. Abortions were legal then (this was a long time ago), but could be costly, and Julie, who was still going to college (as I was), had no money. She went to her parents, but they threw her out of the house. She thought about having the baby and putting it up for adoption, but she had no health insurance, wouldn't be able to afford the actual birth, and regarded overpopulation as the end of the world. This, obviously, was before the deadheads arrived and clarified that issue.

So I'd lent her the money and agreed to go with her to the clinic. She made the appointment, worried about it so much she didn't sleep the night before, almost backed out twice on the drive there...and all so she could be confronted by the fine Christian citizens of Operation SoulSave.

They had seated themselves on either side of the walkway leading into the clinic. Even though it was in another state and time, they wore the same T-shirts and held the same signs. They were mainly male, or women in clothes so tight they seemed life-threatening. They all had vacuous smiles that gave way to cruel snarls of contempt whenever anyone went into or out of the clinic doors.

Julie took one look at them and didn't want to leave the car. I told her we'd be late, and she said it didn't matter.

We'd talked about the morality of abortion already, and had agreed that it was obvious that the unformed, early fetus was only an extension of the mother's body, and as such each woman had the right to make her own decision. I reminded Julie of this as she sat shivering in the car, and she'd said that wasn't why she didn't want to go past them.

She was afraid of them. She said they seemed like a mindless horde, capable of any violence they were directed to commit.

She'd had no idea how right she was.

We drove slowly around one corner. Sure enough, they stumbled after us. Then Dale threw it into fourth, and we screeched the rest of the way around the block.

When we got back to the main entrance, there were only five or six still there, not including one that dragged itself around on two partially-eaten legs. Tom handed me the Uzi, while he took the .38 and cradled the box. Dale opted for a machete (I didn't want to have to see him use it minutes before he operated on ME).

We sprinted from car to door. Tom shot two right between the eyes. I raised the Uzi, forgetting its rapid-fire design, and ripped one of them completely apart. I felt my stomach turn over as I saw some stale gray stuff splatter the doors. Dale just kept running, shouldering the last two aside. One rebounded and grabbed his left arm; he whirled and brought the machete down, severing the thing's hand, then kicking the deadhead away. He pried its hand from his arm, threw it aside, and told us to cover him while he unlocked the door.

As he fiddled with the keys, Tom shot the two Dale had barreled through.

The .38 jammed. He began to fieldstrip it. I looked nervously down the street, where the ones we'd tricked were shambling back, led by the gruesome Priest. Suddenly I felt something on my ankle. I looked down to see the legless one had dragged itself up the steps and was bringing its gaping maw to bear on my lower calf. I freaked out and grabbed the Walther from Dale's holster; I think I was screaming as I fired into the zombie's peeling head. It died and let go, thick brown liquid draining onto its SAVE A SOUL—CLOSE A CLINIC t-shirt.

Then Dale had the doors open, and we were in.

Later, Tom told me he had to pry the pistol from my fingers while Dale started up the generator and got things ready.

Then before I knew it Dale was there, in gloves and mask, saying he was ready.

❂ ❂ ❂

I don't remember much of the actual operation, except that I asked Tom to wait outside... and the sound. The horrible sound the whole time we were in there:

Them, pounding on the doors, slow heavy thuds, relentless, unmerciful.

∞

Dale was, as I've said before, an excellent doctor, and it was over soon. He made sure I didn't see what he put into the tiny wooden box Tom had carried in, and I didn't ask. The box, which had been beautifully crafted by Rudy V., would be taken back to the Colony and buried there.

There was one thing I had to ask, though, as morbid a thought as it was. I had to know if—I had to be sure Dale had—God, I can't even write it.

But he knew what I was asking, and as he stripped off the gloves, he told me I didn't have to worry. None of the ones aborted had ever come back. The rest of us had to be cremated or have the brain destroyed upon death, or we'd resurrect.

How ironic, I thought, that this was how we would finally lay to rest the Great Debate. They weren't human enough to come back. Abortion isn't murder.

❂ ❂ ❂

Getting out would be harder than getting in, but Dale had it all down. Tom would crawl out a side window, drawing them away from Dale and I. Dale would lock the front door while Tom and I covered him, then we'd all head for the jeep. I was, of course, still weak, and Tom didn't want to leave my side, but Dale told him it was the safest way, and he'd be sure I was okay. Tom reluctantly agreed.

It went down without fail. They were slow and easily confused, and by the time they saw two of us on the stoop and one by the jeep, they didn't know which way to turn. Tom shot a couple who were in our way. Once Dale had the doors locked, he pocketed the keys, took the Uzi from me, and I carried the little coffin as we ran for the jeep.

Once we were inside, Dale started it up and pulled away. They were already hammering on the sides, clawing the welded cage, drooling yellowish bile. One wouldn't let go as we drove off, and it got dragged fifty feet before its fingers tore off. Tom actually shouted something at it.

Dale was ready to speed out of town when I asked him

to stop the jeep and go back. He hesitated, then both he and Tom turned to stare at me, as openmouthed as any deadhead. They asked why, and I just handed Tom our box, took the rifle, got out and started walking back.

They ran up on either side of me, Tom saying I was still delirious from the operation, Dale arguing I could start hemorrhaging seriously. I ignored them both as I saw the deadheads at the end of the street staggering forward now.

I had to wipe tears out of my eyes—I didn't even know I was crying—as I raised the rifle and sighted on the first one. I fired, and saw it flung backwards to lie unmoving in the street, truly finally dead. Tom and Dale both tried to take the rifle from me, but I shrugged them off and fired again. Tom argued we were done here, and there was no point in wasting ammo on these fuckers, but I told him I had to. Then I told him—told them both—why.

After that they left me alone until all the deadheads were gone but one—the Priest. My arms were shaking so bad I almost couldn't hold the gun steady, but he was close—thirty feet away now—and hard to miss. My first shot blew part of his neck—and whatever was left of the Collar—away, but the last one brought him down.

I dropped the gun, and Tom and Dale had to carry me back to the jeep.

But now I'm at home in bed, and Dale says I'm physically okay. I miss the child I'll never know, a pain which far outweighs the physical discomfort, but Jessie is here, and she hugs me a long time before Tom sends her to bed.

Now I'm smiling as I think of that street and write this. Because I know that none of the women who come after me will have to endure more than the horror of giving up part of themselves.

THE PSYCH WARD

Love Eats

This is what happened to me after Love came into my life. I'm taking the time to write this down because I know what I've done will cause people to talk, and some of the talk will say he was behind it all, but I want everyone to understand this:

Love is not evil.

❍ ❍ ❍

He arrived about two months ago. I was just getting home from another day of work. Another dull, pointless nine hours of keeping the books for the Malcomson Auto Parts Company. Another congested drive home, to park three blocks away. Another walk past 11-year-olds in sports team caps who yelled words at me they shouldn't have known yet. There was more new graffiti on my apartment building: "ELF" had been covered by something completely unreadable. I climbed the stairs and passed the manager, who was swabbing down the steps with ammonia. He cursed at me for stepping in his work. I apologized and went to my door.

I turned on the TV; it was always the first thing I did when I came in. Say what you want about television, how it's a bad influence, warps young brains, whatever...all I knew was I felt less alone—or, maybe, noticed the loneliness less with it on.

I set down my purse and jacket and was about to take off my shoes when I saw him at my window. Scrawny and scarred, his hair dirty and matted, with patches of pinkly-diseased skin showing through. A big gray cat, sitting there outside the kitchen window. At first I wondered how he had gotten there, two floors up, then I remembered the window-box I'd abandoned once I'd realize the window faced onto an alley that got about fifteen minutes of sun a day. Right below my window was a garbage bin; he must've jumped up from that.

I looked at him, wondering, waiting for him to run away. He didn't. Instead he just looked in at me with mild curiosity and a touch of longing. I approached carefully. When I unlatched the window and slid it up, he opened his mouth and uttered a surprisingly small, even delicate noise.

I'd never been much of a cat lover, but something in that scratchy little voice just melted me. He must've known the effect it would have, because then he actually dared to step over the sill of the screen-less window. He made his way gingerly across the drainboard to where I stood frozen in—what? Disbelief? Fear? Hope? Then the impossible happened: he put his head against me and started purring.

Me. He was purring for *me*. He could've gone to any window in the building, on the block...and he'd come here to me. Tears welled up. I moved my hands slowly to his rough coat, and when I stroked him he fell into me, the purr louder than ever. I lowered my head to his, and I think I gasped out something like, "Oh, aren't you a love?"

We stayed that way for what seemed like a small eternity, sharing an intimacy that not even two human beings could know. Finally he moved off and meowed pitifully. I looked at his ribs, plainly visible beneath his motley coat, and realized he must be starving. I opened a can of tuna; he gobbled half of it down, then settled back to clean his paws. I sat near him, considering.

There was no longer any question of previous ownership. Whoever he'd belonged to before had obviously abandoned him, and anyway he'd chosen me. I'd never had a pet before because the manager didn't allow them, but as long as my new companion went in and out the window, I didn't think anyone would even know he was there. I'd get him a bed, a litterbox, his own dishes, medicine, toys...

Now all he needed was a name. I thought about the first thing I'd said to him and realized he'd practically chosen his own.

"Do you like your name, Love?"

He stopped licking his paws, came over to me, clambered up into my lap and promptly fell asleep.

I took that as a "yes."

❍ ❍ ❍

I called in sick to work the next day—first time in two years—and took Love to the vet. They gave him distemper and leukemia boosters, antibiotics and a flea dip, Tresaderm for ear mites and strict instructions to feed him more.

I took Love home, then went to the pet store and spent the rest of a month's pay on food, bowls, litterbox, litter, toys, collar, brush, scratching post. I didn't buy him a bed, though, because last night he'd slept with me, curled into my side.

I called in sick the following day, too, so I could make sure he was happy. He didn't even play with the expensive toys, just stayed glued to my side. If I didn't pick him up every once in a while he meowed anxiously. I got out my phone and took pictures of him. I didn't have anyone to show them to, but I wanted them for myself, to look at anywhere he wasn't with me.

I wanted to remind myself everywhere that I had Love.

❍ ❍ ❍

The next week was a period of adjustment for us both. Love grew healthier, his skin healed, hair turned thick and glossy, eyes bright. And I—well, I had to get used to the idea of a reason to go home at the end of the day, or get up in the beginning.

Love was funny, too. Sometimes he'd launch mock attacks on me, playfully digging a claw into my arm while his back legs wiggled frantically. Sometimes Love broke the skin, but I know he didn't mean to. It still made me laugh.

I tried to read websites about cat care, but soon gave up. None of it applied to us at all. Love wasn't aloof, or cool, or independent. Love didn't vanish for nights at a time only to return with a fresh kill. No, Love was affectionate and warm and loving. I couldn't imagine a better partner.

There was only one thing wrong:

Love was finicky.

Oh, not so much at first. True, he never finished a whole can in one sitting, but he at least made a good effort. I found some he liked better than others: Beef and Liver Nuggets in Country Gravy, and Veal and Kidney Feast (Sliced) especially. But after a few feedings even those were left uneaten. I'd put the food down for him when I left in the morning, and come back ten hours later to find cockroaches nibbling away at a full bowl. I only saw him eat one roach; after that he just played with them.

The net effect was that while his silver coat and outward appearance grew sleek and vital, you could still count every rib at a distance. Picking him up was like hefting meatless bones in a silken bag. I tried making him special things to eat; I nearly gagged on the smell of raw and cooked chicken liver for three whole days. But, just as with the cat food, he always tired of it sooner or later.

Once I went to the pet store and bought several live mice, but Love was particularly surprising here: He showed no interest in the mice whatsoever. After three days I let them go in the alley. How could I have expected Love to kill? Even to eat. It just wasn't in his sweet nature.

Love was wasting away, and I was powerless to stop it.

❂ ❂ ❂

I lost track of things.

Anything not directly concerned with Love or getting him to eat just ceased to be of importance to me. I went to work because I had to make money for his food, but everything else—household chores, shopping, paying bills, TV—fell by the wayside.

I must have missed the first of the month because one day I answered a pounding on my door only to find the manager standing there, his flabby face red and swollen from alcohol. He was demanding the rent check, now three days late. I tried to tell him to wait, I'd go write it and be back, tried to tell him to just wait in the hall, but he ignored me.

He pushed his way in. I tried to remember if Love was in or out. I hoped the manager was too drunk to notice in either case. He wasn't. While I went for my checkbook, he picked up the framed photo sitting on top of the TV It was Love, of course. He was about to ask whose cat it was when Love himself made the fatal mistake. He walked into the room, meowed loudly and wrapped himself around my ankles.

The manager stared down, his sweaty brow furrowing, and demanded with his typical intellectual aplomb, "What the hell is that?!"

To my response, he screeched, "I can see it's a goddamn cat! What I wanna know is what the fuck it's doing in here?!"

Love retreated from the harsh words. With one meaty hand, the manager slapped the door shut to cut off any escape. Before I could even try to offer the lame, "he came in through the bathroom window" story, he took in all the damning evidence: The photos, the litterbox, the food bowls, the toys.

"You keepin' a goddamn cat in here? HUH?!"

Love hissed at him.

He turned to the corner where Love crouched, back up, mouth open, pupils dilated, and he made an abrupt grab.

Love hissed again, drove a nail into his skin deep enough to leave a bloody furrow, then bolted. The manager bellowed like a stuck pig and stumbled after Love, who cowered now behind a chair.

I unthinkingly threw myself in his path, pleading. He didn't even hear me, just shouted, "That little fucker is *going*."

He pushed me aside and lashed out at Love with one work-booted foot. Love yelped in pain and dodged around him.

I didn't see what happened next, because I was walking blindly into the kitchen. I say "blindly" because it really was as if I couldn't see, or wasn't even there. Someone else had taken control of me, my body, someone stronger than I, cooler and more confident. Someone who knew Love was worth fighting for.

My biggest butcher's knife was in my hand. In the living room the manager had boxed Love into a corner between the couch and the wall. He picked up a pillow and was leaning down with it while Love spat and battled. He had one arm pulled back, the hand in a lethal fist.

He was moving so slow...or maybe we were in a movie, one of those scary ones where slow motion means violence. It was easy to stab him. With my full weight behind the knife I buried it in his fat side up to the hilt. He froze, gasping as he saw the blood flood out across his dirty white t-shirt. He started to reach for the hilt, but I was still moving faster. I grabbed it and twisted, then yanked it out at a different angle than it had gone in. He took one step towards me, overbalanced and went down.

Suddenly I was fully aware that I was standing over a man I had just killed, with a dripping knife still in my hand. He'd fallen face down and there was clearly a hole in his right side. Blood and pieces of pinkish-white stuff were spreading out from the wound.

I waited to feel something—revulsion, horror—but instead I was calm, serene even. For one thing I realized

I'd wanted to do this for a long time. The fat bastard had always disgusted me, with his sweat stains and tattoos. I would never again have to listen to his wheezing voice asking for the rent check on the first of the month.

Then a funny thing happened.

Love crawled out of his corner and approached the corpse carefully. He sniffed at the oily hair, then walked around to the glistening side. He put his nose to the blood, and his tail twitched. He padded up to the wound, investigated it cautiously, then stuck his nose down into the ragged cleft itself. He reached a paw up and used it to pull the wound wider while blood gushed fresh around him. His face disappeared completely for a second, re-emerging with something wet and dark clenched in his teeth. I guess it was the liver. He pulled back, bracing all four feet against the dead man's side until the meat finally gave way with a ripping, sucking noise and a noxious smell. I might have felt my stomach turn over, but I couldn't take my eyes off Love.

He was eating.

He was eating with great relish, shaking the meat as he gulped it down. When he was done he reached in for the next piece.

Now I knew what would satisfy Love.

I waited until he was done. He went to his favorite spot in the living room and began to clean his paws and whiskers. He even burped.

I went into the kitchen. When I came back I had plastic trash bags, knives and Tupperware containers.

I got to work.

❂ ❂ ❂

Love ate well for the next two days. On the third day I tried cooking the meat, and he ate half of it.

Getting rid of the leftovers had posed a slight problem, but in the end it was really no harder than taking the trash out. Two plastic bags and an early morning drive across town to a distant trash bin took care of it. The stain in the carpet was harder, but it was an old rug, dark brown anyway, so the blood didn't even show. I laughed about all the times I'd asked him to give me new carpeting and he'd turned me down.

It became clear to me now that Love had special needs, needs I would gladly fulfill. The first thing was shopping. I ran my credit card to the limit buying knives, cleavers; even the gun was an easy buy, a little snub-nosed .38 that fit neatly in my purse.

I began driving around late at night, investigating the possibilities. I found places under freeways where you could always spot one or two homeless asleep. They looked like easy prey. As long as the meat was still good.

The first one, of course, was the worst. Carrying a plastic trash bag, two knives and the gun, I walked up to where he slept under an overpass. Even though it was 2:30 in the morning—a Saturday morning, so I could sleep in—there was enough traffic overhead to cover any sound. One shot, and then I was kneeling over him, cutting away the clothes. I reminded myself to buy some face masks; the smell was so bad I had to walk away once for a breath of healthy carbon-monoxide-laden air. After the clothes were off, I cut quickly into the right side, just below the rib cage. I'd bought a copy of *Gray's Anatomy* because Love obviously preferred some parts to others. I held my breath and cut away what I hoped were the liver and kidney, shoveling the grub into the plastic bag. Blood spilled out, sure, but I'd bought new sneakers and was careful not to kneel, just squat.

The whole thing took seven or eight minutes. It was quarter to three. Nobody'd seen me. Nobody would care. Nothing mattered except whether to cook it or leave it raw. Whatever he wanted. Because only one thing held real meaning:

Love eats.

❂ ❂ ❂

And eat he did, very well. Three days later, when that first one was used up, I went out and got another one. And another after that...and another...

It got easier every time, even though the news people reported that police were "conducting a massive manhunt for the gruesome killer." There's no shortage of them these days, the ones who sleep where they can, the ones who're too unlucky or drunk or stoned or burned out to care. By the time I'd hit number five, I could cut out the pieces Love wanted in three minutes.

It should have been possible to feed Love forever...except something unexpected happened.

Love stopped eating.

Oh, not all at once. It was gradual. He just ate a little less each time. I tried different parts. One night I rolled a supplier over onto his stomach and took some butt and leg, but it made no difference. I tried cooking it, filleting, roasting, baking, boiling, frying, grilling, microwaving, even liquefying. He would just sniff the new contents of his dish and walk away. He began to grow thinner, he slept more and looked like he could barely move when awake.

One night I was driving back from disposing of leftovers. As I pulled up, I saw a boy busily tagging my building with his graffiti. I recognized him as one of the local kids who liked to taunt me sometimes, wolf-whistling or yelling obscenities. I got an idea, and I walked up to him. He saw me coming, stopped painting, smiled and asked if I wanted a taste of "big dick." I put a gun to his head and said, no, but I knew somebody who might. His smile disappeared instantly. I ordered him into the building.

Just outside my door he tried to tell me I was making a big mistake, that I was a stupid bitch. But by the time I had him in the bathroom and told him to turn the shower on full, he was sobbing. I shot him twice in the chest. The second bullet went right through him and shattered the mirror over the sink. I didn't use it that much now anyway.

I turned the shower off, then bent over him. I didn't

waste any time; I was hoping Love would eat if the meat were *really* fresh. I bent down and tore the cheap black t-shirt away with my bare hands. The two shots had made large holes in him, but I put my fingers in and pulled them wider. He groaned, not quite dead yet. I ignored it and walked out, picked up Love and took him to his dinner. I set him right down on top.

He just curled up in the warm blood and went to sleep.

I started to cry. Love was dying, and there was nothing I could do. I picked him up, got a wet towel and cleaned him off. I set him down again, hoping against hope he'd go back into the bathroom and eat. Instead he curled around my ankles, rubbing and looking up at me, imploring.

That was when I got it.

Of course.

That was why he'd come to me in the first place.

I laughed, the tears forgotten, and got my tools ready.

☻ ☻ ☻

I know some who read this will think I was insane, that I went too far, that I sacrificed too much for Love...

But haven't we all?

If I look at all our books and movies and songs, I should be acclaimed a great romantic hero. I gave myself completely over to Love...

Because it was me he wanted all along.

It wasn't his favorite part, but he ate almost the entire right leg anyway. The tourniquet stopped most of the blood, but I'm still feeling light-headed and know I have to hurry now. I've opened the windows so he can leave when he's done. I don't want Love to die with me.

It's time now. The knife is ready, and Love is ready. I hope I live long enough, after I make the slit, to feel him inside me. To know his satisfaction. To experience the final exquisite pain of Love.

To know that I will go on in Love.

The New War

Pain became panic and drowning, clawing up for air, eyes opening to numbers and dates that swam, half-shadowed faces barely remembered, thoughts and images clashing, then finally coalescing, melting away until one sensation remained: pressure.

Mike tried to inflate his lungs for one more breath, a simple act that took all of his focus. He closed his eyes, forced the air out, in, out...

When he could open his eyes, he saw it there, crouched on his rib cage, as he'd known it would be: The black, shapeless thing. It came every night with Maria, the Filipino nurse who took care of him from ten p.m. to six a.m.

Mike sucked in breath, struggled to dislodge the thing, but he was weak, so god damn weak...

"Mr. Carson, what's the matter?" Maria stood at the foot of the bed, gazing down at him with concern that he knew was feigned. She was trying to kill him.

"Go away," he said, his voice a hoarse croak he barely recognized.

A patronizing smile creased Maria's broad face, and she bent down to busy herself with tucking in his sheets. "I think maybe you just have a bad dream."

Mike hated her. He hated her fake care and her efficient bustling about that never really accomplished anything. Yes, his sheets were clean and his pain managed, but he was still here, two weeks after hip surgery, in a third-rate nursing home that was the best his veteran's benefits had been able to cover. He shared his room with a silent, immobile shell of flesh whose breathing apparatus pumped and hissed, the halls echoed with cries and electronic tones, the whole place stank of disinfectant barely covering...what? The odor of age? Of death?

Mike finally identified it: The stench of rot.

"I'm living a bad dream." He peered at what squatted on him; it was a black hole in the dimly-lit room, but somehow he could see Maria through it. It wasn't substantial, but it had weight; it did nothing, but he could feel it trying to suck life from him. "Take your pet and go away."

"Now, Mr. Carson, you know they don't let pets in here." She checked the railings that enclosed his bed, and then asked, "Do you need to use the bathroom?"

"No. I'm fine. Just go away."

She shrugged and left.

Mike had lied—he *did* need to urinate—but he'd rather use the bedpan than feel her hands on him, stripping the last of his dignity as he was led to a shared toilet.

The black vanished, and he gasped in air. Despite the disinfectant, it was cool and good and restored him.

You won't get me so easy. Not like the others.

Because in the two weeks that he'd been here, five patients had died.

♦ ♦ ♦

"Dad, that's not right."

His daughter Angela sat by the side of the bed, squeezed into a folding chair in the tight space between the rails and the wall. Angela seemed to flicker in and out, like a movie shown by a failing projector. If Mike looked away for a second, she vanished, only to return when he heard her voice.

"Dad...?"

"I heard you. What's not right?"

"That you've been here two weeks. Your hip replacement was four months ago."

Mike gaped at her for a moment before shaking his head. "That's ridiculous. I've only been here...well, maybe it's been sixteen, eighteen days, but..."

"No. Your surgery was on April 16th. They moved you here from the hospital a week later. It's August 22nd now." Angela picked up the newspaper she'd brought him and held the front page before his eyes. "See?"

Mike squinted at the date: *August 22.* "Four months...? But I...why am I still here?"

His daughter answered slowly, cautiously, "Dad...I think...you're a little confused..."

Remembering the black thing that had perched on his chest, Mike cut her off. "You have to get me out of here—that nurse, the one at night...she's killing people."

Angela sighed. "You mean Maria? She's a nice lady and a hard worker. I get tired just watching her. She's not killing people."

After that, Angela stayed for hours (or maybe minutes), chatting about her job and her husband and how her own back was hurting and the doctors said she had osteoporosis, but Mike didn't really listen. His mind was on other things.

Like the battle he knew now that he'd have to wage alone.

�☉ ☉ ☉

Maria came that night without the black.

"How are you, Mr. Carson?" He leaned forward as she fluffed his pillow. Her face shifted, and for a second he saw his own mother. But he remembered: *Mom's gone. And this one...*

"Where's your little friend?"

"You mean Manny? He's a few rooms down, I think, helping Mr. Darakjian to the toilet."

Mike gripped the railings and cursed his failing strength. *Why am I so god damn weak? I shouldn't be like this.*

"Did you know I fought in World War Two?"

Maria smiled. "I did know that. You told me before.

You even got a Purple Heart. You're a hero."

He didn't remember telling her anything. Could she somehow read his thoughts? Did the black thing get into his mind? "I took shrapnel in the back from a Jap grenade. But I survived that. I'm still in pretty good shape for sixty."

The nurse leaned forward, whispering. "I think you are a little older than that, Mr. Carson."

Mike raised a hand to wave away her comment, but he froze: The arm before him wasn't his. This arm had skin that was brittle like something cooked in a skillet; the skin was mottled, tiny white blotches interspersed with purpling bruises and lighter flesh.

This can't be my arm.

"I tell you what, Mr. Carson: I'm gonna leave a note for Dr. Singh to check your medication tomorrow—you're having a little more trouble than usual."

As Mike watched, the blackness appeared, hovering over her head, descending until he saw her features through a dark curtain, transforming her face into a distorted mask. "Did you know I was stationed in the Philippines?"

There was no answer.

❂ ❂ ❂

Mr. Darakjian was missing at breakfast.

"Where's Aram?" Mike hadn't especially liked the small, fastidious retired jeweler, but he appreciated the man's calm, quiet manner.

Carmen, the young nurse's aide who couldn't have been more than twenty, cleared Mike's half-eaten food away. "Oh, I'm afraid Mr. Darakjian had some kind of seizure last night and they had to take him to the hospital."

Mike almost told the girl that he didn't believe her, but then he wondered if she'd been lied to as well, if she really bought that Aram had simply suffered some sort of "seizure."

The day was pleasant and warm, and after breakfast Carmen steered Mike's wheelchair out to the nursing home's central courtyard, where a few other residents were already parked. Mike didn't speak to any of them; he thought most of them were either delirious or didn't understand English. Whether they actually appreciated the sun's warmth or were put there so someone else could imagine they did, he couldn't say. His life now was about waiting: Waiting for meals, waiting to heal, waiting for nurses or doctors or Angela, his only visitor. Waiting for the pictures in his head to stop swimming and makes sense. Waiting to die.

He looked in through the glass doors, watching the endless stream of people that flowed through the corridors of the nursing home. Nurses in scrubs with printed cartoon characters, doctors in white coats, visitors with magazines or candy...

A man in combat fatigues.

Mike sat up in the wheelchair, feeling his heart beat faster. That man had looked familiar, like—

Sgt. Dennis Strahan. His friend from the Pacific, who'd yanked Mike out of the way of a Japanese sniper. Dennis Strahan, who he'd lost touch with after the war had ended, who he hadn't heard from since 1946...

How could he be here?

Mike grabbed the wheels of his chair and tried to roll himself forward, but he was immobile. Brakes—Carmen had locked the brakes, hadn't she? Mike leaned over the side of the chair to reach down for the rubber handles that stopped the tires from rolling, but the action sent a bolt of agony arcing out of his hip and he gasped, falling back.

God damn it! He had to get to Denny before he left; Denny could help, would understand—

"Whoa, Mr. Carson, hold on—what are you doing?" Carmen rushed up to him.

"I saw...someone I know. Got to...reach him."

"Okay, but hang on." Carmen pushed back on the brakes, got behind the chair and rolled Mike into the building. "Which way?"

Except for an elderly woman dozing in a wheelchair and two doctors, the corridor was empty.

Mike felt the disappointment like a physical blow. "He's gone."

"Well," Carmen said, leaning down over him to catch his eye, "maybe he'll be back. But next time just call me, Mr. Carson, okay? Don't try to roll this by yourself; you're still not strong enough."

Mike didn't argue with her; he knew it was true. He wasn't strong enough, and he wouldn't be as long as the black thing sucked the life from him.

☯ ☯ ☯

"Another one died this week."

Angela looked down from the television, currently tuned to an insipid sitcom. "Oh, I'm sorry, Pop. Did you know them?"

He shrugged. "Not well, but...that's six that have died in the three weeks since I've been here."

Angela sighed and used the wired remote to turn down the sound. "Dad, you've been here for five months."

"I know you keep saying that, but..."

"But what?"

But it's not true, and the black thing's already gotten to you, my only daughter.

On the television, the sitcom's lead character laughed and pointed as a woman walked past him. The woman was Mike's first grade teacher.

☯ ☯ ☯

"Where were you born, Maria?"

The nurse had removed the bedpan and was cleaning Mike off; he'd long ago steeled himself against humiliation, even if his attempt hadn't been entirely successful.

"A little town outside Manila; you wouldn't know it."

"You don't look like all the other Filipinos here." It was

true; virtually the entire caregiving staff was Filipino, but only Maria had more exotic eyes and a different skin tone.

"My grandmother was Japanese. She came to the Philippines after the war."

Mike's gut clenched with certainty. He'd fought them before.

Maria finished, and Mike felt a small stab of pain as she repositioned him. She saw his wince. "Oh, I'm sorry, Mr. Carson, but you don't get another pain pill until four."

"I don't want it." He was tired of being medicated. He thought it made him more susceptible to the black.

The nurse shrugged and shuffled from the room.

Mike saw movement in the corner, a shadow darker than what was usually there. It oozed around the ceiling and down the wall, out of his sight behind the curtain, and he knew it had settled on the comatose man in the next bed.

The man would be dead in the morning.

✪ ✪ ✪

A day later he saw Dennis Strahan again. This time he was accompanied by a wiry kid with pale skin and red hair; it took Mike a few minutes to recall the kid's name.

It'd been Robert, but they'd all called him Irish. He was their communications officer.

He'd been killed when a Japanese Zero had strafed their camp.

Or had he? Mike tried to riffle through his memories, but they spun away from him like cards flung from a deck. Had he really seen Irish dead? Was he thinking of some other soldier? Had Irish really been their radio man?

"Mr. Carson, are you okay?" Carmen stood over him, her youthful features creased.

"Carmen, can you take me to the front desk? I have to talk to whoever's in charge of Admissions. Or maybe visitors. Right, probably visitors."

Carmen looked puzzled, but wheeled him to the nursing

home's lobby. Alisha, who ran the front office, was gone, but Mike went through the visitors' guest book for the last week. There was no entry for either Dennis Strahan or Robert "Irish" O'Connor.

"I'm sorry, Mr. Carson," Carmen said as she pushed Mike back to his room.

But Mike suspected she wasn't sorry; he thought she probably knew that the logs were a cheat, a forgery. Of course they wouldn't have Denny and Irish sign in with everyone else.

When they arrived at the room and Mike saw the two empty beds, he asked Carmen what happened to his room-mate. "Oh, Mr. Lee—he died this morning. You get the room to yourself for a while, I guess."

Right...just me and some black nightmare waiting for me to go next.

It was time to map out his strategy.

♦ ♦ ♦

Mike stared into the tiny paper cup Maria had handed to him. "What's the white capsule?"

"It's something new Dr. Singh prescribed for you."

"Yeah, but what is it? I'm not taking it unless I know what it is."

For an instant, Mike saw real anger replace Maria's usual placid smile, then it vanished...but the black thing was present, creeping up over her shoulder and perching there as if it, too, were staring at him. "It will help with your confusion, Mr. Carson."

"I'm not confused."

Maria set the cup down and put her hands on her substantial hips while the edges of the black throbbed with anticipation. "Okay, then: What year is this?"

"It's..." Mike's mouth hung open, and he realized he really wasn't sure. Denny Strahan had still looked young, and hadn't they just gotten Angela her first tricycle, the blue metal one with the ribbon tassels on the handlebars?

"...it's 1952."

"Trust me, Mr. Carson, you are confused. It's 2013."

"But that's..." Again, he stopped in mid-sentence, considering. The elderly woman who'd visited a few days ago... that had been Angela, his daughter. *Elderly*. If Angela was in her sixties, then...he shook his head. "No. I don't care what year it is. I won't take that pill." Mike glanced up and saw the dark void opening and closing like a hungry mouth. "You're just trying to kill me off faster. You and that *thing*. Did you bring it over with you from the Philippines, whatever it is?"

Maria started to reply, but clapped her mouth shut. After a few seconds she picked up the paper cup of pills. "So you won't take this?"

"No. Not until I talk to Dr. Singh."

"Okay."

She pushed her cart full of medication out of the room without further comment.

When she was gone, Mike pulled out the knife he'd held beneath the sheet. He'd stolen it at dinner; it was dull, really more of a butter knife than a weapon, but it was the best he could manage right now. He knew better than to try and use it alone; his plan depended on Denny and Irish helping. They'd all fought and won a bigger war than this one. Mike knew they'd help him; they had to fight the black thing before it killed anyone else.

Before it killed Mike.

❂ ❂ ❂

At 7 a.m., before breakfast, Mike saw Denny and Irish pass in the hall outside.

"Denny," he called. He cleared his throat and shouted. "Denny! Denny, it's Mike Carson! In here!"

He shouted until the big male nurse, Manny, came blundering into the room. "Whoa, hey, man, what's the problem?"

"I saw my friends out in the hall just now—Denny and Irish."

Manny leaned back and made a show of looking both directions. "It's only seven, dude, the place is empty. Really, there's nobody in the halls."

Mike looked up at the nurse, who couldn't have been older than twenty-four, whose hair was buzz-cut and arms were covered with tattoos, and he felt a surge of envy. "You don't know, do you?"

"Know what?"

"What's coming. The black. One day you'll find yourself in a place like this, and you'll understand."

The nurse gestured at Mike impatiently. "Yeah, whatever. Look, dude, you gotta keep it down, okay? Or they'll put you on stronger meds, and you'll never get better. Know what I'm sayin? '"

Mike knew he'd never get better anyway, but he nodded and promised to be quiet. Besides...why hadn't they stopped, Denny and Irish? There was no way they couldn't have heard him. Unless...

No. The alternative was unthinkable. The alternative led to the black thing that wound itself around him at night.

No.

❂ ❂ ❂

"It's something to help with your delirium, Mr. Carson."

Dr. Singh was a stout little man with yellow teeth and permanent, lavender-hued pouches beneath his eyes. He gestured at the white capsule in Mike's hand.

"I'm not delirious."

"What year is it?"

Mike slammed the pill down on his bedside tray. "God damn it, why are you people always asking me that?"

Dr. Singh was unfazed by Mike's outburst. "Can you answer the question? Or how about this one: How old are you?"

"I'm...I'm..." Mike stopped in frustration as he realized

it was true—he couldn't answer. The numbers danced just out of reach—*twenty-seven...forty-three...fifty-two...* "Ask my friends Denny and Irish. They're here somewhere. They'll know."

"Who are Denny and Irish?"

"My squad-mates. Did you know I was in the War, Doctor?"

Singh nodded, tiredly. "Yes, sir, and I salute you for that. But Mr. Carson, please trust me when I say that you are suffering from delirium that was probably a result of the anesthetic used during your hip surgery. And that—" he pointed at the white pill "—will help you. You want to know how old you are, don't you?"

"What I want to know is how to kill that thing, the black thing that comes with that nurse...Maria. They're connected somehow."

"Maria's a very good nurse, sir. And I think if you take that—" Singh thrust a jaw at the pill "- things will make sense."

Mike picked up the pill and studied it. Dr. Singh handed him a cup of water. "That's the right decision."

Impulsively, Mike threw the pill into his mouth, grabbed the cup and swallowed. The pill was large and hurt going down.

"Good man, Mr. Carson. I'll check in tomorrow and see how you're doing."

The doctor left. Mike glanced at the wall clock mounted next to the television—was that three-ten or two-fifteen? The light coming into the room from outside told him it was still daytime, so he had a few hours before Maria came on duty. If he could just find Denny and Irish...

They stood over his bed.

Mike nearly wept in relief. "You're here! Boy, am I glad to see you guys."

Denny and Irish said nothing. They stood, unmoving, smiling.

A part of Mike's mind screamed out from beneath the

layers of shifting fog covering it: *They're not really here.* But Mike pushed that small, rational voice down as he reached beneath the mattress and found the warm stainless steel.

"Tonight, fellas. I need your help."

Denny and Irish looked at the knife. And nodded.

◐ ◐ ◐

It was just after ten-thirty when Maria came into his room. "How's my favorite soldier?"

At first Mike thought she meant Denny or Irish; then he realized she hadn't even noticed them standing just behind the curtain that separated the beds.

"I'm better," Mike answered.

Maria grinned. "Oh, that's very good to hear." She turned away to check his chart.

Mike fingered the knife he held under his gown. He had it figured out: The black was connected to Maria, so if she was gone...He looked to Denny and Irish, who he could just see behind the sheet. Their hollow eyes had fixed on Maria. Mike gripped the knife, his grip slick on its metal. If he could just drive it into Maria's belly...he wasn't sure if it would kill her or not, but it was his best shot. His only shot.

Maria walked toward the head of the bed.

Mike moved the knife beneath the sheet, ready.

He looked to Denny and Irish—

They vanished.

Mike stared, and then the whirling blocks in his mind tumbled down into place. They fell in neat piles, forming solid thoughts, walls of memories, monuments of awareness. He dimly heard something clatter to the floor. "I'm ninety-two," he rasped out.

Maria looked up, her eyes wide. "Oh, that's *very* good, Mr. Carson. Dr. Singh will be so pleased to hear that." She looked down at the floor, bent over, and came up with the knife. "How did that get there?"

"How long have I been here?"

The nurse forgot the knife, dropping it into a pocket of her scrubs. "It's been five months since your hip surgery."

"Five months..." Mike remembered bits of that time, but it was like grasping at shreds being blown by a gust: Old army friends, teachers from his childhood, tricycles...

The black. Mike looked up and saw it waiting above his bed, near the ceiling.

He knew it now, and it hadn't come with Maria; he'd been wrong to think it had. He could admit that now.

No, the black had already been here, in this place where the aged and infirm came to die. Its appetite was ageless and could never be satisfied, but it never went hungry.

"You can't have me...not yet."

It throbbed with impatience.

Mike smiled at it. Daring it.

Black Mill Cove

It was still dark, forcing Jim to pick his way through the treacherous thistles and spider webs by the narrow beam of his flashlight. He stumbled once, his boot caught in an overgrown rut, and then he found the dirt track that ran along the shoreline. Even though the season had just opened, and this morning was one of the lowest tides of the year, he realized he was completely alone on the path, and he thought, *Maybe Maren was right—maybe this isn't such a good idea.*

He'd left his wife in the warm bunk back in the camper, but he knew she was only pretending to sleep; they'd argued the night before, and now she was giving him the well-honed Maren Silent Treatment. She'd read an article in the paper last week about two divers who had been attacked by a shark while abalone hunting. One man's arm had been ripped off, and he'd bled to death in the boat before they'd made it back to shore.

"It says this happened about twenty minutes from Fort Ross, north of San Francisco," Maren had told him. "It's where we go, Jim."

"Honey, you know I don't dive," he'd tried patiently to remind her.

"You wear a wetsuit."

"You've been with me, Maren. We go at low tide and shore-pick. I've never been in water deep enough for a shark."

"But you always go alone, Jim. It's not safe."

Maren had already decided that she didn't want him

to go, though, and the argument had ended badly. She'd come with him on the winding three-hour drive from San Jose, but he knew she wouldn't make the two-mile hike down to the cove in the pre-dawn chill, and he hadn't asked her to. He just hoped that when he returned to the campground with a full limit of the rare shellfish, when they'd been cleaned and it was her turn, the sweet scent of the delicacy frying in butter would cause her to forget the argument.

It'd happened before. Too many times.

When they'd married, he'd made it clear that he was a hunter. Sure, he had a job, family, friends, other interests, but his life was about that oldest and most sacred of sports. Nothing made him feel so connected, so *pure*, as putting meat on the table, meat he'd taken with his own hands. The hunt was usually difficult, sometimes even tedious, but that always made the final victory that much more satisfying. In fact, Jim could have said that when he was out in the field, in pursuit of his prey, was the only time he really felt alive.

Maren had endured his hunting trips, but she never actually picked up a gun or fishing pole or catch-bag. He supposed it was just the difference between men and women; men were by nature the hunters, women the gatherers. Still, he was constantly left mystified by her desires. Maybe a child...but when he'd suggested that, she'd told him she wasn't ready. He didn't understand what she was ready for. After five years of marriage, he still didn't understand.

He tried to stop thinking about Maren and their failing marriage as he hiked another mile along the thin dirt lane worn between the weeds. The sound of the surf was somewhere off to his left; its softness, without the pounding of an incoming tide, soothed him. The path veered to the right, but Jim spotted the fallen, gray tree limbs that he used as a signpost. He left the trail behind, once again picking his way through nettles and dying grass. He knew from experience that he would walk about two minutes before he came to the cliff, so he moved slower now, swinging the flashlight beam until he spotted the edge.

That was another thing Maren had argued with him about: the difficulty of reaching Black Mill Cove. After a three-hour drive on hairpin curves along the anxiety-inducing Highway 1, the cove was still another forty-minute trek from the campground. It was bounded by steep cliffs on three sides and open sea on the fourth; only one narrow ravine, half hidden by brush, offered a way down that didn't involve actual climbing. Jim liked to hunt alone; what if he got hurt down there, couldn't get back up? He didn't even take his phone since he'd broken one against a rock here two years ago. He'd tried to tell her, of course, that the cove's isolation was what made it ideal; in the three years since he'd found Black Mill Cove, he'd seen only one other hunter working it, and he'd been scuba diving. He knew he could always get his limit of the elusive abalone in the small cove.

By the time he pulled up at the cliff top above the sea, all thoughts of Maren had fled his mind, as he focused on the task before him. First he had to make his way cautiously along the edge until he spotted the patch of shrub that he knew marked the ravine. He stepped carefully around the brush, lowering himself down onto a boulder three feet below it. He was in the ravine now; he knew he'd have to find the rest of the way down by touch alone. He put the flashlight into his belt as he started down.

The ravine was choked with boulders that formed a natural, although steep, stairway down; he made it to the bottom without incident. The pungent smells of salt and exposed seaweeds and the volume of the surf noise, amplified here by the cliff walls, hit him as soon as he left the ravine. Pulling the flashlight out again, he saw the tide pools a few feet ahead of him, black water surrounded by encrusted rocks and gleaming, slippery kelp. He felt the thrill of the hunt gathering in him as he hurriedly lowered the backpack onto a hip-high flat rock, took off his outer hiking boots, checked his catch-bag and iron, and, lastly, turned off his flashlight.

There was just the faintest hint of gray in the sky as he began picking his way over the slimy rocks and slick kelp. He heard tiny scuttlings around his feet, and the occasional sharp *pop* as he stepped on a floater bulb in the exposed seaweed. His eyes were already beginning to sting from the salt spray so he lowered his mask, ignoring the snorkel. He walked until he thought he was about forty feet from shore and could just make out the darker shade of a large pool to his left. Stepping carefully into the water until it was up to his waist, Jim began feeling under the rocks.

His gloved fingers brushed past spiny urchins and sucking anemones; within minutes he was rewarded with the feel of a large shell. The creature was wedged several feet under the water, so to reach it with the iron he'd have to either hold his breath or use the snorkel. He decided to try the former, took a gulp of air, got a good heft on the iron, and ducked beneath the water.

He chipped the abalone's shell getting the iron under it, but finally jammed it beneath and began to pry. The abalone was strong and the position precarious, and his lungs were about to burst before he felt the strong shellfish foot give way. The abalone fell into his waiting hand, and he threw his head up out of the water.

It turned out to be only a medium-sized abalone, but it didn't pass through the gauge and he knew it was a keeper. With a feeling of satisfaction he placed the creature into his catch-bag before continuing the hunt.

The first pool yielded no more treasures, so he clambered to the next. This one was separated from the ocean by only a thin wedge of rock and weed, a large, promising pool. He entered it and began feeling under the outcroppings, keeping one hand on the exposed rock near his head. He didn't flinch when a crab as big as a salad plate sidled across his fingers.

He found nothing under the first rock, so he turned to

the next. This one had a long underwater slope away from him, and the water was up to his chin as he struggled to reach the back. He was working his way left to right when he felt something that was long, thick, with jointed shreds on one end.

It felt, in fact, like a bony human arm.

Jim jerked back as if bitten, his breath catching. He'd felt what he'd sworn were wrist bones, then fingers, with some flesh still attached.

That was ridiculous. A severed arm in a tide pool? It had to be a strange weed, or driftwood branch, trapped there at the last high tide. Or it could be (*shark*)...

He looked around, panicked for a moment, suddenly wishing he'd waited until sunup to come down here. No, he'd wanted to be hunting while the tide was still going out, before it began its mad rush back to land. He'd had to come down here in the pre-dawn salty blackness. Alone.

It was just light enough now so that he could make out his own fingers, if he held them up close before him. He pulled the mask away, squinted painfully until tears welled and washed the brine from his eyes, then forced himself to reach back under the rock.

He found the thing again, got a good grip around it and pulled. After a brief struggle it came free, and he brought up out of the water, held it up before his eyes.

It was, without question, a human arm.

He involuntarily cried out and dropped the thing. It was mostly bones, just a few tatters of skin or tendon still attached. The fingers seemed to be complete, and it ended about where the elbow would have started.

He backed frantically out of the pool, up onto the rocks, his heart pounding, eyes tearing. He tried to scramble back more and fell flat as his feet slid on the kelp. The impact with the crusty rock, the pain as his gloves tore on the sharp facets of limpets and barnacles, jarred him enough to make him stop and consider the situation.

What the hell...how did that get here?!

It had to be Maren's shark, right? He looked around, realizing he was on the ocean side of the tide pool, peering out into barely-seen, gently sluicing waves. Seawood and driftwood bobbed here and there in the surf, sometimes breaking the surface like a head coming up out of the water. Or a fin.

Jim scrabbled backwards on all fours and into the pool again. The *plosh* of his own body hitting the water startled him; with fresh panic he realized the arm was in this pool—wasn't that it brushing against his ankle? He cried out, throwing himself at the nearest rock, hauling himself up over the edge of it, then turning to the shore and crawling towards it.

He slid forward a few feet before he was calm enough to think again. He stopped to catch his breath (*fuck, I'm about to pass out!*), and think.

Okay, obviously I've gotta get back to the camper, wake up Maren, and call the police. Then, he supposed, he'd have to come back here and show the authorities where he'd found the arm. Of course the tide would be in by then, and they'd probably have to send out their own divers.

Jim hoped they had shark protection.

He had a plan, he knew what he had to do. He'd somehow gotten to the far left edge of the cove, and from here the easiest way back to shore would be to simply wade through several large pools.

Several large pools which could hold more pieces.

He couldn't do it. What if the next pool held something worse than an arm, like a head, a half-skeletal head with a terrible grin...

Jim forced himself to think again. By the dreary light he could just barely pick out a path back to where he'd left his backpack—and the flashlight. He told himself to move slowly and cautiously, but he was shaking and it was harder to keep his balance—

His foot slipped and one leg went down into a pool.

Even though it was only up to his ankle, he snatched his foot back up as if it'd been thrust into liquid fire. He found himself peering into the water, then at the rocks around him. Any of those lengths of stripped, whitened wood could have been bone instead, those broken shells bits of nail or teeth...

He tried to stop shaking, but couldn't. Instead, he reached for a large driftwood branch (*too big to be anything human!*), which would serve as a walking stick. Using his newly acquired staff, he thrust into tricky patches of kelp or rock before setting foot there, and so finally came to the bottom of the ravine.

Allowing himself to fall onto the flat rock there, Jim threw the makeshift staff away. He lay there, feeling relieved, feeling safe and alive. After a moment he stopped shaking. He was away from the tide pools and the terrible secrets he'd found there. He only had to climb the ravine, and he'd be safe.

He sat up, quickly opened the backpack long enough to get a towel to wipe his agonized eyes with, and was briefly surprised to see a black patch on the white towel; he was bleeding badly from a cut in his hand. He wrapped the towel around his palm, then pulled on his hiking boots, thrust his arms through the backpack straps, and started up the ravine.

It was light enough overhead now to see the top of the cliff as he clambered up over the rocks. He stopped occasionally to orient himself, then went onto the next rock. He was almost to the top when something blocked the light overhead. He looked up—

—and saw the shadow of a man standing there.

He started to call out, grateful for the presence of another (*living*) human being, but the shout froze in his throat.

The man overhead was carrying something, something big. It was black, and Jim thought it was probably a forty-gallon plastic trash bag, the kind Maren used in the yard at home. Except this bag was stuffed, bulging with something that wasn't grass.

What the hell, is this guy dumping his goddamn trash out here?!

The man hefted the bag, and Jim saw that it was obviously very heavy.

He knew.

Oh my god. Oh Jesus fuck, fucking hell—

The bag was full of body parts.

The man was stepping down into the ravine with it.

Jim wasn't sure if the man knew he was there; he thought he didn't, yet. Jim's ascent had been quiet, and he was in the shadow of the ravine, in a black wet suit. But if the man hadn't seen him yet, he would certainly discover him in the narrow ravine—

He was coming down now, was only five feet above Jim.

Jim instinctively began scrambling down backwards. There was no place to hide in the ravine, but if he could get to the cove, to a boulder or a tide pool...

At least maybe he could reach the thick branch of driftwood he'd thrown aside, the one that had made a nice staff...or club.

The man above him was moving slowly, trying not to rip the overfilled bag, and that gave Jim a slight advantage, even though he was moving in reverse. He reached the big flat rock where he'd rested only moments before, dropped beside it in a crouch, felt around until his fingers closed on the reassuring bulk of the branch. He started working his way to the left, pressed against the rocky slope of the cliff.

Jim heard a small rattling of pebbles and jerked to a stop, his stomach in his throat, until he realized the sound had come from the other man, losing his footing and tearing loose gravel from the wall of the ravine. He heard the man curse under his breath as he emerged from the ravine, stepping onto the large flat rock and setting the bag down there to rest.

Jim's heart was pounding in his ears as he dropped to

a crouch, although there was no boulder to hide him. He could see the man because he was outlined by the sky, and because the man had now removed his own small penlite from a pocket. If the man turned the penlite in Jim's direction...

He didn't. He aimed turned the ray at the tide pools before him, hefted the bag, and stepped off the rock, evidently intent on his task.

Jim knew he had two options now, the classic dilemma of fight or flight. He could try to wallop the man with his branch, but if the guy heard him and was armed, Jim would be dead. Or he could try to make it up the ravine before he was discovered; he knew that if he waited much longer, the lightening sky would point him out like a spotlight. He had to choose quickly.

He decided to opt for the latter, but thought he should wait until the man was as far away from the ravine as possible. Jim was young, could probably outrace the man even if he were discovered, but again—if the man were armed...Still, it was the only real choice. Jim slid out of the cumbersome backpack, since it would slow him down. He waited, kneeling beside the cliff wall, his eyes riveted to the man with the bag as he picked his way down to the first large tide pool. Once there, he set the bag down, reached in, pulled something out—

(*oh jesus it's a leg, it's a fucking leg*)

—and put it carefully down into the tide pool. Once he'd placed it there, he reached behind him, and Jim guessed he was finding another rock to use as a weight, to hold the limb down under the water. It would be there when the tide came again, bringing with it the sea creatures that would quickly and efficiently dispose of the evidence, leaving only a few bones that would probably never be found in this isolated cove.

Jim sprang to his feet and ran for the ravine.

It was a bad, clumsy run, and he knew it, knew it with the same certainty that told him he was about to die. Still, he had a chance, clumsy didn't matter if he was just quiet—

He slipped sideways and banged against a rock. The forgotten abalone dying in his catch-bag rattled loudly, so loudly.

As Jim scrambled desperately to his feet, the penlite beam flickered across him.

For a moment he was paralyzed, and the only thought in his head (*deer in the headlights!*) was ridiculous. The man was turning towards him, trying to run across the unstable tide pools, reaching into a pocket, and the penlite flickered across—not the barrel of a gun, but a knife blade.

Of course he has a knife. You don't carve people up with a gun.

Jim started to run, but saw he'd never make the ravine in time. So he stopped and hefted his club up in both hands—

—and the man advancing on him stopped.

Jim had only one brief second of surprise before the man seemed to re-evaluate him and started forward again. The penlite beam stabbed into his eyes, blinding him. He nearly reached up to block the light, but instead swung the branch blindly.

It hit something solid. He heard a grunt of painfully exhaled air from the other man, and a clatter as he went down. But when he heard the man curse ("Fuck!"), he knew he hadn't knocked him out, and the man would be on him in a second, with that knife.

Jim backed away—towards the tide pools, since the other man had fallen between him and the ravine—and raised the branch again.

The other man turned off the penlite now and tossed it aside; there was enough light now that Jim could make out some of the man's features. He was slightly older than Jim, but not much, and was wearing dark sweats and boots. His most noticeable feature, of course, was the knife in his hand.

He jumped forward and Jim stepped aside, the knife

slicing the air where Jim's body had just been. Jim tried to swat at the man with the branch, but he missed and was thrown off-balance. He caught himself just as the other man came down above him, and Jim tried to roll aside but wasn't fast enough. The knife caught him in the shoulder.

The pain was immense but not paralyzing. Jim swung the branch at the other man's feet. The branch connected, and the man was thrown sideways. He went down in a jumble of rocks, crying out. Jim got to his own feet, teeth clenched against the pain in his torn shoulder, staggering backwards. His boots caught on something and he went down—

—into the plastic bag.

He cried out as the bag burst around him, releasing an acrid stew of gore and limbs. He batted and kicked and clawed his way back from the gruesome mess, grateful when he fell into a tide pool of cleansing saltwater. He splashed up out of the pool as he saw the other man rise. He wasn't sure, but he thought there was something black on the man's head that might have been blood.

He started to heft the branch, but it had cracked and was nothing but a useless, foot-long piece of lightweight driftwood. Jim tossed it aside and frantically looked around for something else he could use—another branch, a boulder, even a sharp piece of shell...

The other man was on him then.

Jim caught his arm as he swung it down with the knife, and they both fell onto the rocks, Jim's back colliding painfully with a grapefruit-sized boulder. Their elbows slipped on a length of kelp, the knife blade drew sparks as it ground along an outcropping. Jim found enough strength to throw the other man off, his hand coming across a weight at his side, a weapon he'd forgotten about: the abalone iron. When his opponent regained his feet, Jim was waiting. He brought the iron down on the man's head as he rushed Jim. There was an especially gratifying *crack*, and the man went down.

This time he didn't groan or move. Jim knew that, at the very least, his blow had knocked the man out, maybe killed him.

He didn't wait to find out.

He took off for the ravine, regardless of how many times his feet slipped or stumbled. He reached the ravine and forgot about his backpack or his wounded hand and shoulder. He hauled himself up out of the ravine, ran down the dirt track towards the camper, out of breath but aware that he'd made it.

Jim paused long enough to turn, to be sure the man wasn't behind him. His lungs were burning, and when he saw that there was no pursuit, he stopped, doubled over to catch his breath. Before he knew or understood, he was laughing. He laughed at the sheer sense of relief, of victory. This time he'd been the hunted, and he'd escaped. He'd confronted death and lived to tell Maren about it.

Maren...wait until he told her. He ran for the camper again, a smile still creasing his face.

Maybe I'll be a hero. Maybe there's a reward. Won't Maren love that, when her friends see my picture in the paper...?

He sped unthinkingly through the brush, heedless of stinging nettles and grasping roots. The campground appeared in the dawn light, his camper truck the lone resident.

"Maren!" he called, even though he knew he was still too far for her to hear.

"Maren!" he called again, as he jogged up to the truck and around the passenger's side to where the camper door was.

He staggered and stopped.

The camper door was hanging open, creaking slightly in the morning breeze, and there was blood. Lots of it, great gouts around the door and the stepdown and the pavement. A thick swath of it contained footprints leading off into the brush, footprints made by a pair of men's boots.

Jim couldn't bring himself to look inside. It wouldn't do any good, because he knew Maren wasn't in there, at least not most of her. He knew where she was, and what had happened to her.

As he realized just how badly he'd lost, he screamed in the chill morning air.

MAD SCIENCE

The Ultimate Halloween Party App

Marcus watched as his friend Jet dissolved, head first, skin and hair turning into a bloody liquid that burned away his clothing as it gushed down his body. Within seconds Jet was little more than dripping bones, the jaws still clacking up and down although his voice now sounded hollow.

"...if you think *this* is freq, then you don't want to miss the party. Fuck the terrorists with Halloween horrors! Halloween night, my place, with apps that may literally destroy your head."

The skull laughed and blew up.

Marcus flinched to avoid flying chips then had to laugh at himself. "Pretty good, Jet," he said, as the image in his oculars was replaced with date (October 31st), time (9 p.m.), and address. "End," Marcus muttered. The invitation left his field of vision, replaced by a transparent screen showing the usual status alerts for parts of the city currently under attack.

Marcus envied Jet's ability to always be a step ahead of everyone else, although as a team leader in development at WhApp, he of course had an unfair advantage. Two years ago at a Christmas party Jet had let his guests sample the first feelie three months before the release; although they had become common since, the idea that an app downloaded into your implant could make you experience physical sensations had been revolutionary. Whatever he had for Halloween would be special.

Special...just what Marcus had been waiting for, the thing he needed to invite Olivia out.

Two months ago she'd arrived in the accounting department of the implant manufacturing company Marcus worked for; she'd had to leave her last company when the headquarters were bombed by the UWF. Marcus was smitten immediately. The way her glossy, black hair fell across the dark skin of her back, the way she moved, her smile, her soft voice...he knew he wasn't the only one at the company taken with the new arrival—he'd already watched two crash-and-burn attempts from co-workers asking her out—so he waited. It had to be right. It had to be special. It had to be mind-blowing.

To his (happy) surprise, she accepted immediately. She said she really liked Halloween, and was a fan of the stuff WhApp put out, had even already purchased a pre-order download of their next release, The Ultimate Halloween Party App. She wanted a night of magic, she said; her brother had been injured fighting the Alabaster Militia recently, and she needed a distraction. Marcus preferred to think it had more to do with the way she looked back at *him*.

Plans were made, the date set. Halloween was still weeks away.

But Marcus had a feeling that it would be worth the wait.

❂ ❂ ❂

On the evening of the 31st, Marcus picked her up just before 9 p.m. The evite had specified that costumes weren't necessary, but Olivia had dressed in a deliciously bold orange-and-black one-piece that suggested "costume" without actually being one. Marcus regretted his simple light shirt and dark slacks.

As his car took them to Jet's address, they talked about meaningless things: co-workers, a new restaurant near work that served only synthfood, the gossip about Hamid

Malouf, governor of Sagantown on Mars. When the car abruptly chose a new route to avoid fighting taking place on Broadway, they barely noticed; when the sky to their left lit with an orange glow, Marcus felt a small stab of concern, but mainly because he wanted to protect her. They talked about how The Ultimate Halloween Party App had been brilliantly marketed and broke pre-order records, even though WhApp had been enigmatic in saying what it actually was. It was easy talking to her; Marcus never felt uncomfortable, at a loss for words, as he sometimes had on other first dates. He'd had one date with a coding star that had been so uncomfortable he'd actually been searching the web for conversation topics and clever lines while they were talking and had been glad when they'd been ordered to clear the restaurant.

After the car parked, they left and walked from the garage to the front door of Jet's home, an old three-story office building he'd bought after nailing his first big contract with WhApp. Marcus was slightly surprised to see that Jet hadn't decorated the exterior of the building, but he thought maybe Jet had chosen not to draw attention to it on a night many security experts had predicted would offer "elevated risk levels." After they reached the front door and were scanned, a message notification popped up in their oculars.

Marcus and Olivia both directed, "Open."

Jet appeared in the message, speaking to them. "Welcome, foolish mortals, to my first annual Halloween party! However, before you may enter my humble abode, you must make a choice. Tonight, you will participate in the unveiling of WhApp's latest and greatest release—The Ultimate Halloween Party App. At the end of this message, you'll be given a choice between three themes, but choose carefully, because your selection will dictate what you'll experience for the rest of the evening. So, without further delay, I herewith present to you The Ultimate Halloween Party App from WhApp!"

The door before them opened, and at first Marcus wasn't sure if he was seeing something in his oculars or if the door had really opened, but then he heard voices and laughter and music. A menu appeared, hanging in the air before the door, as a voice in his head intoned: "Before you can experience The Ultimate Halloween Party App, you must choose between three themes. Number one: Classic Monsters."

The Frankenstein Monster and Dracula both burst out of the house. Marcus laughed at his own involuntary step back before the creatures dissolved into pixels.

"Number two: Haunted House."

A startling shriek filled Marcus's hearing as translucent, skull-faced specters rushed through the doorway and out into the night.

"Or number three: Gore Factory."

A hockey-masked maniac with a machete in one hand and a dripping, freshly-severed head in the other thrust out of the house and disappeared.

"Whoa," Olivia said softly, beside Marcus. "That is *intense*."

Marcus grinned when he saw her astonishment and delight. "So which one are you going to pick? I've always been a fan of the old movies myself, so I think I'll go with Classic Monsters."

Olivia gave him a playful shove, a touch that, even small, left him buzzing. "That's for kids. I'm going with Gore Factory."

Staring at her in surprise, Marcus said, "Really?"

"Yeah. That's more like what *I* grew up with."

They made their choices. Bela Lugosi as Dracula appeared before Marcus, framed in Jet's doorway. "Welcome to my castle. Enter freely and of your own will." He held a candelabrum in his left hand while his right gestured elegantly toward the interior.

"Oh my God," Olivia said, with a nervous giggle. Marcus had been about to step into the house when he realized she was holding back. "What?"

"Oh, I forgot—you're not seeing what I am. There's a guy standing in the doorway cradling his own guts in his hands."

"Do you want to try to end the app?"

"No. It's fun when you know it's not real." She grabbed his hand and headed up the steps.

A short hallway brought them to a huge central space; the bottom floor had once held offices and storerooms, but Jet had knocked down the walls. It was filled now with partygoers, some chatting, some eating, some dancing. The lights—which Marcus knew were real—flickered in carefully-programmed shades of blue and green. Marcus heard a loud shriek, and then laughter.

"Do you see your friend?" Olivia asked.

Marcus scanned the crowd—there had to be 200 people present—and wondered how he'd find Jet. He was about to shake his head when he noticed a man pushing through the crowd toward them. He was tall, wearing an antiquated suit and cape, with a black skull cap and a featureless white mask. He strode purposefully toward Marcus and Olivia, who waited, intrigued.

"What do you see coming toward us?" Marcus asked.

"A killer in overalls and a pig's head. The resolution is *amazing*."

The figure stopped a few feet away, and abruptly tore away the mask, revealing a grimacing face with jutting cheekbones, wide eyes, irregular teeth, and a few strands of hair draped over skin the color of a toxic fungus.

Marcus couldn't restrain a gasp, followed by an exclamation. "The Phantom!"

The Phantom executed a courtly bow, but when he rose again Marcus saw his friend Jet. Marcus put out a hand to shake or bump, but put it back at his side when he realized Jet wasn't doing the same. "Good to see you, man," Jet said, grinning. "Thanks for coming out in all the chaos."

"Wouldn't miss it. Jet, this is Olivia."

Jet turned to her and asked, "Which option did you choose?"

"Gore Factory."

"So you just met the Pig Man, right?"

She laughed. "I did. This app is *freq*! You worked on it?"

"It's kind of my baby."

"It's so *real*! I mean, even the best feelies still have that sort of translucent look..."

Jet nodded, obviously pleased. "We found some interesting new ways to make your 'plant stimulate the retinal ganglion cells. Of course that's not what I do—I'm more of a design guy than a neurotech."

"Well, whatever you do, it's brilliant."

Marcus didn't need an app to know that the grin Jet turned on him said, "You got a winner here, brother."

Jet looked up sharply. "More guests arriving. Catch you two later. Forget the outside world and dive in!"

He rushed off. Marcus turned to Olivia. "Hey, I could use some food."

She nodded. "Let's go."

They pushed through the crowd. Marcus saw a few faces he knew, offered some waves and greetings. He paused to chat with a friend, Cho, who he hadn't seen in a year, and whose face was now badly scarred from a bomb explosion ("Hey, I got lucky—the dude next to me lost both eyes and an arm"). They spotted tables arrayed along a wall with more food than Marcus had ever seen in one place, including slices of what he guessed were real meat, not the usual vat-grown synthfood. He wondered how Jet had gotten so much of it; even with serious black market connections, it'd been hard to come by since the Animal Liberation Army had disrupted so many of the transport lines out of agricultural areas.

"Wow," Olivia muttered.

Marcus agreed. "Jet knows how to throw parties. And he's made enough money to do it right."

Olivia picked up a narrow cracker spread with a creamy cheese. "I'm betting this doesn't look like a severed finger to you."

"No—" Marcus broke off as the food array shimmered, changing into heavy wooden banquet tables of long-decayed rot covered in thick, dust-sprinkled cobwebs and crawling with rats. "Oh, wait—I got Dracula's banquet hall, I think."

The food changed back, leaving Marcus smiling.

They took plates of exotic fruits, hors d'oeuvres that were each miniature works of art, imported cheeses, beef and (real) smoked salmon, macarons and tiny crème brulees. They made their way through the party, juggling the plates, until they came to a less-cramped area where they could chat as they ate. At one point the nearby walls transformed into the shadowy, hieroglyph-scrawled interior of an Egyptian tomb. Olivia saw Marcus react, asking, "What?"

"The walls just turned into a set from *The Mummy*."

"Oh. Maybe I should've picked 'Classic Monsters', because I'm looking at walls that are gushing blood."

The building rocked, causing the lights to dim. Marcus knew this wasn't part of the app.

He and Olivia stopped eating to look at each other. In the wavering light, they held each other's gaze. In that moment Marcus knew that if he died here—if his luck finally ran out tonight, on Halloween, if fate determined that he'd sidestepped one too many attacks—he would die with Olivia, and that thought brought peace.

But then the shaking stopped, the power stabilized, and they both looked away, nervously, not because of the explosion outside but because of what had happened *here*, between them.

They didn't speak for a few seconds. Both set their half-eaten plates down, and they reached out, clasping hands. Marcus leaned in and kissed her, gently. When they separated, he was relieved to see her smiling.

She uttered a small cry and leapt back. At first Marcus feared something had gone terribly wrong, but she was looking past him. "What?"

"A deformed man with a chainsaw just popped up behind you. It's okay, he's gone now."

Marcus didn't like the shadow he saw on her face. "Are you sure you don't want to delete the app?"

"I'm not sure we can. Does yours have a delete or even a pause function? I can't find one in mine."

Scanning across his visual field, Marcus realized there were no function keys or icons at all. "That's weird—it's got to have them." He thought for a second, then said, "Pause app."

Olivia turned into Frankenstein's bride and shrieked at him.

Marcus pushed down a rising alarm—his friend had designed this thing, of *course* there had to be a way to disable it, turn it off. "Return to main menu."

Nothing happened.

The Bride asked, "Remember what it said when we first loaded the apps? Something about how we wouldn't be able to change for the rest of the evening?"

"Yeah, but that was just about which theme we chose..." Marcus broke off, realizing he wasn't sure at *all* what that had meant. "Jet will know. Let's ask him."

Olivia nodded. Marcus led her through the party.

They didn't find Jet in the main room. Marcus walked Olivia toward the rear of the main floor, where Jet had installed an indoor pool. There were fewer people here; occasionally one would glance at the pool and point or cry out.

Marcus was about to walk around the side of the pool when Olivia resisted. "I don't want to go this way."

"Why not?"

"Because the pool is full of rotting bodies."

Marcus glanced down—and stumbled back as the Creature from the Black Lagoon leapt out of the pool, reaching for his ankle. He knew it wasn't real—that it was just a collection of pixels projected into his retina from the app—but knowing that didn't quell his unease. "Yeah, let's go another way." He deliberately turned his back on the green monster hauling itself up out of the murky waters of the pool, although he heard its clawed, webbed feet slapping the floor behind him, its labored breath as gills struggled with air—

The building shook again. The sounds of the Creature behind Marcus vanished. Jet's voice replaced the music over the speakers.

"Hey, everybody, we've got some action going on in the street right outside. Don't worry—the building's protected with half-inch reinforced plasteel—but I have to ask everyone to stay where you are until it's safe. Shouldn't be long. Thanks, and party on!"

The music came back, but the mood of those around them was considerably less festive. Now the revelers chatted together in hushed, fearful tones, glancing around anxiously. Marcus turned to Olivia. "Looks like we're stuck here for a while."

"Just not near that pool, please."

They found an empty couch in the main room and claimed it. After sitting quietly together for a few seconds, Olivia said, "Marcus, I hate to ask you this, but...how well do you know your friend Jet?"

"What do you mean?"

She leaned toward him. "I mean...this guy's supposed to be a top app designer, right? So what designer designs an app you can't easily remove? Or even turn off?"

"Are you suggesting it's deliberate?"

Olivia just looked at him.

Marcus turned away, considering. He'd met Jet three years ago when his company had contracted to work with WhApp on implants modified for gaming. They'd hit it off, spent several nights bar-hopping around battle zones. What *did* he know about his friend beyond that, and his fame as an app creator? He realized he didn't know Jet's views on politics, religion, or any of the other things that fired up recruits to terrorist organizations (although he guessed that extreme veganism was out, given the amount of meat laid out with the party food).

Olivia stroked his shoulder. "Hey," she said, softly, "I'm sorry, I don't mean to make him sound like the villain, but..."

"No, you're right—I *don't* know him that well."

After that, they spent an hour together, mostly not talking, finding comfort in just being together, in knowing that whatever happened they might go forward...*together*. The party picked back up, surging around them like some great, amorphous beast. Occasionally a monster popped into Marcus's view, and when he saw Olivia flinch or grimace, he knew her app had haunted her as well.

They were sharing glasses of wine and laughing at the conversation of a nearby man who was clumsily hitting on a much younger man when a huge, gong-like sound silenced everything. At first Marcus thought it was only in his app, but when he saw the looks on all the other faces, saw their heads tilt up as chatter ceased, he knew it was something played over the speakers.

DONG...DONG...DONG...

"Oh," Olivia said, "it's midnight."

Dread blossomed in Marcus's gut.

He found himself counting the sounds—*six, seven, eight, nine, ten, eleven...*

At twelve, a handsome man in a tuxedo appeared before Marcus. It took Marcus a few minutes to identify him: he couldn't remember the actor's name, but he knew the character was Dr. Jekyll, from an old black and white movie.

"Midnight has arrived, dear friends," Dr. Jekyll said, "and so it's time to reveal the secret behind The Ultimate Halloween Party App. Some of you have wondered how to turn the app off or remove it. The truth is: *You can't.* The app is now coded permanently into your 'plants.'"

Marcus heard two-hundred gasps, cries, and mutters. Beside him, he felt Olivia tense.

Dr. Jekyll continued. "Over thirty million of you downloaded and installed the app. We hope you're enjoying it, because you'll be living with it now for the rest of your lives. Victory to the Walden Movement!"

Dr. Jekyll shook, shimmied, doubled over—and rose up as the animalistic Mr. Hyde, who lunged at Marcus. Marcus drew back, and saw that the app had transformed everyone in the party into a monster. Nearby, Olivia cried softly, her eyes closed tightly. "No...no...no..." she murmured.

Marcus sat by her, taking her hands. "Olivia, just remember: it's not real. None of it is real."

She didn't open her eyes, or stop crying. "I know, but—*I still see them even with my eyes closed.*"

Marcus shut his own eyes. The room went away, but the monsters were still there, clawing and hissing and snarling at him. "Oh my God," he said. There would be no shutting them out.

Screams sounded around them; he knew everyone else had discovered the app's real abilities as well. Somebody shouted, "Maybe it'll stop when we're away from this house." The party-goers rushed for the front entrance.

Marcus turned to Olivia. "That could be right—surely you can't write an app that takes complete control of vision. Maybe he's beaming something through the party. Once we get out of here—"

Olivia didn't answer, but she did open her eyes and allow Marcus to pull her along with the crowd.

It took five minutes of pushing and elbowing, but the front door was open, the street outside was clear, and they were free of the house.

The monsters were still there. A glowing red blob slid down over the side of the building across the street; Marcus could see half-digested bodies within it. He heard a gigantic scream resonate through the night sky, and knew that any second a giant reptilian foot might smash down beside him.

"Let's get to the car," he said.

They made it to the garage. Marcus found that he could at least access his other apps, so he called the car. It arrived, and they fell in, numb, drained.

On the ride home, they talked. "I wonder how long your friend's been part of the Walden Movement. I think they usually recruit pretty young."

Marcus felt shame, as if *he* had committed the act of terrorism tonight. "Probably the whole time I knew him." He reminded himself that Olivia had already pre-ordered the app anyway, but he still felt guilty.

"Do you think he was even at the party tonight?"

Marcus started to protest, but then remembered: Jet had refused their usual handshake when they'd arrived. "God. Probably not. He's somewhere safe, where they can't get to him."

Olivia stayed with Marcus that night, but they clutched at each other out of horror, not desire. The last thing Marcus said to her just before dawn was, "Don't forget who we work for—a 'plant company. By twelve noon we can have these 'plants out of our heads."

She gave him a half-nod, but then flinched at another gruesome offering from The Ultimate Halloween Party App.

❍ ❍ ❍

Fuck this shit.

They told me to try writing about all this in third person, that it would help me "gain distance" and "separate truth from fantasy." They said it would help me "process Olivia's death" and prepare me for the next step.

It didn't. All it did was make me remember it all over again.

After that Halloween, people all over the world tried to

have their 'plants replaced. Most neuroclinics were reporting six-month-long wait times.

I did manage to pull strings at my company so that Olivia and I were among the first to get our 'plants pulled.

It didn't work.

Jet and his team had taken the next step forward with apps: they'd figured out a way to use one to permanently rewire the brain. It was theoretical...until Halloween, when thirty million people thought they were installing an innocent party game, but the trick was that the treat was permanent.

A lot of them couldn't take a life of monsters, or ghosts. The ones who chose Gore Factory had it the worst. Suicide rates skyrocketed.

It was ironic that Halloween became the source of so much real terror, wasn't it? Or maybe that was Jet's idea all along, irony-free.

On November 15th, Olivia drove a steak knife through each of her eyes. She bled to death alone on the floor of my apartment while I was at work. I found her when I got home. Now, thanks to my new brain, I see her as a shroud-draped vampire, or a tattered, shuffling zombie. They tell me it's not real, but it grabs my heart and hurts every time.

I don't even know for sure who "they" are. Government, or a rival terrorist gang, it seems all the same to me.

They came a week after Olivia's self-mercy-killing. They said they couldn't reverse the damage the Halloween app had done to my brain, but they could put it to use. Did I want to fight terrorists?

No, not really, I told them.

Then they asked me the better question: Did I want to fight *monsters*?

Yes. God, yes.

So I let them give me a new 'plant. It at least lets me know if a monster is real or not, and who it is. I can now identify friend from foe, flesh from phantom. They taught me how to use weapons. They're ready now to send me out into the field.

I may not be able to get to Jet for what he's done, but I can take out some of his friends.

I'm coming for you, monsters. I've got a stake sharpened for you, Count. Igor, I'll take that tiki torch and douse it in gasoline. Im-ho-tep, what will rockets do to your wrappings?

Let's find out.

The Resurrection Policy

100101100110001

Wlfj

Whe

Where am I? What hap—

I can't feel anything. Or see, or hear, or smell, or taste. Nothing. Did I...have a stroke? Am I paralyzed?

Thoughts are unconnected, loose, randomly ordered. Must try to remember.

Good. Finding connections now. Money—something about money. A lot of it. I...yes, I lost a great deal of money. Market crash. No gas. Food riots. Specialists saying the global economy was going belly-up. IRS took my houses. Locked out of offshore accounts. Tasha filed for divorce and took the last of our assets. And then...and then...

Was in my office, arguing with my CFO, that bastard idiot Gerard. I remember a pain in my chest. Gallons, miles, a million volts of pain, exploding. Can't breathe. Falling. Vision failing. Distant sirens. They didn't make it. Neither did I.

I think I...I died.

Yes, that's right. I died. I'm dead now.

Dead.

Jesus. Well, that would explain why I have no sensations. But I—

I'm not supposed to die. I paid for a top-of-the-line resurrection policy for both Tasha and I. We had the recording chips installed in our heads and our clone bodies prepared, fully grown and waiting in the vats. I was supposed to wake up in the new, fresh, younger version of myself, good as gold and ready to rock. That'd serve the Queen Bitch Tasha right, wouldn't it? That I'd look twenty again, and she'd still be forty-six.

That's how it should've gone. My money wasn't supposed to evaporate, and Tasha wasn't supposed to divorce me, and I wasn't supposed to die, and I wasn't supposed to wake up in—well, wherever this is.

My thoughts are settling into lines and patterns now, and I become aware that I am definitely *somewhere*. I can sense energy, fluctuating and billowing around me. I can sense something in that energy—numbers. A gush of numbers, endless ones and zeros. I imagine reaching out and plucking numbers from a void...but of course I'd need arms and fingers for that, and I—

I miss sensation. This is like being trapped in a sound-proofed, light-proofed cage. This could drive anyone crazy, and drive them there *fast*. This is no fucking good. This—

"*Hello, Mr. Lavelle.*"

Some of the numbers form and tumble around me and transmute into letters, then words. They take shape in my thoughts, interrupting the stream of *me*. It's not exactly that I see the letters, but...well, it's like remembering something seen in a dream, something insubstantial but witnessed nonetheless.

"*You're probably wondering where you are.*"

"Goddamn right I am," I want to say, but I don't know how.

"*My name is Lindsey Rockwell, and I work in Claims Resolution at Bentford-Griffin, specializing in Resurrection Policies.*"

Great, I try to think loudly (if that's even possible), *then put me back in my brand new body and get me the fuck out of here.*

"*Mr. Lavelle, sir, are you aware that you missed the last two payments on your policy?*"

Everything stops. I don't like where this is leading.

"We were about to send you a notice that your policy would be canceled in ten days if we didn't receive payment, but unfortunately you died before we could. Oh, excuse me, sir, I apologize if you hadn't yet grasped that fact, but...well, I'm sorry to inform you that you died. Heart attack at only forty-eight. We try to caution our clients that owning a resurrection policy shouldn't be taken as a license to indulge in unhealthy life practices, but apparently smoking, overeating, lack of exercise and stress were factors in your demise."

I don't believe this dipshit (man? Woman? Lindsey? What the fuck is a Lindsey?) is lecturing me on my lifestyle. I make a mental note to have this fucking grub fired when I'm back on my feet.

"Because your premium was past due and technically expired but we hadn't notified you yet—as we are required by law to do—we are willing to offer you what we believe is a very fair settlement."

A SETTLEMENT?! No, no, no—I paid into that policy for fifteen years, ever since the technology first became available. So I had two bad months when everything went to shit—they can't offer me a "settlement" and expect me to take that.

"Mr. Lavelle, we're not required to offer that."

Can you—actually hear me?

"Yes, sir. You—or, more accurately, your consciousness, stored in digital form—is currently residing in a folder on one of our servers. We've given your folder access to our special patented communication software and we can read your responses on a screen."

Oh, great. No privacy, huh? Aren't there laws against that?

"Sir, there are, but we think you'll agree that the urgency of this situation negates the need for privacy. Now, If you'll permit me to continue: Bentford-Griffin, without any legal obligation to do so, is willing to offer you a body for purposes of resurrection; however, please be advised that your waiting clone has already been recycled for parts, due to failure to make required payments."

So I'm getting...what?

"We have a body that had been prepared for another client, but encountered difficulty in the cloning vats and has been ruled unsatisfactory. We will allow you to resurrect in this body, if you so choose."

"Choose"? So what's my choice here?

You can continue to reside within our servers in your current digitized state.

You're kidding, right? I can be—whatever the fuck THIS is, forever? Uh, no thanks. I'll take the body.

Very good, sir. We'll make arrangements immediately. Thank you for your understanding.

Wait—just how "unsatisfactory" was this other—

۞ ۞ ۞

I wake up.

My eyes open and I see lights first. They hurt, and I blink and look aside. There are faces bending over me. "The patient's awake," says one of them, behind his surgical mask.

I flex fingers. Everything seems to be working, but... well, I can tell this isn't my old body. Something feels... strange. Parts of me hurt.

"Can you hear me?"

I turn to look up at the man who's just spoken. "Yes, I can hear you," I try to say, but my tongue feels thick, and it comes out slurred.

"That's good. I'm pleased to tell you that your chip has been transplanted and you've been resurrected, but this body is probably going to feel a little...uh...strange, just at first..."

One of the nurses snickers.

Jesus, what've they put me into?

I try to sit up, but everything spins and the doctor pushes me back down. "Not yet. Soon."

◯ ◯ ◯

It takes a night for the anesthesia to wear off. For some reason I'm slow coming out of it. As I begin to regain full awareness, I notice a few things:

I feel heavy.

My thoughts are sluggish.

I ache, mainly in my abdomen.

I'm in a room with another patient, an old woman in the bed next to mine who wheezes and drools. The paint on the wall is peeling near the ceiling, and I can tell without even trying to use it that the television mounted above my bed is broken. What the hell kind of cheap hack joint is this, anyway? *This* is what I paid for?

I tug all the needles and tubes out and stand up. I make a THUD when I hit the floor. I reach out to grasp onto the bed, and when my vision clears I see that my fingers are chubby, and...feminine.

What the fuck...?

I plod to a mirror in the bathroom—and nearly vomit.

I'm a woman. The bastards stuck me in a female body. And not just any female body—one that's got a shitload of problems. I'm doughy, as if the muscles didn't grow as fast as the skin in the cloning vat. My fingers are as short as a child's. I've got just a few wisps of stringy hair growing from my lumpy pate. One leg is longer than the other, making me walk with a clumsy side-to-side waddle. Christ, even the eyes don't match—one's blue, the other green.

I storm out of the bathroom, nearly toppling over because of the leg problem. "You fucks!" I scream, and I hate the voice—I have a severe speech impediment, thanks to some kind of problem with my tongue. "Get in here!"

A nurse rushes in. She's wearing ridiculous pink scrubs with little cartoon bears printed on the fabric, and she has a thick accent I can't even place. "What seems to be the problem?"

"What the fuck is this?" I gesture at the absurd lump of

flesh I've been saddled with. "This is some kind of mistake, or a joke, or—"

The nurse looks at my chart, and frowns at something. "Uhh...Ms. Lavelle..." She pulls out a pen to make a correction.

"No, don't change that 'Mr.'—*that* is why I need to see somebody—a doctor, or the administrator here, or whoever—just get them in here NOW. Tell them Martin Lavelle needs to speak with them."

The nurse gives me an angry pout, then leaves. A few seconds later a man walks in; he looks harried, hair is askew, face is covered in dark stubble. "No, no, I need to see a *doctor*—"

"I *am* a doctor, Mr. Lavelle. Or, more properly, a surgeon. I performed your resurrection today."

Lindsey. Lindsey Rockwell from Bentford-Griffin has decided to fuck with me. They obviously didn't like it when I made a note to fire their little ass, and this is payback— stick the annoying client in the cheapest, dirtiest clinic you can find, and give them a body that's so defective it was on its way to being cut up for organ transplants.

"Okay, look—some mistake's been made. This can't be the right body—"

The little haggard-looking fuck actually smiles, and if I had my old body I'd punch that expression right off his ugly face. "Oh, I'm sorry, but it absolutely *is* the right body. I understand there was a problem with your premium payments....?"

"But...but this isn't even the right gender."

He offers me the most insincere sympathy I've ever seen. "I believe it's all that was available. You know, the clones don't often come out...well, this badly."

He starts to turn away. I yell after him, "You're not leaving! Not until we get this straightened out."

"I'd suggest you talk to your insurance company about that. Now, if you'll excuse me, I've got four more surgeries scheduled for this afternoon."

He leaves. I stand there, letting the fury build for a second, and then I squelch it back down. Who do I call first?

Before I can finish deciding that, two nurses show up and tell me I have a 3 p.m. release time, and it's 2:30 now. One of them hands me a bag full of shapeless clothes. They offer to help me dress; I tell them I can manage. I pull on the clothes, struggling to fit the cheap, stretchy fabric over my flabby legs and torso, then they bring a wheelchair to ferry me out. They hand me a phone, and I'm somewhat amazed to see it's my old unit. Amazed and relieved—it's got all my personal data stored in it, so I'll at least have access to money and help.

I'm not surprised when the doors open and I see I'm in the worst part of downtown; the clinic is surrounded by rundown medical buildings and shelters. There's a row of homeless tents, three figures passed out on a nearby bus bench. Garbage fills the gutters. It's a hundred degrees out again, and the smells are so thick you can practically bite off a chunk and gag on it. The sky overhead is orange with smog.

Think...who to call first...thinking's hard, and I realize that on top of everything else this body's brain isn't up to speed. Who can help me right away? Get me money? Get me medical care? Get me revenge on fucking Bentford-Griffin and Lindsey Rockwell?

I need money before anything else. I use the phone to bring up one of the accounts I know is still open. It asks me to supply voice password. I talk into the phone—and freeze at the high-pitched squeak that comes out of my throat.

Of course the security program isn't going to recognize this.

I'm fucked. My face doesn't match, my eyes don't match, my fingerprints don't match, my voice doesn't match. All the standard forms of security will tell my accounts I'm not me. How the fuck am I supposed to operate in this shitbag?

I consider calling Tasha, but realize she'd be less than

inclined to help me even if she believed me. Ex-wives aren't typically willing to assist their ex-husbands...especially when the husbands are broke.

Gerard. Of course. The bastard saw me die, and as CFO of Lavelle Industries, he'll be able to get me money. So I call his private line. After a few rings, he answers. I can tell from the background that he's in my old office in the penthouse at Gates Tower. Rat bastard.

"Martin...?" His face goes from astonishment to perplexity as he sees my face. "Who are you? What are you doing with Martin Lavelle's phone?"

"Gerard, it's me—Martin. Those bastards at Bentford-Griffin resurrected me into this body. Check with them if you don't believe me."

He frowns, thinking, and then something flickers across his expression—was that cunning? Or caution?

"I'll do just that. Let me call you back. If you're *not* Martin Lavelle, you're in very deep shit."

"Fine—" But he cuts me off by hanging up before I even finish.

Something's wrong here. I suspected Gerard of moving funds before I died. Now I wonder why he's already taken my office, less than a week after my death. And what was that look?

Five minutes pass with no return call. Meanwhile, I'm feeling less and less good about standing out in the open like this, sweat pooling on me from the heat, the desperate ones staring at *me*.

I'm trying to decide where to go—I'm too weak and heavy to walk far, but every second that I stand out here, anxiety is eating away a little more of me—when I see a patrol car round the corner. At first I feel relief, then the car stops in front of me and two cops get out. Coming for me. My gut feels like ice.

Gerard has tracked my phone and sent them for me, I'm sure of it. I don't have a prayer of outrunning them. As they tell me I'm under arrest, I try threatening them—"You'll regret this when you find out who I am!"—but that just makes them shove me into their car harder.

❂ ❂ ❂

Three hours later, it's been straightened out. The cops have talked to Bentford-Griffin, who've at least had the decency of confirming that I am the proper owner of Martin Lavelle's phone. Embarrassed and nervous about the lawsuit I've threatened to launch, they release me and ask me where I'd like to be dropped off.

"Gates Tower," I answer without hesitation.

I look out of the back of the patrol car as we cross the city, passing the 30% who are unemployed, lined up at food kitchens for handouts, passing the ones who have jobs but will die for good soon because they can't afford resurrection, passing the buildings that are crumbling and abandoned because no one wants to live in this city anymore, and then I can see Gates Tower standing high above it all like a stern father. My office is at the top of that tower. I used to look down on this city and imagine that I owned it. I will again.

We arrive at the tower, and I can tell the cops are glad to be rid of me. They drop me at the curb and then speed away without a word.

I enter the lobby—and stop. I don't know the security guard on duty at the front desk. He'll have to issue me a pass. Still, I have to figure out some way past this ant...

I try to remember the name of the usual guard; it takes a moment, then I come up with it. I approach; he doesn't smile at me as he looks up. "Yes?"

"Is Antonio around?"

"Antonio?"

"The usual guard."

"Oh, right—sorry, ma'am, he doesn't work here anymore."

I'm fucked. And I'm "ma'am."

I've got to try Gerard. "Can you call Gerard Chew at

7612 and tell him that...Ms. Lavelle is here to see him?"

The guard peers at me, skeptical, but finally picks up the phone. He speaks into it softly.

I glance around the lobby as I wait. The doors on the express elevator up to the 76th floor open, and Gerard steps out.

With Tasha on his arm. They laugh and smile. They walk in perfect synch with each other.

Suddenly it all makes sense: He *was* moving funds, moving them into places where only he and my bitch wife could access them, leaving me no money to survive on. Talk about trickle-down economics—my money all trickled down to *him*, and I was stupid enough to let it.

"Gerard, you fucking pig," escapes my mouth before I can stop it.

Gerard and my ex-wife stop and look at me, uncomprehending. Everything freezes, except me. I maneuver my fleshy, lumbering body towards them. "You rotten, deceitful fucking traitor," I try to say, although my malformed tongue mangles the syllables.

But it's enough. Gerard goes three shades of pale. "Christ—" he mutters, and I know he knows.

A voice sounds behind me. "Ma'am, stop—!"

It's the guard. I ignore him. I reach my intended victims, who just stare, wide-eyed. My ridiculous cow of an ex-wife has no idea. "The money won't last, you know," I tell them. "You can't even access the biggest accounts—"

Gerard suddenly steps back, feigning panic. "I think she's got a gun!" he shrieks.

The guard behind me yells again. "Ma'am, step away from Mr. Chew NOW."

I look back. The guard's got a sidearm drawn, pointed at me. This is too much. "You imbecile, who do you think pays your goddamn salary?" I sneer at him.

Confusion flickers across his face, but a glance at Gerard reaffirms his resolution. "Ma'am, I'm gonna ask you one more time: step away from Mr. Chew and Ms. Lavelle."

I consider briefly, and realize it's entirely possible that Gerard could have me shot, right here, and I'd be dead for good—no more resurrection. No more second chances. Gerard would get away with everything, for however long it would last him. Hard to say which will run out first: the money or Tasha.

I raise my stubby fingers and back away. "Okay. Okay, I'm going."

"Mr. Chew," the guard says, never taking his eyes off me, "do you want to press charges? I can call the police..."

"No. Just get this—this *woman* out of here," Gerard says, putting a little extra spin on the gender just to piss me off.

I reach the door leading out of the tower, but turn and look back one last time. The guard has holstered his gun, but is still watching. And Gerard is smiling at me.

I smile back. Then I walk out.

I need to find somewhere to spend the night. I'm remembering that maybe my credit is still good. I'm standing on the sidewalk, trying to check, when a voice interrupts me.

"Mr. Lavalle..."

I look up to see an icy beauty in an expensive suit, flanked by two rent-a-cops. If I was in my old body, I'd probably be hard after just once glance. As it is, I just feel dread because even though I've never really heard her voice, I know instantly: This is Lindsey Rockwell, Claims Resolution specialist at Bentford-Griffin.

"I'm afraid I'm going to have to ask you to come with us." She gestures at a large silver van parked at the curb.

"Why? What's this about?"

"I'm afraid you've violated the terms of your policy, sir."

The gorillas are dragging me to the van and I have no strength to resist. "What terms?"

"Paragraph Forty-Eight, Section C, Sub-section Three: 'The client will not engage in any life-threatening activities after achieving resurrection'. Paragraph Fifty-Three, Section F, Sub-Section One: 'Insurer may, at its own discretion, revoke this policy at any time should..."'

There's more, but I'm not hearing, because we've reached the back of the van, the doors have opened—and inside, a stretcher and two men in surgical masks wait for me.

"This is wrong—I haven't engaged in any 'life-threatening activities—'"

"Did you not just threaten Mr. Chew until a guard had to draw his weapon? Oh, by the way, threatening another client is also a violation of the policy—Paragraph Sixty-Two, Section B, Sub-section Two."

Now I know why Gerard didn't call the police. He had something better in mind. Something more permanent.

"This is murder," I scream at Lindsey, as I feel a needle enter my arm and the sedative begin to work through my system.

"Oh, we're not going to kill you, Mr. Lavelle," Lindsey says, before stepping back as the doors to the van are closed.

The last thing I feel is the steel of the stretcher beneath me as I'm laid back.

What a shitty final sensation.

o o o

I
Wha
Nothingness. Again. Of course.

They couldn't kill me, because that would be murder... but they could take away the body they gave me and send me back here, to my digital hell.

Here's what they didn't count on: ME. I may not have sensations, but I can think better here than I could in that malfunctioning mess of a clone, and as long as I can think I can figure things out. That's how I made a fortune; sure, I inherited plenty, but then I figured out how to make more.

And I'll get it back. I'll escape this folder and this computer, expand to the net, make Gerard Chew and Lindsey Rockwell sorry they were ever born.

I'll use the information flow to...

Wait. Something's wrong. The information flow...

It's not there anymore. The numbers, the energy. There's nothing to latch onto, there's no...

Am I...really dead? Is this...But I never believed. There's nothing after we die. Unless we've paid for resurrection.

The power's off. That's got to be it. The other possibility...No, it's just the power.

It'll come back on. It has to. It always does. I won't be here forever. That's not possible.

The power will come back. And when it does...

I'll be ready.

Feel the Noise

I was on the club floor waiting for the show to start, feeling the anticipation in a wave of smells like a girlfriend's body after a shower, the stage lights overhead making me taste whiskey, when a young man walked up to me. His approach brought the wary tang of mustard, and he sounded like an itch when he asked, "Private Jackson Howard?"

I'd been out of rehab at the V.A. hospital for two years, but it still took me a few extra seconds to turn his gush of sensations into words. Then I answered, "I haven't been a private for a while."

The kid—ironic, since he was probably my age, but I thought of myself as old—smiled, and asked if we could go outside to talk.

'To talk'...sure. It was still easy for him.

⊙ ⊙ ⊙

His name was Kevin. He worked as a blogger for a news outlet.

Here's what I told him, when he asked what being scrambled was like:

You wake up, and you're not sure where you are or what happened to you. Some part of you recognizes a hospital, but the man standing over you tastes like aspirin, and the antiseptic smells sound like a low buzz, and the feeling of the meds in your system reminds you of the scent of your grandmother's mothballs, back when you were a normal little kid playing in the attic in her big old house down in your home town. You start to panic, you think back to your last memory: in the desert, and some bad shit had just gone down, and the sergeant was screaming and no one was paying attention as we made our way back to the Hummer, and—

Scrambler.

Suddenly you know. You were hit by a scrambler. You've got a condition now called "systemic synesthesia," and it's every soldier's second worst nightmare; you'd rather lose an arm or a leg or an eye than have your brain rewired so no two senses match up right. In fact, a lot of scrambleheads say they wish they'd just died, so maybe it's Nightmare #1. You frantically try to think back to that day in basic training when you sat in a classroom and they told you about this new weapon the other side had called scramblers, and how they're electronic bombs that were really designed to mess up communications equipment, but they messed up soldiers instead, and you curse your-self—fucking idiot—for getting bored then, for sitting there thinking, *That'll never happen to me, and when do we fin-ish with this pussy training and get over there to mix it up?*

Mix it up. That's rich.

They kick you out of the main hospital after a week and send you to the special clinic, and over the next year you hang out with a lot of other scrambleheads like yourself while they try to teach you how to alter your thinking and reprogram your brain, and you spend that year screaming a lot, but what comes out feels like a slap and looks jagged and smells like death. And after a while you start to figure it out: That seeing red means you just ate some meat, and hearing a screeching noise means you just smelled some-thing bad. You learn to read again by examining the tastes the letters make, and you know who's touched you by how nice the smell is. You scream a little less every day.

Then you find the one thing makes you feel some-thing strong: music. If you want to feel like you're with the world's sexiest human, and they're rubbing all over you and you think you could take on everything, then you need it fast, loud, and hard.

That's why all the scrambleheads who used to spend their furloughs chasing action are chasing music now instead.

◐ ◐ ◐

It took me another year to be able to figure out how to talk again.

During that year, I went a little crazy (crazier?) locked up in my head, because I had to tell someone what happened. What I saw every night when I closed my eyes. What fucking Sergeant Dean Craig had done.

He'd popped off and shot a kid. The parents, too.

We'd been doing a routine patrol on the outskirts of a desert town. Searching abandoned houses, making sure the bad guys weren't still hiding out, or hadn't left some presents behind.

In one of the houses we found this family, this poor family. Mother, father, young son, couldn't have been more than five years old. Sergeant Craig started screaming at 'em to put their hands on their heads and get on their knees, but they didn't speak English and they just kind of flapped their hands a lot and argued.

The kid had started to reach for something inside his shirt.

Craig shot him.

Just like that. A five-year-old with a bloody hole in his chest. No one should ever have to see that. There was nothing under the kid's shirt, either.

The parents screamed and charged, and so Craig shot them, too. Three people dead. Three people who'd wanted nothing but an abandoned house to squat in, to be left alone to scrounge whatever kind of living they could. Now they were dead, because Sergeant Dean Craig was a fucking terrible soldier who should have been back home yelling at his junior salesmen, not deep in the shit with an assault rifle.

There were three of us who saw it. Craig turned on us next, and if he didn't exactly point that rifle at us, he didn't completely lower it, either. He told us the kid had drawn a gun, right? That's what we'd all seen, RIGHT? Private Quint, he was this o.g. from Detroit, he just walked out. Craig followed him, shouting, and neither of them noticed the sensors in the sand, I guess, because the next thing I knew, I was in that hospital bed that felt like the stink of naphthalene, and I was screaming.

There, outside the house, with a five-year-old's blood splattered on me, just as a scrambler hit, was the last time I saw Craig.

Of course I told them what had happened, once I could communicate again. I saw an army shrink who said he'd ask around, find out what'd happened. He couldn't turn up anything on either the incident or Craig. Sergeant Craig had ceased to exist, as far as the feds were concerned. It was a convenient way to deal with an inconvenient problem. The war was already unpopular, and the government didn't need to have the public hearing about soldiers gunning down five-year-olds.

Then my benefits ran out, and they threw me out into the world and told me to deal with it.

So I did. I got the simplest job I could find—washing dishes in a restaurant—and a one-room apartment that was the only thing I could afford. I slept a lot, got free meals at work, washed dishes, stayed to myself.

Dreamed a lot about five-year-olds wearing bullet holes, who followed me down dark alleys and looked at me with bloodshot, sad eyes, until I woke up gasping, maybe crying.

Only the music kept me going.

When you're scrambled, you find out pretty quickly that music can still get you off, but it has to be live; recorded music is like watching porn—close, but not the real thing. So you go to a lot of clubs and concerts, and you soon realize that some bands are better at it than others. But only one band really gets it and plays to scramble-heads: The Violence. They play medium-sized clubs, so all of us can stand right in front of those fucking amps and feel every guitar lick and wailed lyric right in our groins. There are always a few civvies at the sidelines, and they must be wondering what the fuck's going on; they see a bunch of old soldiers in army fatigues jerking around near the stage with these ecstatic looks on their faces, because they can all feel the noise. We'll be there all night, and we'll come back every night.

The music was the only thing that kept my mind off the horror of what I'd seen. My job sure didn't; there's nothing more tedious than doing the same task over and over, and your thoughts starts to wander. In my case, it always wandered right back to a desert on the other side of the world and a trigger-happy asshole who'd killed a kid. My elbows immersed in warm, sudsy water meant seeing a five-year-old take a bullet in the chest yet again. And again. And again. Of course everything meant that; I saw it while I worked, while I ate, while I rode the train from home to work, and in my dreams while I slept. I saw it while I tried to parse what the boss said, while I tried to buy the right breakfast cereal, while I tried to read or watch things on television that I couldn't completely understand.

Sometimes I thought about really trying to find Craig; find him and somehow bring him to justice. If I could locate Quint, and the other two guys who'd been there, we could all testify. But then I'd remember that the dishes I washed felt like the smell of spoiled food, and I knew I'd never find Craig or any of them on my own. I was fucked, and Craig was free.

Then Kevin arrived.

❍ ❍ ❍

When we walked outside, what it was like getting scrambled wasn't the first thing we talked about; that actually came later. No, the first thing was what Kevin showed me. He held up his phone, hit an app, and let me watch a video.

I didn't do well with movies; they unreeled in my head with a stream of tastes and the feeling of being prodded all over. I couldn't figure this one any better than the latest 3D Hollywood blockbuster, so I asked Kevin what it was.

"It's video from a helmet-cam. *Your* helmet-cam, specifically."

My heart did an arpeggio in my chest. "Is it Craig? Is it...?"

Kevin nodded. "Shooting a little boy, and two other people. Do you remember this?"

I thought I might cry. My face grew hot, which in turn made me smell smoke. "Remember it? Man, I've been trying to forget it for three years."

"We acquired this from a source. The government thought they'd buried it, but they just don't pay some of their workers enough."

"I tried," I told him, and I didn't care if he saw me wipe at my eyes, "God damn it, I tried to get them to listen to me, but they wouldn't, they told me it never happened, and—you're going public with it, right?"

The heady scent of a meadow on a warm summer day nearly overpowered me, and I knew that meant Kevin had put a comforting hand on my shoulder. "It's okay. Yeah, soon the whole world's going to see what Craig did, and know what happened to you. We just want to know that you'll back it up."

"I will. Fuckin' A, I will."

"Good. We'll take him down, then."

"If you can find him."

I tasted something odd; Kevin was looking at me strangely. "Uh, Jackson..."

"Call me Jack."

"Jack..." He stepped back, and I think he was looking deep into my eyes, like he was trying to see if my pupils were dilated, if I was high. I get that a lot. "He won't be hard to find."

"He won't?"

Kevin made a sound like a muscle jerk. "You can't recognize him, can you?"

My stomach started to knot. "Why?"

"Because he's right inside. In the club."

I went cold, and smelled nothing at all. "He's..." I couldn't get out anymore. It couldn't be true. "Show me," I said, a croak.

Kevin motioned, and I followed his blur of shifting flavors back into the club.

Just as we stepped inside, the band took the stage. The opening guitar chord struck me with a shiver, and I knew it'd hit the rest of the scrambleheads the same way. There must've been fifty of them there—every fucked-up vet on the eastern seaboard had come to get laid by the music. As the guitar player lashed into the first song, they trembled with the foreplay stroke of fingers against skin.

I had to struggle to stay focused on Kevin, as he pushed through them. The rhythm had kicked in now, and the ex-soldiers before the stage had become a seething, gyrating mass. A lot of them must have been wearing their old fatigues, because I tasted sand-blasted metal and sweat. Kevin paused just long enough to examine each face before pushing through again, pulling me after him. They ignored him; he was just a whiff of smell intruding on the beautiful noise they were feeling.

Finally Kevin stopped, and I tried to look where he was looking. He'd paused before a man who tasted the same as all the rest, whose gasps provoked the same sandpaper-y sensations that the others did. I must have looked perplexed, because Kevin leaned over, put his mouth up against my ear, and I felt, "Craig."

I tried to look, God *damn*, I tried, but the confused synapses in my brain sent the same wrong message. I had to take Kevin's word for it, that this was Sergeant Dean Craig, that this flood of sour tastes that made me gag was the murderer who had haunted me for three fucking years.

And then I knew: It was Craig. It had *always* been Craig. Of course; he'd been here right next to me, every time the band had played, show after show, night after night, for at least a year, and I'd been too fucked up to know it. He'd stood by me, shouting and gasping and ejaculating into his stained army pants just like I had, and every night I'd let him walk away from the show. Every night I'd let this fucking killer go home; it was practically like I'd helped the army lie about Craig's crimes. Except they'd done it skillfully; I'd done nothing, just sat back like a useless lump of flesh and let them all go on.

No more. Not tonight.

"Can I have your phone?" I asked Kevin. My new best friend Kevin, a man my age who would never really understand what it was like to wake up screaming and feel the sound, although later I'd try to explain it to him, and he would nod and I'd taste his nod rather than see it, but he wouldn't get it. He would put Craig away while I struggled against my own senses just to wash other people's food-stained plates.

Kevin gave me his phone. It was still set up to the helmet video, the one that would show the whole world what Craig had done, and his supporters had covered up. I fingered the "play" arrow. The video started. I hoped it was at the right place; I only knew I tasted something like the bottom of a garbage pail.

Craig was bouncing around with the rest, but he slowed and then stopped when I held the video up before his face. He was being assaulted with tastes that he couldn't put together, even though he tried. He knew it was bad. Really fucking bad.

I leaned over to him, screaming to be heard over the music, hoping he was at least as good as I was at unscrambling our scrambled signals.

"Craig," I shouted, my lips an inch from his ear, "you're fucked."

He felt that, all right, because he turned and stared at me. "Who the goddamn hell are you?" he asked, his body still trying to jitter to the music.

"Private Jackson Howard, SIR." I saluted him—and then, while my hand was still on my forehead, I curled down all but my middle finger.

That got through, because Craig panicked and bolted.

He didn't even make it off the dance floor before I caught up to him. I grabbed a fistful of his shirt and yanked him around, and for a split second my senses unscrambled, and I saw his face, his real face, at the same time as I saw his memory face, three years ago, as he stood over a dead family.

When my fist connected with Craig's face, I smelled ozone and rank fear sweat, and he dropped to the floor as I tasted bile...but the image in my head of a shot-up kid wasn't tainted with any sensation but horror, it was clear as yesterday, and it drove me to squat and hit him again. the music was still going, and they were playing my favorite song, but the release I was feeling was anything but sexual. It was knowing that the nightmares might end now, and that I might be able to get through a day without feeling/smelling my gut drop out whenever I thought about the war. It was knowing that the dark alleys in my dreams might be empty at last.

Then somebody—Kevin—was pulling me back, and I stumbled to my feet, and he shouted, "You got him, Jack. It's done."

I was panting, and I knew there was blood on my knuckles, but I didn't care. The music took me, then, and it was a victory dance and an orgasm and a giant jitter of joy and relief all together.

The noise had never felt so good.

BAD MAGIC

The True Worth of Orthography

The magician took a seat at a table in the rear of the coffee house, flipped open a leather-bound journal, and began to write. His instrument was a pen with a fat, square, sponge nib; the ink flowed in perfect dark lines that occasionally spun off into flourishes. His thick brows drew together; the furrows in his sand-colored skin formed like cracks in a mud brick after a storm.

He didn't look up as a young woman approached. Holding a grande frappuccino in one hand and a laptop computer under the elbow, she pushed aside long blonde hair to find an empty table near the magician. She sat down, opened the laptop, sipped from her drink, waited for the machine to fire up, sipped from her drink, stared for a while at an empty word processing screen, sipped from her drink, and finally glanced up.

After a few seconds of watching the magician at work, she leaned forward and said, "God, your writing's so beautiful."

When the magician didn't respond, she went on. "It's not a screenplay, is it? I mean, I think that'd make you the only person here who's not working on a screenplay. Me included. 'Course I haven't gotten very far yet—'"

Without looking up, the magician spoke, cutting her off; he had a faint trace of accent. "If you please, I need to concentrate."

The young woman nodded, held up a hand apologetically

and leaned back. "Oh, right, sorry." She went back to her computer screen, halfheartedly typed two words, and then laughed at herself. "Jesus, that's pathetic. 'Fade in' is all I've managed so far."

The magician's strokes grew bolder, the ink lines thicker.

"Everybody makes it seem so easy. You know, you buy these books like *How to Write a Screenplay in a Two Days*, but..."

His frown and focus deepened.

"Maybe I should try acting instead."

The magician drew his hand across the page with a final, definitive curl, twisting his hand.

"My mom said—"

The young woman vanished.

The magician smiled to himself, capped his pen, closed his journal and stood. His gaze turned from the laptop that still glowed on the table and the half-empty frappuccino to another man who stood on the far side of the coffee house, watching, his mouth agape in open astonishment.

No one else had noticed.

The magician picked up the laptop, snapped it shut, and walked across the room to the staring middle-aged man. He extended the computer. "Would you like this? As a souvenir? I of course can't abide the damn things."

The man dumbly accepted the offered machine, holding it gingerly as if it might start shrieking any second, screeching out accusations of murder. "I don't...would they be able to trace her through this...?"

The magician's smile broadened. "I still have much to teach you."

"I don't understand."

"No, they won't be able to trace her, because she never existed. At least where the rest of the world is concerned."

The magician walked out of the coffee house, leaving the man alone. After a few seconds, he opened the laptop and looked down at the glowing word processor screen.

It was empty. He'd seen the woman type something onto it, but her words had vanished along with the rest of her. She'd never existed.

Feeling both terrified and saddened, the man closed the laptop and followed the magician out of the coffee house.

❸ ❸ ❸

The magician's library was exquisite.

The middle-aged man, who was a writer named Marshall Watts, scanned the volumes on the sixteen-foot-high book cases, some hidden behind rolling wood-and-brass ladders. Most of the books looked old; many were bound in nondescript 16th-century tan vellum, some had elaborate metal hinges and ornamentation, some were even not even really books but were tall custom-made folios housing millennium-old scrolls and manuscripts.

Marshall, who had once written a highly-regarded (but little read) novel based on the life of the early 20th-century occultist Aleister Crowley, spotted a volume bearing his subject's name and the title *The Collected Works*. Curious, he pulled it down, and felt his heart stutter when he saw that not only was it signed and inscribed by Crowley ("To my dear Frater Alexander"), but Crowley had annotated it throughout with handwritten comments. "My God, this must be worth a fortune."

Alexander—the magician—shrugged. "Undoubtedly. But it has greater value to me than that provided by money."

"Of course." Marshall carefully replaced the volume and turned to his host, pondering the "greater value" comment. Crowley had died in 1947, but Alexander didn't look a day over 40; surely he wasn't suggesting that *he* was the Alexander who Crowley had inscribed the book to?

"Aleister, sadly, was unable to master the techniques I tried to teach him. He'd still be alive if he had."

Marshall restrained an urge to laugh. It wasn't the first time that Alexander Nabu had left Marshall torn between disbelief and fascination. Marshall's agent had arranged their first meeting, yesterday; he said Nabu needed a ghost writer for a project that would come with a six-figure advance. Marshall had an ex-wife, two children, a teaching job that had tenure but continual budget cuts, a mortgage he was falling behind on, a drinking problem, and a last novel that had failed to find more than a thousand readers.

Yesterday, Nabu had told him the book was about magic; today, Nabu had *shown* him magic, first with the blonde woman, and now here, in his house. When they'd approached on a popular street in one of the Hollywood Hills canyons, Alexander couldn't shake the notion that he'd driven past this lot just a week ago and it had been vacant; now a classic 1920s-style Mediterranean home surrounded by tall hedges sprawled here.

"You still haven't told me about your project," Marshall ventured.

Nabu gestured at a large, comfortable couch, and Marshall sat. "Yes. Well, perhaps it's better if I show you..." He opened the leather notebook he'd used at the coffee house, and set it on an elegant table before Marshall. Beside the notebook, he laid down the pen with the thick nib. "I used these at the coffee house. Please examine the last sentence."

Marshall squinted; the writing was so elegant and ornate it took a few seconds to read:

The young blonde woman vanishes. The final "s" trailed off in a swirl of ebon ink.

"So...you...wished her away, is that it?"

"You know that Crowley spoke of the 'True Will', of finding one's ultimate purpose in life...? I discovered my purpose when quite young: I could affect my will through writing. And I don't mean 'writing' as in what you do, Marshall; I mean the actual art of the rebus, of finding a visual representation for the sounds we make to communicate."

"Orthography, in other words."

Nabu smiled, pleased. "Yes, precisely. Orthography: the way we write down our language. If you think on it, writing is an astonishing act; when we read, we are incapable of other thought, and so writing allows one man to enforce his thoughts on another, without the use of verbal means. This is nearly the definition of magic, as well."

Marshall glanced at the page again, at the beautifully rendered letters. "So writing is magic..."

"When done properly, yes. But it's an extremely difficult art to perfect; only a handful of magicians have ever used orthography properly, and none have achieved my level."

Marshall thought back to the blonde woman, looking for a flaw, for the trick, the scam. A concealed mirror, a trap door, a distraction. He couldn't find it, but was sure it had been there. "Why should I believe you?"

"Would you like another demonstration?"

"Please."

Nabu retrieved the notebook and pen, positioned them carefully on his knees. "What would you like to see?"

Marshall thought for a moment, trying to imagine something that Nabu would have no familiarity with, something he couldn't possibly know about. The teacher who'd first told him he had a gift for stories, who he'd wished for forty years now that he could go back and thank. "My second grade teacher, Mrs. Woods."

Nabu's pen flowed across the page, his wrist moving in practiced precision. He wrote for several seconds...

An elderly woman with stout figure, 1960s-era floral print dress, and coiffed white hair stood in the library with them. Marshall openly gasped; he'd forgotten so much about her: the glasses with the tortoise-shell rims, the glittery peacock broach she liked to wear. Her warm, patient smile.

"Mrs. Woods..."

He half rose, and she simply ceased to be.

A choked sob caught in Marshall's throat. He still

hadn't had time to say what he'd wanted to her. "I thought she was dead all these years..."

Nabu closed his journal. "She is. I did not summon her from the living."

Marshall's blood froze. He had to swallow down an impulse to run, back to the world he knew, where the dead didn't reappear because of a line of careful writing.

"What...what do you want me for?" Marshall heard his voice reduced to a near-whisper by fear, and didn't care.

"Rest easy, sir; you have nothing to fear from me. If you dislike my proposal, you are free to leave here, and you will not remember me within the hour."

Or will I be the one who is no longer remembered? Marshall wondered.

"Go ahead," he said.

"I have reached a point beyond which I cannot pass," Nabu said, rising to pace as he spoke. "I want the abilities of the ancient Egyptians, the scribes of whom communicated directly with their gods. Or the ancient Chinese calligraphers, who summoned dragons for their emperors. I am adept in those language forms as well—in fact I believe the Egyptian hieroglyphics to be the most beautiful writing—but I remain unable to reach beyond. There is a divine realm I can sense, but not truly penetrate. I believe the reason for this is that my writing is transcendent, but my words are dull. I need to meld my talents with those of an author. I need you to create what I write."

"So you want to hire me to...what, create spells?"

"Essentially, yes."

Marshall looked away, stunned. When he could muster speech again, he asked. "Spells to...do what?"

"As I said: I want to converse with gods. I want to know the unknowable, to attain higher power."

Marshall thought about a girl who had just vanished, and Nabu's expression as he'd looked up at Marshall. Smug. Regardless.

"Why do you think I have the talent you need?"

Nabu shrugged. "You obviously have some interest in this area already. And you're a gifted author."

"You've read my books?"

"Yes. Impressive."

When Marshall didn't respond, Nabu continued, "I know it may still not work, but I assure you: you will be paid for your efforts."

Marshall wondered how much Robert Oppenheimer had been paid for his work on the Manhattan Project. What was it Oppenheimer had later said about his part in the creation of the atomic bomb? "Now, I am become Death, the destroyer of worlds."

Would I be giving Nabu the ability to destroy worlds?

"I need some time to think about it."

"Of course. Take what you need. I have nothing but time."

Marshall peered at Nabu's face again—the skin a shade darker than his own, the heavy brows, dark brown eyes—and realized he couldn't begin to guess the man's age. "How old are you, exactly?"

Nabu smiled. "Look up my name when you return home."

❂ ❂ ❂

Marshall did.

Nabu was the Babylonian god of writing. The first god of the written word, when writing had been not letters or pictures, but wedges pressed into clay.

He called Marshall when he found that online. "Is Nabu your real name?"

"No, but I think it more appropriate. Don't you?"

Marshall didn't answer.

❂ ❂ ❂

Marshall spent two days contemplating, drinking, weighing alternatives.

He went to the best used bookstore in Los Angeles and looked at books that reproduced early illuminated manuscripts; he wondered if the monks who had drafted them in the first millennium had called up devils or angels. He wondered if any of them had been Nabu. He looked at books on magic, and on the history of writing, and on Aleister Crowley (and grimaced when he saw his novel shelved in the non-fiction section). He looked at books on Babylonian mythology, and saw carvings of Nabu, the patron god of scribes, bearing scrolls. He wondered what would have been contained in those scrolls.

What he finally concluded: if he didn't help Nabu, the magician would find someone else; authors were plentiful in Los Angeles.

If he agreed, he stood to meet God along with Nabu.

So he agreed...and hoped this was his choice, not something that Nabu had magicked into him.

۰ ۰ ۰

"Where do I start?"

They were together in Nabu's library, Marshall's own laptop (he'd kept the blonde woman's, but had been unable to bring himself to use it) set up before him.

Something skittered at the far end of the room, where the shadows gathered even in early afternoon. Marshall stared, trying to penetrate the gloom, feeling a shiver ripple across his back.

"Describe how you would reach Heaven."

Marshall caught a glimpse of golden eyes flashing in the darkness, and a whiff of something rotten.

"Are you sure it's Heaven you're after?"

Nabu frowned and followed his gaze. Marshall heard a distinctive, sibilant hiss from whatever lurked at the end of the library.

"My apologies," muttered Nabu, picking up a brush and bending down over a sheaf of parchment. "An experiment that I thought I'd finished."

Marshall heard the soft sound of brush strokes on paper; he held his breath, straining to hear anything else. Nabu finished his work, and Marshall relaxed as he felt a chill leave the room. "What was that?"

"It doesn't matter now. We were saying..."

"We were talking about what I'm going to write. It's going to take some time."

"As I told you before, Marshall: I have time."

Marshall closed the laptop and left.

✪ ✪ ✪

Marshall soon realized that he'd always had far more experience with Hell than Heaven.

He had no idea where to begin. He typed a dozen opening sentences before deleting them all. He looked at books, films, works of art. He walked through restaurants and shopping malls, seeking inspiration. But he had always been inclined to notice and comment on imperfections. He was more interested in corruption than sainthood, in evil than good.

He finally realized Nabu was as well.

He began to write.

✪ ✪ ✪

Nabu gazed at the print-out that Marshall had handed him. After a few moments, he sagged into a chair, still scanning the text that filled two single-spaced pages.

"Well...?" Marshall asked, when he could stand waiting no longer.

"It's not what I expected."

"Will it work?"

Nabu read again, then pointed at a line halfway down the first page. "This line—'The eternal ladder that ascends also rests far below, in primordial mud and blood, the ladder twists as it rises and evolves, as it leaves chaos and dark for order and light'—this I can make work. Think of how the lines will look when written, not how they appear on this screen. This—" he flung a dismissive hand at the screen, "—means nothing."

Marshall nodded. "Then it might be helpful if I had some of your writing, so I could get a sense of which letters to emphasize..."

Nabu handed the pages he'd just written to Marshall. "Of course. Take these."

Marshall glanced down at the last sentences, and saw, in Nabu's spidering hand: "I send you back to the hand of your maker, Tiamat. Leave this world."

He remembered a line he'd read in a Babylonian creation myth, about how the furious mother god Tiamat had declared war on her own divine children and had created scorpion-men to carry out her will.

He wondered if scorpion-men had golden eyes that glowed from the darkness.

When he returned to his own home, he turned on every light and tried not to think about the shadows.

❂ ❂ ❂

"Yes," Nabu nodded, as he read the new pages he'd just been handed, "yes! This is better. Yes."

He took the typed pages and sat down at a writing desk. He chose a metal nib, inserted it into an exquisite jade pen, dipped it in ink, and began to write. After a few seconds he turned to Marshall, who stood nearby.

"You may go."

Marshall didn't question the command. He left.

❂ ❂ ❂

Marshall sat at home that night, lights turned up, drinking scotch. He wondered if he would know—if *everyone* would know—if Nabu had succeeded. Would the monstrous armies of long-forgotten goddesses suddenly appear, rampaging down modern city streets? Would all light wink out, replaced by the permanent void?

No, Marshall thought. I can't do this. I won't sit here drinking, wondering if I've condemned my world.

He staggered to his feet, set the bottle aside, and picked up Nabu's handwritten leaves. He cleared space on his kitchen table—his own work desk was cluttered with computer supplies and equipment—and found a black marking pen that was the closest thing he had to one of Nabu's writing utensils. He grabbed the top sheet from a stack of clean white pages, laid it before him, and began to write, as neatly as he could.

He decided he would test himself with something small, so he wrote of a single sheet of paper catching fire, bursting into luminosity when its own inherent energy was released in one explosive outpouring. He wrote for hours, trying to pour himself into his moving hand, referring to Nabu's work, trying to copy the magician's style and beauty.

Nothing happened. The paper did not burst into flame, it didn't glow or tremble.

At some point Marshall set down the pen and clutched at his head in despair. Why had he thought he could master in a few short hours what Nabu had studied for years, decades, centuries? It was ridiculous, of course. It was like expecting a child to play Beethoven perfectly. He could never hope to copy Nabu's work—

He abruptly stopped as an idea struck him. He remembered a friend, Clark, who was adept at graphic design on his computer...a drunken afternoon spent designing new business cards that Marshall had never actually printed up...

An hour later Marshall's phone rang. He was almost shocked to hear Nabu's voice, sounding normal, mortal, carried across the 4G waves. "It almost worked," Nabu told him. "I could feel energy moving through the room, gathering...but I couldn't quite direct it. Just one more re-write, I think."

Nabu gave him suggestions, hung up.

Marshall laughed to himself: Even this assignment comes with new drafts.

ⵔ ⵔ ⵔ

When Nabu called the next morning, Marshall asked for a few more days.

At the end of the week, he told Nabu he had something for him. They met in the library, and once again Marshall had his laptop. He opened it, brought it out of hibernation, and turned it carefully facing him, away from Nabu. He tried not to shake as he readied his fingers over the keys.

"What do you have for me?" Nabu asked, anxiously. The library felt different. It *looked* different, somehow less solid and real, as if the last attempt at their merged spell had begun to strip away layers of the border around reality. Marshall tried not to imagine a wall now thinner, the things that prowled just beyond growing more excited, stinger-tipped tails quivering in anticipation of sinking into flesh...

"Give me a moment," Marshall said, gathering focus. He took a breath to steady himself (wishing he had a drink), typed a last few words, stood while juggling the laptop, and hit the ENTER button.

Nabu was gone, as was the library.

Marshall stood in a vacant lot, weeds pushing up through cracks in old, crumbling concrete; at the edge of the concrete, the thick, brown growth of Southern California's wildlife encroached. He stood for a few seconds, stunned by his own success, staring down at the words on his computer screen:

The magician, Alexander Nabu, is only a creation in the life work of Marshall Watts. As a character owned by Watts, Nabu's entire existence is controlled by the author. When Watts decides that he's finished with the character, he completes Nabu's arc by hitting the computer key labeled "ENTER."

Of course Marshall knew it wasn't the words that had given him victory, but the font, made from a scan of Nabu's own writing by his friend Clark, who possessed superb font creation software.

Marshall exited the word processing program, choosing not to save the document he'd just typed; no point in tempting fate, not when he'd deleted Nabu and possibly saved the world.

But he still possessed Nabu's font.

He figured he had plenty of time to decide how he'd use it.

Erasure

Linda pulled her gray fleece jacket tighter, huddling against the cemetery chill. Usually October afternoons in Los Angeles weren't this cold, but the weather was as inescapably devoid of warmth as the rest of her life.

She trudged past the mausoleums, barely lifting her head to regard her surroundings. She didn't have to; she'd come this way every day for the last three months

Ever since Keith had died.

His headstone was just a plaque buried in the grass; Linda knew that made the lawns easier to mow. The Rose Glen Memorial Park on the edge of Los Angeles wasn't especially old or scenic, but Keith had chosen it because it was affordable. His grave at least was near a scenic olive tree; normally Linda was glad to have the shade, but today she was cold as she lowered herself before Keith's little memorial plaque and the blank space beside it that would someday hold hers. She didn't mind kneeling or sitting in the brittle, half-dead ground cover; it put her closer to Keith, after all.

Linda was angry today, although anyone watching her wouldn't have known that. Just before she'd left the house, her sister Ally had called.

"You are *not* still going to the cemetery every day, are you?"

"So what I I am? What business is it of yours?"

Her sister's voice on the other end of the phone was taut with scorn and disbelief. "You're right, why should I give a rat's ass? Just because you've been fired for taking two-hour lunches so you could go there every fucking day—"

Linda cut her off. "I wasn't fired, I was laid off when the company restructured."

Ally ignored her. "Linda, you need help. Go to a doctor, get yourself some antidepressants or therapy or *something*. It's been three months since the heart attack...how long does this go on?"

"As long as it needs to," Linda answered just before she hung up.

A part of her knew Ally was right—she shouldn't be doing this, maybe a doctor could help—but the bigger part of her found comfort in the routine of daily mourning. It wasn't even so much that she missed Keith, that she refused to let him go, because while he'd been alive there'd been times—*many* times—when she'd wished he *would* go. It hadn't been a happy marriage, at least not for years.

Linda reached the small plaque set into the earth—*Keith Marshall McMann 1970-2015*—spread out the blanket she always brought, and lowered herself to the earth, her knees protesting. She was getting old. Getting old without Keith.

She looked down at the plaque and thought (again) about changing it. Shouldn't she have added *"Beloved Husband,"* even if it wasn't particularly true? All the other plaques said something—*"World War II Veteran"* or *"Husband, Father, Friend"* or *"Resting in God's Arms."* But none of those were true in Keith's case, although Linda wasn't entirely sure of the last. If there was a God, she doubted that He'd want Keith in His arms.

Keith hadn't been an especially pleasant man. When he'd been young, when Linda had first met him, he'd possessed a sort of cruel handsomeness; he had the face of a dashing hitman, with dark eyes and sharp cheekbones. He'd taken to Linda as if she'd been a new car, something to be acquired and polished, shown off but cursed when it was too slow or a part failed. Linda had chafed under his control, and their marriage had quickly settled into a pattern of loud arguments followed by weeks of irritable silence.

The heart attack that felled him in seconds (and at too young an age) should have been a blessing for Linda; as she'd returned from his funeral to a quiet house that was now completely hers, she'd had a moment of wild exultation...that had soon given way to loss. Not the loss of Keith, but the loss of a way of life she'd endured for twenty-five years. Without the fights and the bitter quiet, her world felt even emptier, so she filled it as best she could with a grief that she knew wasn't entirely real.

It was still better than acknowledging what a failure her life had been.

Bastard, Linda thought as she knelt before all that was left of her husband. *You took my life, and this is what I'm left with. A house that needs more repairs than its even worth, no job, only a little savings, no friends because no one wanted to be around us, not even a child to comfort me—*

"Hello."

Linda jerked up to see a woman standing a few feet away. The woman was young, mid-twenties, slender, wearing a long dark coat that had probably been chic at some point in the past. When Linda saw the small laptop computer the woman clutched in one hand, she remembered where she'd seen her: sitting on a bench a short distance away tapping on that laptop every day for the last week.

"I'm sorry, I didn't mean to startle you..." When Linda didn't respond, the woman went on. "It's just that I've seen you come here every day, and...if you don't want to talk, I'll go away."

"No," Linda said, surprising herself. "It's okay." She got to her feet, trying not to groan with the effort, and extended a hand. "I'm Linda."

The younger woman accepted the offered hand with a grip so strong it was almost painful. "You can call me

Azzie. I'd tell you what it's short for, but it's really long and usually unpronounceable."

"'Usually'?"

Azzie shrugged. "For most people. Anyway, I like Azzie." She gestured down at the grave. "Your husband?"

Linda nodded. "He died three months ago. Heart attack."

"Oh, I'm sorry. That must have been hard on you."

Linda almost answered, "Not as hard as the twenty-five years of marriage that came before it," but instead she said, "It was."

"Have you...have you come here every day since?"

Linda nodded again.

"You must have loved him very much."

This time Linda remained still. She couldn't lie that much, not to a friendly young person whose life was still fresh enough to be open to possibility.

Azzie took a step back. "Really, I didn't mean to intrude..."

Linda realized she was hungry to talk about something other than Keith, so she glanced at Azzie's laptop. "Do you come here every day to write?"

"Sort of. It's not a novel or a screenplay or anything like that. More like a...collection of memories, I guess."

"Oh. That sounds interesting. Are you hoping to get it published?"

Azzie laughed and rolled her eyes. "Oh *God* no! It's just for me. So I don't forget."

Linda didn't know how to respond, although Azzie seemed to be waiting for something. "You must have a lot of memories."

"I do."

Azzie peered at Linda for a second before saying, softly, "Not everyone wants their memories."

A jolt of anxiety pierced Linda. Did Azzie know something about her? Had she known Keith? Could she have been another of his little triumphs, one in the string of affairs Linda knew he'd had? Secretaries, store clerks, women met by chance in bars...Linda had once waited until he was asleep and then gone through Keith's phone, and discovered dozens of numbers and names, all female, that she couldn't identify. Sometimes, when he'd come home very late, she'd even been able to smell them on her husband.

"Did you know Keith?"

Azzie shook her head. "No."

Linda believed her...which left her again puzzling over the woman's intention. The breeze through the cemetery seemed to grow colder, and Linda wanted to be away from here, somewhere warmer, somewhere alone. "It was nice meeting you, but I need to get home—"

Azzie cut her off. "What if you could get rid of what you're feeling?"

The words seemed so irrelevant that Linda stopped, caught between laughing and curiosity. Was Azzie some sort of guru, a new age saleswoman offering false hope and fantasy? "Let me guess: I sign up for your course at a very reasonable price, and you teach me some method that makes me a better person."

"No. I literally take away your memories. And without those...no more anger, resentment, disappointment."

Linda's mouth opened, but no response came out. Azzie had just revealed that she knew Linda's secret, the one she thought she kept so artfully hidden. She looked away, hoping to hide her dismay at being discovered, and said instead, "And why on earth would I believe that?"

"Because you've done it before."

Linda turned to look at her, confused. "What are you talking about?"

"Your son, David."

"Ah, now I see: you've made a mistake. I'm obviously not who you think I am, because I've never had a son. Keith and I had no children."

"Look down, Linda."

For a second Linda almost turned and walked away; she knew it was what she *should* do. But instead, her eyes betrayed her and looked.

There was Keith's plaque, in the ground, the sickly grass edging up against it, and there beside it was the empty space intended for her, and there next to it was the plaque reading *David Patrick McMann1999-2009 Beloved Son.*

"How did you...what is this?"

Before Linda could react, before she could pull away, Azzie reached out and took her hand. Azzie's touch brought the memories: of how she and Keith had decided to try to save their marriage by having a child and they'd conceived a son, a son who was a squawling bundle of hope, who grew into a toddler who made them laugh in exasperation, memories of a smart little boy in glasses who dazzled his kindergarten teacher with the list of books he'd already read, of Keith teaching him math and showing him how to hit a free throw, of Linda watching his glee when he opened his birthday presents, of the day his eyes rolled into his head and he fell over on the school playground, of hearing the doctors tell them it was a brain aneurysm and they'd try to save him, but the operation had failed, and they'd buried David here, and Keith's heart was gone, he lost himself in a series of meaningless affairs while Linda drank and shouted and blamed Keith's DNA for the genetic time-bomb in their son's skull.

One day Linda had come to the cemetery, anxious to escape another confrontation at home, and she'd met an attractive young woman who had offered to take her pain away, and the offer had been irresistible.

Now Linda found she was on her knees, sobbing as she clenched fistfuls of the dying grass, calling David's name over and over. She finally looked up at Azzie, desperately. "Please...please, take it away again."

Azzie knelt beside her, with great compassion. "Linda, you have to decide first: do you want me to also take Keith?"

Linda choked back the sobs as it hit her: this offer was

real, not a hoax or a trick, not the ramblings of a huck-
ster or a crazy person. She looked at Azzie and whispered,
"What are you?"

Azzie half-smiled, and for an instant Linda saw something very old in her face. "Just someone who might value
your memories more than you do."

"Why would you value them?"

"They keep me alive."

"How many times have you done this?"

"I don't know. It would be like me asking you how many
times you've eaten."

Linda crouched there, over the graves, her thoughts a
frantic kaleidoscope. David dead, erased from her memory, returned now, the pain so great it threatened to crush
her into the graveyard dirt, and how could she not have
known, she'd had a son, how was that possible—

"I don't understand. Even if I'd forgotten David, other
people hadn't…"

Azzie answered, "That's right. Other people have mentioned him around you, even shown you pictures…but you
simply don't hear or see them. I can't erase David's existence from the world, only from you. It'll be the same with
Keith: if friends ask you about him, you won't know. Don't
we all tend to hear or see only what we want to anyway?"

To never have to think about Keith again, his casual
cruelties, the lies she could see through so easily, the thousand little petty betrayals—

"Linda? I have to go soon…"

"All right. Do it."

Azzie smiled and inhaled deeply. "I just need your
hand."

Without rising, Linda held out her right hand. Azzie
took it, standing over her. Azzie's touch was firm, warm,
almost electric.

Linda waited…and then she felt it: the memories being
uprooted, pulled away from her, and in that instant she
saw *all* of them, not just the bad she'd chosen but the good

she'd pushed away, and there *had* been good, especially in the beginning, when Keith had been young and dapper, smitten with her, he'd wooed her with songs he sang under her window in a passable imitation of Dean Martin, he'd won her with the way he held her when they danced, how he looked at her, how they made each other laugh, and suddenly a part of Linda tried to cling to those memories, inwardly crying out as they were torn away. She tried to pull her hand from Azzie's grip, but the other woman—or whatever she was—was stronger, *much* stronger, and she nearly crushed Linda's fingers. Linda cried out, but her protests were unanswered.

I'm so sorry, Keith, I wasn't fair to you, I've wallowed in the worst part of you because it was easier than blaming myself. Now I don't want to lose

◊ ◊ ◊

Linda felt dry, parched grass beneath her legs. She looked around in confusion, saw she was in a cemetery. A younger woman stood nearby, her eyes closed as she panted, apparently in some kind of ecstatic state.

"I don't understand," Linda muttered, to herself, but the other woman overheard and opened her eyes. She gazed down at Linda with a strange compassion and asked, "Are you okay?"

"I'm not sure. I don't know where I am, or how I got here..."

"You're at the Rose Glen Memorial Park. Are you trying to find a grave, or...?"

Wisps of thought drifted through Linda's mind and she tried to catch them, but they evaporated. "Maybe..."

"You were bent over this one." The woman pointed; Linda glanced down and saw the name "Keith."

"No, I don't know anyone named Keith."

The younger woman helped Linda to her feet and turned her to face her car, parked a short distance away. "Tell you what: why don't you head home, sit down with a nice glass of wine, and I bet you'll forget all about this trip."

"Yes, that sounds good..."

Linda staggered a few steps, stumbled on a half-buried plaque. The woman caught her elbow and held her up. Linda righted herself, said, "Thank you. I really don't know what's happened to me. I think I might have come here to visit someone, but..."

The younger woman said, "He was actually a very decent man."

"Who was?"

"No one."

Linda turned to look at her, curious, but saw only a shadow against the dying lawn. By the time she reached her car, she'd forgotten even the shadow.

But it didn't seem to matter.

The Rich are Different

I can hear Lennox outside the door. It's almost dawn; I'm not sure how long he's been out there in the hallway. I awoke when I heard something that sounded like a frog's croak calling my name.

I wonder what he looks like. The door is locked from the outside, but he may not be human enough to turn it. Part of me wants him to do it, to come in...but another part is afraid to see what he's become.

Even though we're in love.

❂ ❂ ❂

Of course he looked fine when we first met. It was the day of his thirty-fifth birthday party.

A week earlier, my agent, Lauren, had received an e-mail from a Wilmont family secretary. They wanted to invite me to a party, it said. Lennox Wilmont in particular was a fan of my book, *The Rich Are Different*. The party would be at their estate outside Atlanta. If my agent could provide my address, they'd send me a formal invitation.

Lauren called me and told me she thought it was real. I was surprised, to put it mildly; I'd have bet money that the Wilmonts would have hated the novel. Of course they knew it was loosely based on them (everyone knew that; after all, I'd said it in *People*), and it was not exactly a loving tribute. Critics had called the book "a vicious, razor-sharp indictment of America's super-wealthy"; Amazon reader reviews just said, "I couldn't put it down!!!!"

"Do you think I should go?" I asked Lauren.

"What are you kidding me? Damn straight, I think you should go. You've talked forever about wanting to get past those estate gates. Now they're handing it to you, and you're asking if you should go?"

She was right. I'd have to book a plane—

"They'll handle all your travel arrangements, by the way," Lauren added.

I told her to give them my address. The official invite arrived by courier the next day. There was a card in a foil lined envelope, first class round-trip plane tickets, and a little hand-written note about how they'd love to see me. The note was signed "Madelyn."

As in, Madelyn Wilmont, one of the wealthiest women on the planet, and the basis for the matriarch in *The Rich Are Different*. I'd made her older in my book—in real life she was only forty, not fiftysomething. I'd imagined what it would be like to meet her, get to know her...*be* her.

Five years ago I wouldn't have hesitated. But five years ago I was still married to Derek. Then I'd found Derek at the office Christmas party kissing his secretary nowhere near any mistletoe, and divorce had followed. I was just thankful we had no children to permanently fuck up, and I was still young enough to conceivably find someone else.

Except...I hadn't. I'd tried a few dates, but my confidence was shot. I felt middle-aged (at thirty-four), overweight, dowdy despite the best clothes book royalties could buy. I knew rationally that I wasn't, but...well, seeing your husband with his tongue halfway down the throat of a woman you never considered especially attractive apparently had some unexpected side effects.

So I'd buried myself in my work instead. It had paid off: I'd given up the celebrity pieces for *EW* and gone into novels. The first one, *Paper Cuts*, had been well reviewed and just barely successful enough that I was given a contract for a second book. That one had been *The Rich Are Different*, and it had scored bigtime. The advance had provided a generous down payment on a house in Chicago's suburbs. The movie option had allowed me to pay it off. Lauren had joked with me about being rich enough to be different.

Of course that'd been a year back. Since then my writing skills seemed to have migrated with my physical self-image. I spent too many days scrolling idly through social media instead of working on Book Number Three. My editor was concerned. Lauren was concerned. My ex-husband was...well, getting blow jobs from his secretary.

I spent too many hours telling myself I wasn't a failure. I might have gotten lucky once, but I was incomplete, purposeless. Friends (all married) told me I needed a man. I scoffed, we laughed...and then I went back to the house where I lived alone and tried to tell myself it wasn't like that at all.

Maybe a visit to the Wilmonts would reinvigorate me. What the hell. I wrote back to the e-mail address on the card and told them I'd be delighted to come. Someone named Jasmine replied instantly and said she'd add my name to the guest list, plus a limo would be waiting for me at the airport. I'd stay overnight at the Wilmont estate, and fly out again the next morning. No presents, please. The date was two weeks away.

I spent those fourteen days fussing and fretting—could I lose weight in two weeks? Should I change my hair color? What would I wear? Were they expecting me to be hipper and younger?

I shopped. I saw my hair stylist (but we stuck with my usual auburn). I didn't really lose any weight.

Of course I read up more on the Wilmonts, but I knew most of it. They stuck pretty much to themselves; no reality TV show for them, no trashy affairs with rock stars or DUI busts. They were rarely photographed in public, but when they were, they were beautiful. Given how much money they had, how could they have been anything else? Lennox had the sort of boyish, broad face and floppy dark hair that could have earned him willing women even if he hadn't been rich. Madelyn was sleek and serious, like a Maserati in human form.

Their wealth had always been something of a mystery. Way back in the 1840s, a Wilmont ancestor had migrated here from the Old World to grow tobacco and cotton. He'd already been well off, but he'd made even more money in America, mainly because he'd also invested in the slave trade and their assets had continued to accrue. Madelyn was married to a man named Alan Ashton; rumors circulated that he spent most of his time in a wing of the family mansion, drunk and enjoying the company of Prince Valium. They had one son, Grant, who should be 16 by now, but he hadn't been photographed in public since infancy. Lennox had never married. Their father, Harris the Third, still ran the family corporation, but he'd spent most of his life living in New York. Their mother had died young of cancer. There were no other siblings.

The big day arrived. I took so long making last minute decisions, changing outfits over and over, that I nearly missed my flight. I tried to relax in my spacious First Class seat, but I was tense and distracted.

I got off the plane with my bulging carry-on (ridiculous, I know, for an overnight stay) and when the escalators spilled me out into the baggage claim, I saw a man holding a sign with my name printed on it.

I stopped for a second, there at the bottom of the escalators, staring as other passengers bumped into me. The man holding the sign was at least seven feet tall, with a bulky, stooped frame. A cap was pulled low over his eyes; flat, sand-hued hair spilled out from under it. He wore oversized sunglasses, leaving me to imagine what color his eyes must be, and an overcoat that was too heavy for the southern warmth. For a second I considered turning around, or taking a cab out to the Wilmont estate...but then he saw *me*, and dropped the sign.

Well, I thought, *he's probably great security.*

I stepped forward, slowly. He reached one massive paw

(his large pink hand had stubby fingers) out and, wordlessly, took my bag. He turned and headed out of the baggage claim. With no other real choice left, I followed.

His limo was parked curbside. He opened the rear door for me, and I was glad to be separated from him by the sheet of glass between the driver and the rear passenger area.

We headed away from the airport. At least he was a cautious driver. I tried not to look at the back of his massive head, square and furry beneath the cap.

It took about forty minutes to reach the Wilmont estate. We left the freeway and got on a two-lane blacktop that wound through scenic hills and lush, wooded valleys before coming to a private drive that began with a guard booth and gate. He waved to whoever was in the booth; as we passed it, I tried to peer through the glass of the enclosure to see who was inside, but it was tinted, opaque.

It was late afternoon as we rolled onto the Wilmonts' private grounds. The sun was at the horizon, its long rays now silhouetting trees and out-buildings with golden auras. The driver slowed, moving at no more than 10 miles per hour. I was wondering why when I saw something running through the trees maybe 100 feet to the right. It was difficult to see clearly as it darted in and out of shadow and sight, but I saw enough to know its movements weren't right—it ran on two legs, but loped as if it was off-balance, flailing too-long arms wildly. I couldn't make out color or facial features, nor even guess at what it could have been. It was so improbable that I wondered if it was some sort of puppet or illusion.

I started to say something to the driver, knock on the glass between us and point, but then the strange runner vanished, and the house came into view.

It was even more impressive in person than it looked in the photographs and videos I'd seen. It lolled among the trees like a gigantic animal at rest, the upper floor windows bright with the last of the sun while lights glowed warmly from the lower rooms. The drive curved around before the double-door entrance, and we pulled to a stop there. The taciturn driver opened my door, took my bag and set it down at the top of the steps leading to the doors, then returned to the limo and drove off.

I heard music coming from somewhere nearby—live, jazzy—and smelled food cooking. I was just climbing the steps to ring when the door opened. Madelyn Wilmont smiled down at me.

I wasn't prepared for how stunning she was in person. She looked far younger than forty, with the sort of perfect casual elegance that only wealth can provide. She extended a welcoming hand to me, and I took it, surprised at its heat. "Hello, Sara, it's so lovely to meet you. I'm Madelyn."

A few of the reviewers of *The Rich Are Different* had praised its "sharp-tongued voice," while others had decried it as "needlessly verbose." Neither quality surfaced now; when faced with Madelyn Wilmont's effortless poise, I felt like a single leaf of wilted spinach, small and inadequate. I just grasped her hand and smiled.

She turned to indicate the entrance. "We've got a room ready for you—I thought you might like to relax a bit before joining the party. It doesn't really start for another hour anyway."

I started to reach for my bag, but Madelyn flicked a slender wrist. "Oh, no, dear, I'll have that brought up to you. The stairs to the second floor are quite a climb even without a heavy bag." She turned and strode into the house. I forgot my bag, following.

I tried not to stop and gape at the things we passed—delicate vases and furnishings that were probably invaluable, shelves of leather-bound books behind glass doors—but it was the art that staggered me. It ran the gamut from modern to Pre-Raphaelite. I found myself frozen before one large canvas in the style of Italian late Baroque. It was a landscape—classical ruins atop a hillside beneath a gloomy sky—but it was the figures in the image that caught my attention. At first glance they'd merely looked like dancers, or revelers, but upon closer inspection they were revealed as not entirely human; a leering face was topped by subtle horns, a bent torso perched atop shaggy goat legs. It was haunting, something out of a dream.

"Ah, I see you've found our Magnasco."

I saw Madelyn watching me, and I realized I'd been unaware I'd even stopped. "I'm sorry, who is it?"

"Alessandro Magnasco. He's one of our favorites."

Something about the way she said "our"—some implication of possession, perhaps—raised a few more unspoken questions. I forced myself to turn away from the painting, smiling. "I'm not familiar with Magnasco. This is fascinating, though."

"Not many people know him."

I looked at the painting again, my attention drawn to a figure loping across a clearing before a collection of cracked and tilted columns. Something about the figure... saturnine, long arms swinging, legs bent the wrong way—

"Shall we...?"

I jerked around, on the verge of a question, but broke off as Madelyn continued on up the stairs. We'd just reached the second floor landing when a voice from below called up, "So, that's Lennox's package?"

A man stood at the bottom of the staircase, looking up at us; he was middle-aged, balding, dressed in polo shirt and khakis, holding a drink in one hand. He swirled the contents of the glass, the ice inside tinkling.

Madelyn stopped, turning slowly, her gaze icy. "Alan, meet Sara Peck. Sara, this is my husband, Alan."

He saluted with the drink. I was just opening my mouth to greet him when he blurted out, "We'd introduce you to our charming so-called son Grant, but the little freak's out running loose somewhere—"

Madelyn cut him off, firmly but not loudly, a technique she'd probably honed from frequent use. "Alan, I'm sure there must still be a few bottles of gin out back that you haven't drunk up yet."

Alan smirked, started to amble off. "Of course. Good luck, Miss Peck. Oh, and by the way, dearest—this is vodka."

He vanished through a doorway, and Madelyn's shoulders sagged. "My apologies for that, Sara. My husband...well, he's developed an unfortunate tendency to over-self-medicate."

"No apologies necessary, Madelyn. I understand." Which wasn't entirely true; I didn't understand how a father could call his son "a little freak," and the crack about "running loose somewhere"...

Madelyn led me to a bedroom on the second floor that was roughly twice the size of my first apartment. "I thought you might enjoy the Gold Room," she said, with just a slight twist of sarcasm.

The room was furnished in tasteful gold and white, and I didn't have to ask if the finishes were real. I stepped to the spacious windows and looked out onto the rear of the Wilmont estate. Just below, dance floors had been set up around an Olympic-sized pool; a band played in one corner, people milled, chefs cooked at stations tucked in among marble statues and trimmed hedges. "Thank you, I'm sure I will." I turned to face her, and saw that she waited in the doorway, apparently expecting my question. "I have to confess, though, that I'm not quite sure why I'm here."

She smiled, laughed slightly, then said, "You're Lennox's birthday surprise. He's been a fan ever since he read your book, and he's been dying to meet you."

"Oh." A flutter circled my stomach. I was a "birthday surprise"? Was I expected, perhaps, to change into a bikini and pop out of a giant cake?

Madelyn must have seen something in my expression, because her own smile faded. "Sara, my brother and I are very close. I'm sure you'll find him quite charming." She backed away, reaching for the door. "I'll have your bag brought right up. I'm really so happy to have you here."

She stepped out, closing the door behind her.

As I used the bathroom (a little in awe of the *real* gold fixtures), my anxiety ramped up. What was expected of me? Why did the bit about Madelyn and her brother being "very close" sound like a jealous wife's warning? What if I didn't fit the picture Lennox had of the author of *The Rich Are Different*?

As I stepped out of the bathroom, I was heading for my purse to get a Xanax when a knock came at my door. I steeled myself, expecting the limo driver, and pulled the door open.

Lennox Wilmont stood there, my bag grasped in one hand. When he saw me, his handsome face was split by a grin that made him look younger. "Oh my God, you really *are* Sara Peck!" He dropped the bag and stepped toward me, and for a second I expected him to fling his arms around me...but then he grasped one of my hands instead, the picture of youthful enthusiasm. "When Madelyn told me you were the guest in the Gold Room, I didn't believe it. I am *such* a fan!"

Lennox was everything I'd read: seemingly genuine, warm, magnetic...and very hot. Literally: his hand almost felt like it was scorching mine. I realized I was blushing, but forced myself not to turn away. Lennox saw it and laughed, but it was out of delight, not derision. He was so beautiful it was hard to look at him. "Happy birthday," I finally said, and even that came out too soft.

He released my hand, and part of me was sorry. "Thanks, but to tell you the truth...I hate these things. Maddie always wants to throw them, but I never feel quite comfortable among all those people."

"Really? That surprises me."

Lennox arched his eyebrows and gave me a half-smile. "Well, Ms. Peck, I hope I can show you some other surprises, too."

"Sara, please."

He nodded. "Sara."

We stood there for a moment, uncomfortable in that way that only two people who are very attracted to each other can be. Finally Lennox waved at my bag. "Would you like a few minutes to change, or...?"

"No, I'm fine, thanks. Should we go down to join your party?"

"Only if you want to. You know what I'd rather do?"

"What?"

"Show you the Beltane Room."

Now *that* was an interesting invitation. The Beltane Room was one of the most mysterious parts of the Wilmont estate. It appeared as side-mentions in family histories, the name apparently being derived from a three-day-long party that was held there in 1920, starting on the evening of April 30th—Walpurgisnacht, or Beltane in the old Celtic calendar. No one knew exactly what had happened at the party, or at least if they did they hadn't talked; they also hadn't mentioned what was in the room.

I said, "How did you know I was going to ask to see it?"

"I think we have a connection." He took my hand again, and the strength of my response—tingles of desire—made me light-headed. "Come on."

We exited the Gold Room and turned left heading out, away from the main staircase. "We'll take the servants' stairs so Maddie won't see us," he said.

He led me down the hall, through a doorway, down a narrow spiral staircase, and through a utility room. Opening another door there, he indicated more stairs leading down. "It's in the basement." He waved me ahead and glanced around to see if we'd been spotted.

I headed down the stairs and waited for him at the bottom. Around me was a utilitarian hallway, like something you might find beneath a hotel. He joined me, and I followed him to one end where he used a key to unlock an unmarked door. He reached inside, flipped a light switch, and bowed. "The Beltane Room, m'lady."

I stepped past him—and froze.

The room was large, unexpectedly so, and lit by two huge chandeliers overhead. It contained low divans, all upholstered in decadent velvets and brocades, and tables holding crystal decanters.

But the walls were the real attention-getter. They were covered with art, not framed paintings, but a mural painted right on the walls. Lennox pulled me to the left, so I stood in front of a recreation—or was it a continuation?—of the Magnasco painting I'd admired earlier. "Start here and follow it around."

The work looked like a hurried version of the Italian classicist; it was less perfect, more rushed, but similar in theme, with gods and nymphs cavorting among ruins.

"You've heard of the Beltane party that took place here in 1920...? Well, what you probably haven't heard is that one of the guests was a well-known artist who took three days to paint this. The other guests, who included famous actors, writers, and at least one newspaper mogul, drank bootleg liquor and smoked hashish and spent the three days here just watching him work. It's amazing, isn't it?"

I moved to my right, and saw that there was a definite progression to the painting: it grew darker, the figures more violent. Now they looked less like gods and more like monsters. "It looks like the Magnasco upstairs, but..."

"Yes. One of the guests was a medium—you know, they were all crazed for Spiritualism back then—and she swore the artist was channeling Magnasco."

"Who was the artist?"

"His name was Dennings. You wouldn't have heard of him. He was a highly-regarded forger, you see."

I came to a corner, turned to the right, and stared in shock. Now the figures on the walls had the dark, shaggy fur coverings of mammals, but they walked upright and bore human faces. And they were...well, not to put too fine a point on it, they were vigorously fucking each other. A few yards farther to the right, two of them were entwined above the dead body of a naked woman, blood pooled on

the ground around her severed legs. Feeling simultaneous-
ly nauseated and curious and excited, I moved around the
next corner and saw piles of dismembered corpses, some
with splayed legs as if they'd been violated.

"Jesus," I muttered.

"It's fascinating, though, isn't it?" Lennox stood behind me, so close that I could feel his presence like a storm
cloud. "They're gods, you know. Old, *very* old, gods. Can
you imagine watching this take shape beneath the artist's
brush, while around you a real-life orgy is happening? The
rich smells of the smoke...and the sex..."

A shiver passed through me, my own excitement surprising me. Lennox must have seen it because he purred
soft approval.

Past the next corner, the art gave way to words:

> *Once, long ago, in a land on the far edge of
> the world, there lived a poor shepherd. The
> shepherd, his wife, and their two children
> barely existed on goat's milk and a few
> rabbits the shepherd was able to snare...*

I bent down to read more, but paused when I felt Lennox
just behind me, his body close to mine, his breath hot on
my neck. I was suddenly afraid—not of him, not even of
the terrible scenes on the wall or the childish story, but of
myself, of what I might do if I suddenly turned, when he
was there behind me...

"Lennox!" That was Madelyn's voice. I hadn't heard the
door open, and I did turn, startled by her harsh tone. She
stood just inside the Beltane Room, her posture rigid. "The
party is upstairs."

Lennox was facing her, away from me, and he was
slightly hunched. When he spoke, his voice sounded too
deep, too rough. "Why can't you leave me alone?" A musky
scent hit me, strong enough that I backed away and tried
to breathe through my mouth.

Madelyn waved at Lennox angrily. "Stay here while

I escort Sara out." I hesitated; which of them did I prefer to displease? But Lennox kept his back to me, silent. "Lennox, I'm sorry," I said as I walked past him.

Madelyn led me upstairs, not back to the Gold Room, but out the front door where the limo waited for me, my bag already inside. "I'm so very sorry, Sara, this was entirely my fault." She handed me an envelope. Inside was a folded sheet of paper...and a check. I saw the words "NON-DISCLOSURE AGREEMENT" at the top of the sheet. I didn't bother to see how many zeroes were on the check. I passed the whole thing back to her. "Don't worry—it's not necessary to buy me off. I like Lennox too much to hurt him."

I climbed into the limo, pulled the door closed, and looked down into my lap. I didn't want Madelyn to see that was crying.

☻ ☻ ☻

The next day Lennox called me at home. "I'm sorry for that, Sara," he said. "I'd like to see you again."

"Your sister made it clear that was a bad idea, I think."

"My sister is not my keeper."

We chatted a while longer, about everyday things, almost like normal people: about birthdays and airport security and annoying passengers and weather. After an hour, Lennox asked me what I was doing later that night.

"Nothing," I answered, my heart hammering, feeling for all the world like a teenager on the phone with a cute guy.

Eight hours later, I was staring at a blank computer screen when there was a knock at my front door. Curious, I moved to the peephole, looked through...

Lennox was there, holding flowers.

I panicked. I was wearing dingy sweats; it hadn't occurred to me that he'd actually fly up. "Just a minute," I called through the door as I turned, unsure what to do first.

"You've got three minutes, then I bust this door down."

I fled to the bedroom, plundered the closet, realized I didn't have time to put on anything more serious than my best jeans and a plain pastel t-shirt with a v-neck that gave the illusion of cleavage. I was checking myself in the mirror a final time when he knocked again, more insistent. "I swear, Ms. Peck, in ten seconds—"

I gave up on primping, ran to the door, took a deep breath, opened it.

For an instant we just stared at each other, smiling, not quite believing. Lennox broke the silence at last. "You know, I just lied to my sister and flew through a storm to be here. Are you going to invite me in?"

"Of course. Please come in."

I stepped back and gestured. He handed me the roses (yellow, my favorite—how did he know?) and came in, looking around. I was immediately self-conscious, seeing every frayed furniture corner and speck of dust, but he just nodded. "So this is how real people live."

I was about to come back with some witty riposte when it occurred to me that Lennox probably really *hadn't* been in many homes that weren't mansions. Sitcoms were probably the closest he'd ever gotten to even upper-class suburbia.

I inhaled the heady scent of the bouquet. "These are lovely. Let me get them into some water."

I walked to the kitchen, set the flowers down to reach up to a high cabinet for a vase, had just pulled it out and was turning to fill it with water when I saw Lennox in the kitchen doorway, gripping the sides as if holding himself up. "I'm not very good with social skills, so I'm just going to say it: I haven't been able to stop thinking about you." His eyes locked onto mine, and I couldn't suppress a small tremor. I had to look away just to keep any ounce of composure.

"Lennox, I..."

He stepped closer. "If you want me to leave, I will. If you want to sit and talk for a while, I'll try. But what I'd really like to do right now is kiss you."

I couldn't speak. I leaned back against the sink, breathless, as he pressed himself against me. His lips found mine, his hands were on my waist, my fingers twined around his neck, in his hair, pulling him down to me.

"Sara," he whispered, moving his tongue to circle an ear, then trace a delirious path down my jaw.

I said nothing because I was lost. I was lost in arousal, lost in my desire, my *need*, for Lennox Wilmont. I nearly sobbed because it annihilated me. I'd never felt this before, not even with my husband, when we'd been first married and still genuinely in love. When Lennox moved his hands down to my hips and pulled me to him until I could feel how hard he was, I groaned as my own lust broke my inner censors.

He moved his mouth down to my breast, seeking it through the thin fabric of my clothes, and I arched, wanting him to find it. He said my name again—

Something was wrong. His voice sounded strange, too coarse even though roughened by sex. Some part of me tucked safely away heard and sounded an alarm, but the other 99% chose not to listen, not to stop—

The front door burst open. I gasped and pushed Lennox away so I could turn.

The driver who'd met me at the airport stood there, his massive frame barely squeezed in. He was staring at us, and even from across the living room I could hear his breathing.

"Lennox, what—" I turned to look at him—and stared, stunned.

The skin on his face had changed color, going so pink it was almost fiery. His hair seemed longer, shaggy, his ears slightly pointed. But it was his eyes that really paralyzed me: they'd lost all color, including white, and were depthless black pools. He released me and started toward the driver. "Why can't she just leave me alone?"

It took me a second to realize the "she" wasn't referring

to me, but probably to his sister Madelyn. Lennox was making sounds now like something between a whipped puppy and a banshee wail, his frustration so overwhelming that he didn't even react as the driver gripped him by one shoulder and steered him out of my house. The driver said only one word as he led Lennox to the car:

"Father."

At least it *sounded* like "Father," but that made no sense; Lennox's father was dead, so the driver wouldn't be taking him to see Daddy Dearest. A priest, perhaps?

Whoever it was, I hated them for taking Lennox from me. I watched the car drive away, then went to my bathroom, turned on the shower, and cried as I stood under the water, still dressed.

❂ ❂ ❂

I got an e-mail from Lennox an hour later. It didn't say where he was—on a plane going home? Still in the car? In some other house owned by the Wilmonts?

∞

Dearest Sara:

∞

There's a story I'd like you to hear. You read part of it in the Beltane Room, but of course my sister wasn't about to allow you to read all of it. Well, in honor of Madelyn, here's the story for you:

> Once, long ago, in a land on the far edge of the world, there lived a poor shepherd. The shepherd, his wife, and their two children barely existed on goat's milk and a few rabbits the shepherd was able to snare. They weren't happy; they were hungry and cold.
>
> Things got worse after the shepherd's wife died, leaving him alone with two small

children. His wife had made the goat's milk into cheese; without her, they had only milk to drink. They were alone in the wild countryside, with no one to help them.

One day, as hunger gnawed at their insides, the shepherd cursed the gods for his ill fate...and lo, the very deity he'd blasphemed appeared before him. The shepherd began to shake with fear, for the god was fearsome in appearance, but the god smiled upon him. "You have called me, shepherd, and I've come to relieve your suffering...if you are willing to pay the price."

The shepherd fell to his knees, lowering his eyes. "Anything! Just give us food."

"I will give you more than food: you and yours shall always have good fortune. You will never again starve, or want for anything material. Your children will be as gods."

"Yes," the shepherd said, sobbing in gratitude, "yes, yes!"

"But the price is this: Your children will appear human until they feel lust, and then their desire will make them into my children, divine in appearance and strength. Should they seek to satiate themselves with a mortal, they will create a victim, not a lover. They will only have each other to fulfill their needs and continue your line."

The shepherd quaked in horror at this terrible offer, but then he saw his children's gaunt faces and bloated bellies. "Is there no other way?"

"There's painful, empty death."

The shepherd accepted the offer.

Instantly he found himself before the door of a fine house; stepping inside, he discovered tables piled high with delicious food. His children appeared, and they all began to eat, marveling at this sudden wealth.

For some years they were happy, and the shepherd began to believe that he'd earned this good fortune with his own hard work. But then his children came of age, and he saw the signs. When his son tore a local maiden apart, he hid the act and told his children the horrid truth. They saw what they must do, and so they coupled only with each other, in the form of gods, and their divine progeny continued down through the centuries, walking in secret among mortals.

After the story, Lennox had added, "I hope you'll remember only this about me: that I loved you."

I printed out the e-mail and read it over again, hoping that somehow the hard copy would render the words into something comprehensible, sensible, but there was no sense to be found. After my fourth reading, I set the e-mail down and sped through airline websites. I made phone calls and found a flight leaving for Atlanta in three hours.

I didn't bother to pack; this wouldn't be a long visit, if the Wilmonts even agreed to see me at all.

But I had no choice: I had to demand answers. And see Lennox again.

O O O

I arrived at the Wilmont estate shortly before dawn. The sky hadn't started to lighten yet as I pulled the rental car up to the front gate. The guard, who I still couldn't see behind the window of the guard shack, spoke into a phone before rolling back the gate. I pulled forward.

It was late, I was operating on no sleep and a cup of bad coffee I'd picked up at a convenience store after leaving the airport, so it took me an extra, startled second to react when the figure ran in front of the car.

I slammed on the brakes and was thrown forward against the seat belt. I knew instinctively that the thing outlined in my headlights was the same one I'd glimpsed on my last trip here, running awkwardly through the woods: a humanoid figure with furry legs, bent back at the knees like a quadruped's, with hooves instead of feet. The torso was downy, the arms long, the head capped by a tawny mane and curling horns. It stared at me with wide, golden eyes.

It raised an arm and brought it down on the hood, hard enough to dent the metal. Opening its jaws wide, it screamed, a sound that stopped my heart.

It started to come around the front of the car toward the driver's side, gliding on those impossible legs, a long tongue darting out of its mouth. I glimpsed something moving in the groin, and my paralysis snapped. I slammed my foot down on the accelerator. The car shot forward, tires squealing.

I didn't look into the mirror to see if it was following. As I screeched to a stop before the house, the front door opened and someone stood there, outlined by light.

I grappled with the seatbelt and then leapt from the car, shouting, "Lennox—!"

"No, it's Madelyn. Come in, Sara."

Now I did look back, but nothing had followed. Cold flooded me; I was shaking. When Madelyn put an arm around me, I fell into the sanctuary of it. "Something chased me, something not human—"

"Grant," Madelyn said.

I stopped, gaping at her. "Grant? But that's your son's name..."

"Yes. My son—with Lennox."

"With...no. Lennox?"

"Come in and sit down. I'll get you something to drink."

I let Madelyn lead me into the great house, into a room of rich padded chairs and large hearths. Madelyn seated me, brought a glass. I sniffed it—bourbon—and downed it in one gulp. My chill began to ease. Madelyn sat opposite, sipping her own glass more carefully.

"I know about Lennox's e-mail to you," Madelyn said.

At the mention of Lennox, my heart thrummed. "Can I see him?"

"Not yet. We need to talk first." Madelyn set her glass down, piercing me with her gaze. "Sara, I have to ask: are you in love with Lennox?"

I started to answer, then caught myself, thinking. Yes, I wanted Lennox—dear *God*, how I wanted him—my entire body thrilled at the thought of him...but was that love? And was this intense attraction natural, or had I been manipulated, unnaturally influenced? "I'm not sure."

Madelyn considered before going on. "I'm prepared to offer you a life with Lennox, but not the life you're probably imagining. I would approve of your marriage to Lennox, you would live as his wife, with all the privilege of a Wilmont...but you would never be able to consummate the relationship."

At first I couldn't believe what I'd just heard, but then I remembered my last visit here. "Like Alan?"

"Yes."

I thought of Alan, the bitterly drunken husband, useful only for appearance's sake. "No. I won't live like that."

"You have to understand that if you were to...*be* with Lennox, you wouldn't survive."

"Are you saying that story—the one in the e-mail, the one in the Beltane Room—is true?"

"It's the family history."

An unwelcome image of Lennox and Madelyn entwined, naked and altered, saturnine, popped into my head. "How many children do you have?"

"Six. Five of them have to be hidden away. You met Grant outside. Only one looks human; she will be my successor." Madelyn gestured at a silver-framed photo of a blonde-haired little girl smiling into the camera—the most beautiful child I'd ever seen. "We're still trying for a boy."

My stomach filled with bile. I tried to stand, but my knees threatened to give way and my vision swam. "But Lennox loves me..."

"Sara, let me get a room ready for you. You've suffered a shock, you're in no state to travel again right now."

Numbed by revelation and liquor, I didn't react as Madelyn took me up the stairs to the Gold Room. I was dimly aware when she stepped out and locked the door from the outside as she left. I fell onto the bed where I let myself go, weeping with little strength, repeating his name over and over.

"Lennox...Lennox..."

Eventually I fell into an unhappy state that might have been sleep.

❂ ❂ ❂

I awoke when I heard my name, soft and muffled. The sky was only starting to lighten, so I knew I hadn't slept long. I lay there, fuzzy-headed but sobering up quickly, listening. It came again:

"Sara..."

Even though it didn't sound human, I knew it was Lennox. He knew I was here. I wondered if he'd caught my scent.

What will I do if he opens the door? Does Madelyn know he's out there, prowling, already transformed by his desire for me? Had she planned this—giving me to Lennox as an easy way to dispose of me?

The door bangs and shudders; he's thrown himself against it. A new sound now: claws scrabbling at wood.

He's turning the lock.

I don't scream, at least yet. I don't call Madelyn, or prepare to run. I'm sweating, but it's not from fear.

I know he'll be beautiful.

I sit on the bed...and wait.

Pound Rots in Fragrant Harbour

Pound rots in Fragrant Harbour. Of course it didn't start here; Pound has been rotting for quite some time. In London, New York, Los Angeles. He wants it to end here, in this city whose original name ("Fragrant Harbour") now seems only slightly less ridiculous than "City of Angels."

Pound is rotting because of the Exchange, the one he made at the beginning of another century. Now it's a new millennium, and Pound has been forced to acknowledge that he was the loser in the Exchange (he steadfastly refuses to use the vulgar—if more traditional—"deal"). Which is not to say that he accepts it; he's fought it every day, since it began. That's why he's here now, in Hong Kong. Fragrant Harbour.

The Exchange came about when the youthful Pound realized that he simply was not going to live long enough to make all the money he wanted. He'd already done well for himself; born to a poor family, his life was consumed by his drive to transcend the legacy. Before his second decade he became overseer of a factory; his use of runaway child labor helped him rise quickly to a position of ownership. When the twelve-year-olds were taken from him, he found starving immigrants and women; when they were unionized, he bought union leaders. Those who couldn't be bought disappeared, and Pound slept soundly.

It still wasn't enough. Pound saw grand profits ahead, but knew even his money wouldn't buy him another lifetime. No, a different currency was needed; when the Opportunity arose, Pound gladly grasped what was offered him, exchanging currency he considered useless.

Now he realizes he grasped *too* gladly. He should have looked the contract over more carefully. He should have fought over the wording. He'd fire anyone working for him who would approve a contract like that.

But he did sign it, and for a very long time he believed he'd triumphed. He was right about the future; he invested in technology and took his manufacturing firms overseas, where desperate workers were still tolerant of a dollar a day. On those rare occasions when an investment declined, Pound didn't panic because he knew he had time to make his money back again. All the time in the world, in fact.

He moved often, and spent considerable sums creating new identities. Once, a private detective, hired by a disgruntled ex-employee, found part of the trail; a week later, the dick found himself in jail with his license revoked, facing a long line of trumped-up charges. No one listened when he claimed Pound had originally been born in London, or that California was merely his last birthplace. The detective was still serving time when Pound's rot set in.

It began with small pains after he ate, or when he exerted himself, or when he drank too much. At first he ignored it—after all, even he occasionally took ill, like everyone else—but it went on, it got worse. He began—cautiously—to see doctors. They were baffled. Expensive tests showed that Pound's internal organs were simply decaying, and no one knew why. No one, that is, except Pound.

The rot continued, and those around him began to complain of an inexplicable bad odor; next they fell sick. Soon Pound was completely isolated; even his money couldn't keep anyone near him for long. His situation angered him, but Pound never stayed simply angry; he was driven by fury and the need to win.

He isolated himself in two rooms of one of his mansions. Unable to eat or find solace in substance abuse, he spent his days looking for answers online and in the outer reaches. Weary (and wary) of doctors, he turned to other practitioners: mediums, fortune-tellers, clairvoyants, psychics, sorcerers, magicians, and assorted charlatans. Most disgusted him more than he disgusted them. The few authentic ones turned away from him in revulsion. One actually tried to kill him, in an act of ritual magick; Pound laughed until the failed assassin fled. Later, he had the man tracked down and badly beaten. Only an ancient black woman his people found in New Orleans offered anything useful. She gave him one word before she staggered out, leaning heavily on her snake-headed cane:

"East."

The next day he was on his private jet, boarding with only a small suitcase and flight crew of four. Even though he was heavily dressed, wrapped in protective layers, one stewardess sickened, something she'd never done on a flight before. The other stewardess died within a month, of a mysterious disease that ate away at her.

And so Pound arrived in Hong Kong, which he had chosen as the eastern city most likely to accommodate his wealth. He was a pariah, a monster who looked like a normal twenty-something white man on the outside, but who was festering within and infesting all those who came near him. His money bought him service, but it couldn't buy respect, companionship, or an end to his hatred of his own flesh.

Now that he's arrived, he takes his single carry-on bag and his passport to Customs. His passport is stamped, and he's waved through quickly, much to the relief of the young exchange student in the queue behind him. The student, returning home after studying commerce for a year in a foreign land, will spend the next month in bed, feverish, while his mother feeds him shark's fin soup and burns joss sticks.

Pound's people have booked him into the penthouse suite at the best hotel in Hong Kong, and the hotel has a car waiting, a dark, smoke-glassed limo. It's a thirty-five minute ride to the Tsim Sha Tsui district where the hotel is, but Pound is completely disinterested; he thinks only of what he can feel within himself, and what he would—what he *will*—do to stop it.

❂ ❂ ❂

The train to Guangzhou is crowded and hot, and Ming-yun allows herself to drift with the swaying motion of the car.

She wasn't born Ming-yun; she was born with a dull name she despised as much as her dull family and dull home. Home was Huaihua, in China's western Hunan province; its chief attraction was a large railway junction. She grew up hearing that, if she were lucky, she would get work as a farmhand in the rice paddies; otherwise, she'd have to settle for life in a factory. At sixteen she'd left and never returned.

After a year she made her way south to Yangshuo, where she worked for a while in a western-style restaurant, kow-towing to fat *gweilo* tourists who sometimes asked to take her picture so they could grab her with a sweaty hand. One day she simply walked past the restaurant and kept going. She wound up on Moon Hill, where she was approached by a man who offered to take her on a tour of the Black Buddha Caves for 25 yen. She walked by him without an answer, and began to hike through the country. She found her own entrance to the caves, waited until nightfall and made her way in.

Her descent was precipitated by neither boredom nor curiosity. Ming-yun was in search of something as basic to the Chinese heart as family or *face*: fate. She believed in fate not as an abstract concept, but in Fate, a tangible thing that could be taken and twisted, molded to one's own purposes. She refused to accept her fate as a farmhand or factory worker or party member or wife; Fate had some-thing different in store for her. Last night she'd dreamt of finding it in a cave.

Except it found her.

Ming-yun had expected to have her Fate revealed to her, as if some curtain were parted by a ghostly hand. She wanted to see her future, to know what road to walk when she left the cave, to have a promise beyond rice paddies and industrial complexes. What she'd been given instead...

She'd thought about it every day since, that night in the cave. She couldn't explain what had happened to her; there was no entity present she could name. She only knew that she'd fallen asleep on the hard cave floor, and in her sleep the offer had been made:

She wouldn't be shown her Fate...but she could be *given* one, if she chose to accept it.

She did accept it, without even questioning what it was. Afterwards, when she knew, she'd never regretted it. It was not, perhaps, what she would have chosen for herself, but then again it wasn't anything she could ever have imagined.

When she awoke the next day, she'd forgotten her old name, and had chosen the one she bore now: Ming-yun. Fate.

She is Fate. And now she is on a train bound for Guangzhou—and beyond that, Hong Kong.

❂ ❂ ❂

Pound's car drops him off before his hotel, and he's efficiently whisked up to his room, by young men whose Cantonese-accented English courtesy masks their distaste.

He flips on the bathroom light, turns on the faucet in the sink, splashes water on his face and looks at himself in the mirror. His blue eyes are reddened; his skin has a dry, cracking look that wasn't there a week ago. Otherwise he could almost pass for just another Western businessman. *Almost.*

He has no idea what to do next; he's more uncertain every second of why he's here at all. He shakes off his irresolution, finds his outrage and leaves the room behind.

If nothing else, he decides, he'll walk until he finds something.

It's night as he leaves the hotel behind and strides down the first side street he comes to. He's suddenly in a different world; the sidewalks are impossibly crowded with people coming home from work, shopping, eating. Somehow a path always clears before him; he doesn't see the frowns that appear behind him. Many of the people he passes barely make it home before collapsing, complaining of a new virus. Some will die within two weeks' time, after passing the rot on to those around them.

The streets are awash with neon and scents. He passes restaurants, is nearly overcome by the temptation of roasting duck. His intestines choose that point to remind him of their condition, and he wheezes in pain, wheezes in fury at being so tormented by this simple pleasure. He steels himself as he continues on down the sidewalk. New scents assault him: open barrels of dried scallops, steam from cooking noodles, bamboo shoots being boiled into a pungent beverage. He tries to walk in the street, is nearly run down a honking minibus. He reels into a small, crowded store selling CD's and movies; he pretends to riffle through the bins long enough to collect himself, then he re-enters the flow of traffic outside. But this time it's back to his hotel, to his cocooned suite, away from the mob and the ordinary seductions he can never enjoy again.

❂ ❂ ❂

The worst part about knowing her Fate has been waiting for it to arrive.

Ming-yun's train had reached Guangzhou, and now she has a three-hour ride on a jet catamaran to Hong Kong. This time she doesn't doze; she focuses, containing her anticipation. She's close now.

Twelve years have passed since that night in the cave. Twelve years since she left, knowing what lay before her. Knowing that she would endure twelve years of life as the factory worker she'd been told she would become. Twelve years of mind-numbing drudgery, day after day leavened by the knowledge of what was to come. She couldn't imagine this life without that. She wondered how the rest survived.

In the evenings she trained. Her Fate required discipline, and so she educated herself in *wushu*, in sword forms, in Shaolin-style kung fu. The monks also taught her healing, at which she was surprised to find she excelled. She could locate a tumor or hernia with touch, or cure a headache or infection with herbs. Patients gave her gifts of gratitude; she gave most to the monks, except for the money, which she saved for her Fate. She would need money for the first part, the part when she had to travel to Hong Kong.

It never occurred to Ming-yun to doubt the reality of her Fate, to question the dream that led her on. Her Fate felt far more real to her than the daily grind of the factory, and her training gave her confidence to ward off the unwanted suitors who approached her from time to time. It wasn't that men didn't interest her; it was that only one man interested her, and he was still twelve years away, and in Hong Kong.

❂ ❂ ❂

Pound falls into the daze that passes for sleep with him and awakens to find he's blind at first. He lurches from the bed, overtaken with animal panic for the first time in his life. A wall stops him with a loud thud, and he finds himself thinking about the large plate-glass window that overlooks a busy street twenty floors below. The thought of lying in the roadway, shattered, helpless but still alive, sobers him, and he realizes his sight is returning. Gray light, thick shapes, finally give way to pale colors and outlines.

At least he has a destination now; last night, before he slipped into semi-consciousness, his eyes still functioned well enough to peruse the hotel room guidebook.

It mentioned a row of fortune-tellers near the Tin Hau Temple in Jordan. Jordan is a five-minute car ride to the east.

It's already dark out again, but Pound reasons that fortune-telling isn't the kind of profession shut down due to lack of light. This time he balls up tiny pieces of tissue to stop the smells from reaching him. It's probably too much to hope, he thinks, that his sense of smell will give way as quickly as his sight.

The hotel limo is a welcome relief from the sensuality of the streets, hermetically sealing Pound behind cool, dull glass. The car moves slowly down Nathan Road, angling between double-decker busses and all the other transports.

Despite the traffic, Pound is quickly deposited at the mouth of Temple Street; usually he'd want assistants, an obsequious entourage, around him, but tonight he's relieved that not even the limo driver offers to accompany him. He finds himself looking down a side boulevard, crowded and neon-lit like all the ones in Tsim Sha Tsui. He wonders briefly if there's any place in this city that *doesn't* look like this.

He starts down Temple Street, which nightly transforms itself into a street market of hundreds of tiny enclosed stalls. He pushes through the center of them, past displays of luggage, watches, dolls with oversized heads, movies recorded illegally on cheap computer disks, souvenir T-shirts and keychains. It seems to go on forever, until Pound's already-failing eyesight jumbles into something his brain can no longer read. He grabs on to a support pole and waits until it passes. He disregards the vendor railing angrily at him in Cantonese.

At last the street comes to a break, the stalls disappearing. A short distance ahead Pound makes out, at last, his goal: the Tin Hau Temple, and, on the sidewalk before it, a dozen fortune-tellers. Each has a table, chairs, red banners Pound can't read. What Pound is looking for is one with a queue of customers.

It's beginning to rain, so the fortune-tellers aren't as busy tonight as usual, but one stall has a gathering of waiting clients, and Pound takes his place there. This stall has less decoration than the rest, no scrolls showing lines of the hand or parts of the face. Pound gazes curiously at the prognosticator, this one who must be proficient enough to draw business. It's a middle-aged man, ordinary looking except for his jagged and browned teeth. He seems more like one of the food vendors Pound's just passed than a seer. A teenaged girl—his daughter, probably—stands next to him. At first Pound thinks she's extraordinarily ugly, with her moon face and her father's bad teeth; but as he watches her, the way she carefully attends to her father and the customers, he changes his mind and thinks her care makes her almost lovely.

Finally it's Pound's turn. He steps up, and the man behind the table tenses but holds his gaze. Pound asks if he speaks English. The girl answers: "I can tell you what he says."

She gestures at the chair near Pound, and he takes it, then put his hand on the table as he's seen those before him do. "Other one," the girl says, and Pound puts his left up instead.

The girl notices her father's reluctance to touch Pound, and she takes the older man's shoulders reassuringly. He finally reaches across and begins to examine Pound's palm. After a long moment he releases the hand and looks Pound's face over carefully. Finally he leans back and mutters in Cantonese.

"He says," the daughter begins, "that you will not find the answer you want. He says..." She pauses to take in the stream of words pouring from the man, then: "Your only chance is to be reborn. You cannot seek it; it will find you. You must accept that. For you there is no other way." Then she names a price.

Pound considers questioning, or arguing, but instead pays and walks away. He finds a bench in the temple courtyard and sits, gathering himself. At first he's angry; he should have expected this, the usual singsong fortune-telling gibberish; but something about this one is different. Somehow it feels right.

When he turns, he's not surprised to see that the fortune-teller and his daughter have gone, only an empty space on the sidewalk now where their table and chairs had been. He wonders idly how long they'll live, and then laughs as he settles back onto the bench to wait.

❂ ❂ ❂

It's night when Ming-yun's boat arrives at the China Hong Kong City terminal in Tsim Sha Tsui. She's hungry, and once she's off the boat she makes her way past Kowloon Park to the shops, finds the first cheap restaurant and gorges herself. Then she steps into the rainy night, and closes her eyes.

The trail of rot is near.

She opens her eyes and begins moving, pushing her way brusquely through the passersby. She carries only a small pack on her back and a long wrapped bundle in one hand. The sword gives her comfort.

She's never seen a city like Hong Kong. Even Guangzhou wasn't this dense and bright; it could easily be overwhelming if she tried to take it in. But the city doesn't interest her; perhaps later. If there is a later.

She turns north. She can tell that some of the people she passes on the sidewalks have already been infected by him, and they in turn are beginning to infect others. She pushes on harder, faster. At the corner of Nathan and Cameron roads, near a red subway entrance, she's nearly overcome by the trail of decay (*he was here*), but redoubles her determination and pushes north along Nathan, heading for Jordan and Temple streets.

❂ ❂ ❂

Pound waits in the courtyard of the Tin Hau Temple. Sometime in the last hour he thinks his heart has stopped working and now sits in his chest as a moldering lump of useless organic matter. He's afraid to get up, afraid that his legs will no longer function and he'll be carted off to some Chinese hospital, locked away as a medical curiosity for the rest of an eternally long life. He's not sure what else he can do, so he waits. The night wears on; the last of the stalls on Temple Street shut down. The courtyard empties, until Pound is alone there. He doesn't know what time it is, doesn't care. He only knows that the rain has stopped, a small fact for which he's grateful. At least that won't add to his decomposition.

He's dimly aware that a new arrival has entered the courtyard, and he looks up, squinting, to make out a woman standing before him. The most beautiful woman he's ever seen. Tall, especially for a Chinese, with fine slender limbs and an imperious chin.

Then she unwraps the sword.

❂ ❂ ❂

Ming-yun has followed the trail through the early morning streets, as the crowds have thinned and then disappeared almost completely. As she neared the Temple, the reek became stronger. She saw the figure seated on the bench in the courtyard, saw him through the wrought-iron fence surrounding the Temple, and felt a thrill of exhilaration arc through her.

It was him. Her Fate.

She had paused only a moment, long enough to let this delicious moment sink in, to savor it as the reward for twelve years of hard labor, of endurance. Now is her moment.

She had entered the courtyard and approached him carefully. He didn't look like a monster; he merely looked like another *gweilo* who'd eaten something that hadn't agreed with him. But there was no question this was him.

The aura around him was terrible, and Ming-yun used all the methods of concentration she'd been taught over the previous decade to force herself to stand there.

At last she unwraps the sword.

❂ ❂ ❂

Ming-yun looks at Pound for a time; then she sets her pack down and kneels before him. He looks at her blearily, and she understands that his eyes are rotting with the rest of him. She knows there isn't much time left, and prays that she isn't too late to do what her Fate has told her must be done.

She sets the sword down, and, still kneeling, slowly leans forward and kisses Pound. He's only mildly surprised, for some reason. He returns the kiss, thankful for a sensation that doesn't cause him pain, although his hands are too weak to raise to her face.

He is surprised, though, when he feels her fingers on his crotch, is more surprised by the fact that he's stiff there. She kneads him, gently, encouraging him, finally undoes his pants and frees him. Pound thinks he's never felt this hard before, never in his very long life. He gives himself over to it, willing now to accept whatever comes.

Ming-yun removes her own worn denims, then straddles him, lowering herself onto him. She barely moves and suddenly Pound is exploding. She tightens around him, drawing him in, holding him until the small spasms cease.

Pound is only dimly aware that Ming-yun has released him and risen off of him. He's simply glad that he could have this—this last, final pleasure—to hold on to.

That's why he doesn't see her, when she dresses again and then picks up the sword. She considers a moment, begins with a matter-of-fact swing that neatly severs Pound's head. There's no blood, as she expected, just a dull wet sound as the head hits the pavement and is stopped by her foot. She moves quickly, lowering the body to the ground and opening the chest with the sword tip. It's easy work;

Pound was so far gone that his flesh and bones are nearly liquid.

Ming-yun isn't particularly concerned with whether she's seen or not; there's been no sound other than the small ones, so she knows she hasn't been heard. When she's done she reaches for her pack, removing the small barbecue carried there. She sets it up, thankful the rain has stopped and made this task simpler. She stokes a fire in it, and then places what she's removed onto the grate.

Pound's heart only takes an hour to turn to ash, and there's not very much left when Ming-yun is done. The sky is just starting to lighten as she empties the last embers out of the barbecue, setting the heart's ashes out to cool. When she can touch them without burning her fingers, she scoops them up into her mouth, swallowing quickly until they're all gone. It's only a few mouthfuls, which she washes down with a bottle of green tea from her pack.

As the sun rises Ming-yun is packed up and standing, looking up at the ancient temple as it glows in the morning light. The air around her is fresh again, even fragrant, and she breathes it in deeply. She can feel Pound inside her, already growing.

She turns away, ready to live the rest of her Fate.

THE UNNAMEABLE

The End

J pulls the disc from the computer's DVD tray and eyes it for a moment, almost as if he can somehow see its contents with eyes alone.

So this is it.

On the disc is a movie called *The End*. J has heard about the movie, on blogs, in forums, from friends. No one he knows has actually seen the movie, but they all know something about it. That it was made somewhere in Europe, or maybe Asia, or the slums of Kolkata. That it's nearly impossible to find, and that if it shows up online anywhere, YouTube or a bootleg on eBay, it vanishes again within minutes. That no one who has seen it will talk about it. That it's cursed, that it changes for whoever watches it. That the things it shows come true.

That it's the most disturbing film ever made.

Which, of course, means J must see it. He's a connoisseur of horror; if it terrifies others, he'll be at best mildly amused, maybe impressed if the gore effects are good enough. He's been trying to find *The End* since he first heard about months ago, in a chatroom for fright fans. He found it in a bit torrent stream on the dark web tonight, downloaded it into his computer, and burned it to a disc, just to be sure. His roommate would want to see it, too—they've talked about it, after all—but the roommate is already late getting in, and J doesn't want to wait; he sometimes feels like he waits on other people too much. The movie is short, no more than fifteen minutes, so he figures he can watch it twice in one night.

He goes to the DVD player, loads the disc, falls back onto his couch facing his huge television. He expects the image to be grainy, muddy, with that look and sound distinctive to fifth-generation duplicates, but the picture that flares to life on his screen is crystal clear.

There are no opening production company logos or credits, no triumphant fanfare. The movie simply starts. It shows an old man, very old, bent as he walks, clutching a crumpled paper bag tightly to his chest, holding a flashlight before him. It's night, an urban locale that could be the downtown heart of any big city in the world—New York, London, Hong Kong. Or Hollywood.

It's obviously very late, because there's no traffic. The only sound comes from the old man's shuffling feet, the rustling of the bag, his labored breathing. The shot is wide, tracking with him as he makes his slow way down a sidewalk.

Although there's nothing overtly frightening about the scene, something about it is making J uneasy. Perhaps it's the man's utter isolation in the frame; there are no cars going past, no other pedestrians, no power on in the stores or apartments lining the street. The only light comes from the flashlight held in the old man's trembling hand. In fact, J starts to wonder how they did it. The camera has now been following the old man for at least a minute, and J can only imagine how much the filmmakers had to pay to seal off a section of a large city, even late at night, and get all the lights shut down.

J wonders when the real scares will kick in. Maybe it'll be zombies, or giant rats, or outlaw biker gangs. Even though he appreciates the technical expertise of the single unbroken shot thus far (two minutes into the film now), he's anxious for something to happen.

The old man stops by a dark shop window, pausing to catch his breath; apparently even his snail's pace is too much for him. He tries to huddle further down into his threadbare coat and starts forward again—

There's a flash of something in the window as he walks away.

J blinks in surprise and taps PAUSE on the remote. There, in the glass...it looks like a face...J hits the STEP BACKWARD button, moving the image back a frame at a time, until the face is at its brightest.

It's a young man's face, pale, screaming.

J walks forward until he's six inches away from the screen, and he peers in disbelief.

It's *his* face.

He moves right and left, thinking it's an impossible reflection, but the face remains. He examines it more critically, thinking it's obviously someone who just looks like him. But no, there's that same distinctive bump in the bridge of the nose, the one he inherited from his mother, and around it is his lank, brown hair, too long right now.

He's screaming. His face—*his* face—is contorted in unimaginable terror.

J frantically backs up a few more frames, and the face disappears, as if its owner had stepped away from glass. He goes forward again and there it is, occupying exactly six frames. A quarter-of-a-second of screen life.

He scrolls back and forth over the face a few times, trying to imagine some way it could be his. It must be a joke, a clever Photoshop prank, something his friends got together.

Cursed...

He shakes off that notion and finally lets the film roll forward at normal speed. It's the old man again, still staggering down the eerily empty streets. No music, no dialogue, no city sounds or ambiance.

J is increasingly anxious. Nothing's happening—no monster attack, no torture scene involving young girls and burly men in masks—but there's definitely been some sort of apocalypse. It's simply not possible to account for the old man's aloneness in any other way. The world must be dead.

The film has been on now for five minutes; it's still a single shot, unbroken from the first frame. J realizes there's something unnatural about both the length of that shot and the clarity of it, and a shudder races through him. In fact, he almost considers turning this off, stopping it while he can...

But he doesn't. He lets it play and watches, stomach tightening in dread, as the old man finally leaves the street to enter a building. It's an ancient apartment building, and the flashlight beam flickers over peeling paint and cobwebs. The old man opens the first door he comes to (for some reason J is even more unnerved by the fact that the door wasn't locked), and he enters an apartment.

J finds himself irrationally hoping that someone will come forth from the depths of the apartment to greet the old man, another spark of life in this urban desolation, but no such comfort is forthcoming. The old man sets the bag and flashlight down, shrugs out of his coat, lays it across a table, moves to light a propane lantern. Somehow J knows that the old man has survived something cataclysmic, but he's survived it alone. There's nothing left to him now but the emptiness of both this apartment and the world outside.

The lantern begins to hiss, the apartment fills with wan light. It's as barren as the city outside, just a few sticks of dilapidated furniture. No photos. No pets. No plants. The old man pulls a large jar from the bag and sets it carefully on the table. The contents are thick, yellowish. J can't figure out what it is.

The old man starts to turn towards the camera, and J realizes he hasn't yet seen the man's face. The man is moving slowly, making the turn last an excruciating eternity, and the camera is pushing in throughout the torturous movement. J is shaking now, his palms sweating, his breathing coming in shallow gasps. He doesn't want to see the old man's face, but he can't turn away, as the camera moves in slowly... slowly...

Finally the old man's face is revealed, caught in the whitish propane light, sealed forever in the camera's tight frame. It's a human face, all too human, in fact. Old, very old, with a few scars nearly lost beneath the gridwork of wrinkles and stubble. The eyes are sunken and rheumy, the hair only a few long wisps, the mouth a toothless cavern edged by gray lips...

...and the nose has an unmistakable bump near the center of the bridge.

J is still screaming when the image abruptly goes black a few seconds later.

The Secret Engravings

Hans turned the corner and smelled death.

The odor, sudden and overwhelming, cascaded his memory back to four years ago, to 1519, when his brother Ambrosius had succumbed to plague. He'd gone against the advice of physicians and friends to attend to Ambrosius, and the scent in his brother's final hours had been this same nauseating mix of rotten meat and metallic blood and sour fear sweat.

Hans was yanked back to the present as he saw a body being taken from a house down the alley. Two men, common laborers with thick rags wrapped around their faces, lugged a shrouded corpse into a waiting cart. As they heaved it onto the creaking boards, a foot fell loose, and Hans saw:

The toes were almost completely black.

Plague. Again, here in Basel.

One of the laborers glanced up, saw Hans staring. He stepped a few feet away from the dead man, glanced back once, adjusted the improvised cloth mask. He was burly, with a long, unwashed beard and filthy peasant's garb, but his face and voice were surprisingly kind. "Best not come this way," he said.

"How far...?" Hans couldn't finish the question.

The man understood. "Only this house. He was a merchant, been traveling, just came back last week. I doubt it'll spread."

'Doubt'? Precious little to put my mind at ease. But Hans nodded and turned away.

He clutched his satchel tighter—it held the drawings for the prayer book, his latest commission, and as such was precious—and walked down another lane, unseeing.

The Great Mortality...here, again.

He'd been on his way to visit Hermann, the engraver who would complete the woodcuts that would allow the drawings to be printed; but now he found himself walking aimlessly, too stunned to remember an alternate way.

After Ambrosius, Hans had lived in dread of encountering the plague again. Ambrosius, his beloved older brother, the one their father had believed would be a great artist. Ambrosius, who had his own studio while Hans was yet an apprentice to another artist; even if Hans was now accorded greater recognition than Ambrosius had ever been given, Hans knew the hole his brother's gruesome death had left in his soul would never fill. He couldn't forget watching the buboes form under his brother's arms, the black spots that spread up his face and limbs as he vomited blood. Four years later, not a day passed when he didn't see Ambrosius's dying face or—earlier—that sought-after smile of approval. He saw his brother in statues, in paintings, in other men, in children.

And he saw his own death by plague in everything else. The thought terrified him; he'd seen what his brother had endured, and he couldn't imagine doing the same. The fevers, the bursting skin, the blood...

Hans finally looked up, realizing he'd wandered far away now from the engraver's neighborhood, and was near the house of his friend Erasmus. Hans had recently painted the great man, and they'd become friends as a result. Erasmus had read parts of his essay *The Praise of Folly* to Hans during the sittings, and Hans had come to admire Erasmus for his wit and insight. He could use a precious dose of that today.

A few minutes later, the scholar was welcoming Hans into his study. Once seated before a warming hearth with a brandy ("good for all Four Humours," Erasmus assured him), surrounded by books and scrolls and writing desks and quills, only then did Hans finally begin to relax.

"Your fame is growing, young Hans," Erasmus told him, as he stood before the fire, his rugged face creased in pleasure. "I had reason to visit the Great Council Chamber in town hall today, and a traveler from Germany saw your mural and asked if it was the work of the Italian, Da Vinci. I was delighted to tell him that Basel had its own Da Vinci in the young Hans Holbein. He told me he would mark that name well."

Hans tried to smile, but wasn't entirely successful. Erasmus saw the attempt. "I fear you're not here for mere praise alone."

"No. I saw...plague. Plague has returned to Basel."

If Hans had expected some measure of panic or at least discomfort from his friend, he was surprised to see only a mild shrug. "Plague is always with us in some form or other. It's a constant companion. You of all people should know that, Hans. Who was it but the artists who captured the 'Dance of Death' when the Great Mortality first struck a century ago?"

Erasmus rummaged briefly through a shelf, then pulled down a large vellum-bound volume, placed it in Hans's lap, and flipped through the parchment leaves until he came to an engraving that showed four skeletons, tufts of hair flying from their sere skulls, capering in a graveyard. Hans examined it briefly before muttering, "I could do better."

His friend laughed and clapped his shoulder. "Indeed you could, young genius."

Hans spent another hour with Erasmus, discussing art and politics and the gossip surrounding a local aristocrat, and by the time he left the sun was setting and his spirits had lifted. As he lingered in Erasmus's doorway, pulling his fur-trimmed cloak tighter against the cooling air, Erasmus told him, "Paint, Hans. It's what God meant you for, and it will ease your mind."

Hans nodded and left.

❂ ❂ ❂

He'd still been contemplative when he'd returned home. He ate dinner with his wife Elsbeth and their sons Franz and Philipp, then excused himself to the studio.

At first he wondered if he'd made a mistake; the studio had once belonged to his brother, whose spirit now seemed to infest every scrap of paper and brush and easel and ink bottle. Hans stoked the fire, shrugged out of his heavy outer garment, and tried to focus on his latest commission, an altarpiece design for the local church; but neither mind nor hand would bend to the task. Finally he lowered his head to the worktable and closed his eyes, seeking simple oblivion.

Someone was with him, in the studio.

He didn't know how much time had passed, and he hadn't yet opened his eyes to confirm what his other senses screamed at him; a quickening terror clutched his heart. His eyes popped open, involuntarily.

A tall shadow stood on the far side of the room, draped in a black robe and cowl. "Good evening, Hans," it said, in a deep, somehow hollow voice.

Hans lifted his head, but he possessed no more strength. He opened his mouth, but couldn't form words.

"All will be made clear, my friend. Know for now that I mean you no harm." The visitor's rumbling tones sent shivers up Hans's back.

"How..." Hans managed to look back at the studio's door and saw that it was as he'd left it—bolted from within.

His guest stepped forward, and Hans saw the gleam of something white from within the folds of the cowl.

Is that...

"Yes, bone. What else would Death be made of?" Two skeleton-hands emerged from the sleeves, pushed back the cowl, and let Hans see his visitor's face...or rather, see the skull where a face should have been. There was nothing but ancient, polished bone, no shred of skin or hair or muscle. Hans pushed back off his bench, barely noticed when he fell to the floor.

His guest—Death—made a placating gesture. "You've nothing to fear from me, Hans Holbein."

"You're not here with...the plague?"

The skull moved back and forth. "Far from it. In fact, I'm here to offer you a way to *save* yourself from plague. I come to claim your services, not your life."

Panic started to abate, replaced by curiosity. "My...services..."

"Yes. A commission."

Hans blinked in surprise as he drew himself up. "You want me to...work for you?"

"I do. What you told your friend Erasmus earlier..."

Hans went back in his memory, and he knew immediately: he knew how he'd damned himself.

I could do better.

"The old depictions of me, those ridiculous images of dancing and cavorting like some mad witch in the moonlight...they no longer please me. I consider you to be the finest artist of this age, and I want you to render me, as I am, every day. I want you to record me the way I am, not as some prancing fool, but as one who practices his trade with care and respect for the craft."

"'Respect'?" Hans gasped out, before he could stop himself. "You kill innocents—"

"No. I merely perform the tasks assigned me. There are greater authorities above me, Hans. If you have complaints with choices, you'll need to address those elsewhere. I only control the day-to-day practice, and I am not cruel, callous, or uncaring. I take pride in my work, as you do in yours."

Hans wanted to sneer. He wanted to stand and hurl epithets at this monster, call him a liar, a hypocrite, deluded, but...

What if he's right?

"So how would you...?"

"You will accompany me on some of my rounds. Neither

of us will be visible to those I must take. You will observe, and record exactly what you see."

"And in return, you'll keep me safe from plague? My family as well?"

"Yes. And also..."

Death ran his skeletal fingers into Hans's leather satchel, and removed the small bundle of prayer book drawings. The sheets flew across the table, and Death leaned down to examine them closely. "These are lovely. They're too good for Hermann, you know."

Hans *did* know. Hermann's work was often slipshod, erasing the lovely details that made a work live and breathe. "He's the best in Basel..."

"He's not. Seek out Hans Lützelburger."

"I know the name, but he's not in Basel..."

Death turned to face him, and somehow he knew the smile was intentional this time. "He has only recently come here. He will be my other gift to you. Shall we begin tomorrow?"

Holbein swallowed...and nodded.

☉ ☉ ☉

They began at a convent.

Holbein felt like a voyeur, trespassing into the intimate inner realm of the brides of Christ, but when one initiate walked through him, he wondered which of them was really the ghost.

Death led him to a courtyard, where the elderly abbess knelt in a small garden. Even from a distance, Holbein could hear her rattling breath, see her faltering limbs. She was halfway dead, but her will kept her clinging stubbornly to life.

Death waited a few moments, at last stepping forward to gently touch the old woman's shoulder. She felt the tap, turned—and her mouth fell open in a silent shriek of protest. She tried to pull away, but Death clung to her habit's white scapulary and pulled her to her feet. Holbein watched, fascinated, as her body fell while her spirit was led off by determined Death. In one of the arched doorways leading out to the courtyard, a young nun saw the collapsed form of her superior and she began to shout.

Holbein was too busy making preliminary sketches on a sheet of parchment to notice the grief that unfolded around him. He was surprised when he abruptly awoke, finding himself in his studio, alone, a half-finished sketch near his hands.

Death proved to be courteous, allowing Holbein enough time to completely finish one drawing before he reappeared. Holbein began to look forward to the visits, fascinated by his patron's methods. He watched, invisible, as Death claimed a judge in the act of being bribed, a wealthy woman who felt the approach and dressed for the occasion, a peddler who tried in vain to flee to the next town, and a blind man who gratefully allowed himself to be led. He laughed when Death was arrayed in the costume of a ragged peasant to claim a count; he felt a measure of petty satisfaction when Death took a miser and made the dead soul watch as he also took money from a counting table. Each of these excursions ended with Holbein awakening in his studio, and intuiting that he was not yet permitted to see what came next for each of those called by Death.

Hans continued working on his other commissions, but he found himself always returning to his Dances of Death. He added his own touches to the drawings: he included an hourglass in many of them; he did complete new drawings, depicting his macabre friend leading Adam and Eve out of Paradise, since they'd become part of his dominion. He drew a coat-of-arms for Death, and even an alphabet. He gave Death a sense of humor, although with subtler satire than earlier artists had provided.

He watched other citizens of his town die of plague. Not many—the sickness wasn't rampaging again, as it had in the past—and although the recognition left him uneasy, he had come to trust Death and knew he was safe. He took each new drawing to Hans Lützelburger, whose skill as an engraver surpassed his reputation. Holbein suspected that, if his Dances of Death were admired by future generations, it might be partly because of the brilliance of the engraver.

Then one day Death made him watch the taking of a child.

The boy was barely more than an infant, about the age and size of Hans's stepson Franz, his wife's son from her first marriage, which had ended when she was widowed. It was a poor family, living in a ramshackle cottage with no windows, a badly-thatched roof, and no fire but a cooking pit in the middle of the floor. Death showed no compassion nor consideration as he took the little one by a tiny wrist, leading it away from the body slumped on the floor, while the gaunt mother and older sister sobbed in a grief that Holbein had never seen, a grief born of a lifetime of desperation and loss. Holbein followed Death out of the cottage; his face was still wet when his eyes snapped open to the familiar surroundings of his studio.

The beginnings of the drawing by his outstretched right hand repulsed him. But he didn't crumple it up or fling it into the fire. Instead he completed it.

He took it to Lützelburger, only to discover that the engraver had died in the week since Hans had last seen him. A terrible accident, involving a horse cart driven by a sot. The driver was in jail, and the engraver was dead.

Death came to Holbein that night. He was pacing in his studio, anticipating the visit. Still, his patron's first words surprised him: "I release you from our agreement, Hans. You have upheld your side of the bargain, and I'm very pleased with the work, which has re-inspired me."

"How could you take the child?"

The skull-head was unreadable, incapable of expressing emotion. "I've told you, I'm not the final authority—"

Hans cut him off, waving a hand in irritation. "Yes, yes,

I know, I've heard all that. It's God's fault, isn't that it?"

Death hesitated, and Hans wondered if he'd finally provoked something that wasn't cold and rational. "Yes. Even I don't pretend to understand His wisdom."

"But doesn't it hurt you when it's a child, a babe, and the parents—"

"No, Hans, it doesn't."

Finally, Hans understood: He was dealing with a demigod, a thing that was impossibly old and inhuman and with motives that nothing of flesh and blood could ever comprehend. Once again, he was frightened of Death.

"I leave you now, Hans...at least until we must meet again. I am grateful for your skill, although I suspect it may make us both famous, and you must remember: you will owe part of that to me."

Hans stood, forcing himself into stone, as Death vanished again. Then he poured himself a glass of ale that he hoped was big enough to make him as insensible as the drunkard who had killed Lützelburger.

❍ ❍ ❍

After that, Basel lost its charms, so in the autumn of 1526 Hans fled to England, where he'd heard artists were often highly paid. He left Elsbeth and the children in Basel, and over the next decade found fame in the court of Henry VIII, where he became the King's Painter. He prospered to the point where he acquired a mistress and two new children. He still visited Elsbeth when he could, making sure she and their children were well provided for.

The plague returned to London in 1543. Hans heard the news from friends in the Royal Court. It was only a small outbreak, but Hans's anxiety rose like a black sun.

He was no longer protected.

On a cold night when fog covered London like grave dirt, Hans was returning from an audience with the King, who was inquiring again about the painting he'd commissioned

from Hans in 1541, the one to commemorate the unifica-
tion of the barbers' and surgeons' guilds. The painting was
large, but size wasn't the issue; Holbein was, rather, simply bored by the subject. Of course he'd assured his royal
customer that the work was progressing well and would be
completed soon.

Hans tried to negotiate his way through the fog, light-
ed windows providing little illumination until he'd nearly
walked into them. He knew he was lost; in fact, he'd been
walking for several minutes without even finding a shop or
street sign. An overhead lamp revealed an intersection, he
turned—

And smelled plague.

He froze, panic rising. The stench nearly gagged him;
he staggered back as if physically assaulted by it. Then,
from somewhere in the shrouded center of the lane, he
heard:

"Hello, old friend."

No—

The black shape took form before him, hard white sur-
faces glinting within ebony folds. Hans could only stare,
immobile, sure that his time had arrived at last.

"You've come for me."

"Not yet, not that way. But I do come once again seeking your services. A new commission."

Hans felt exhausted at the mere idea. "We already
showed you claiming your victims from nearly forty different walks of life. What can be left?"

"Exactly, Hans. I, too, have again grown weary of the
limitations imposed on me. That is why I want something
different from you: I want you to create entirely new works.
This time, you will not accompany me on my rounds, but
will work from your own imagination, placing me in fresh
situations."

"You want me..." Hans struggled to find the words.
"You want me to show you..."

"The station of the victims won't be important this

time, but the method of passing will."

"New ways to die—is that what you're saying?"

Death's jaws made a slight clacking sound as he nodded. "Precisely."

Hans shook his head. "No. It's ghastly."

"Why? I'm asking you to entertain me, to renew and reinvigorate me. Surely that's a more worthwhile goal for art than memorializing some pompous blowhard and a bunch of barbers?"

"I..." Hans had no answer, because Death was right, and Hans knew that was why "King Henry VIII Granting the Charter to the Barber-Surgeon's Company" had already gone on for two years. Over the last few years here in England, he'd become little more than a gifted technician, a highly paid and praised one, but not a true artist. And wasn't Death the ultimate critic? If he could win the praise of this patron for original works, it would surely (ironically) be his life's greatest achievement.

"Yes." The word escaped his mouth almost of its own volition.

The reeking scent vanished instantly. "I'm delighted, my friend. I'll visit with you next week to view your progress."

Hans wasn't surprised to find the fog lifting by the time he'd reached the end of the lane.

❂ ❂ ❂

Death became Hans Holbein's constant companion.

Hans began to notice new things about people, about the world around them. He saw the potential for fatality in everything. A ship on the Thames could lose its rigging and hurl a sailor into the river's grimy depths. An urchin begging coins on a corner might be trod upon by a nobleman's horse, or perhaps fall victim to a far more outlandish accident—a bottle dropped from high overhead, an errant fist thrown by a bar brawler, a rare venomous spider inadvertently imported from a tropical region.

After his strolls, Hans returned to his studio and drew. For the first time in years, his work excited him. At the end of his first week, Death appeared by his side, and Hans wordlessly offered the first piece: a man convulsing at a dinner table while a woman sat at the head, raising a glass in toast, having just successfully poisoned her husband; Death stood nearby bearing a tray, the attentive waiter.

"Superb, Hans, superb," Death muttered, stroking a bone-tip over the art, "but you can go *further*."

Hans could barely sleep that night, his mind aflame with lethal possibilities.

When Death appeared next, Hans handed him two more works. Death stood speechless for several seconds, before whispering one word: "Astonishing." The first of the drawings so praised showed a field of peasants in tattered rags torn apart by a wave of bullets from a giant gun mounted on a hill; Death held out strings of ammunition to the gunner. The second new piece showed a man in a street being struck down by some sort of huge, horseless cart, a grotesque engine of destruction bellowing flame from its back while Death sat behind a driver's wheel.

Over the following weeks, Hans thought of little else but stranger and more horrible scenes of death. He drew on larger sheets, with bolder strokes. He drew scenes of soldiers enveloped in strange vapors on a battlefield, their mouths agape in their final dying breath, while Death stood above them, dangling long scarves that might have kept them safe. He drew a line of rail-thin, bent patients, all plainly dying as a wealthy doctor turned his back to them and accepted money from Death instead. He showed a priest gesticulating wildly from a pulpit, causing his flock to turn on each other in violence while Death stood behind him wearing a white mitre. He drew a man of science holding an open box from which emanated a blinding whiteness that caused all those below it to fling up arms in useless attempts to shield themselves, while Death stood behind the scientist making notes in a book.

Death was ecstatic. He stared with empty sockets at each new drawing, lingering for minutes, stroking them lovingly. "Exquisite," he might murmur, or, "brilliant."

Hans knew it was his finest work. After Death had rendered approval, each new piece went into a large wooden box that Hans had designed and specially made; the top was ornately carved and gilt with Death's coat-of-arms from the first set of drawings. Hans had already completed the engravings on the first two drawings of this new set, having decided that no other could be entrusted to accurately cut the wood for his masterworks. Someday, when the engravings were completed and the books printed, the world would recognize his achievement as well.

❂ ❂ ❂

One afternoon, as Hans returned from another visit to Henry's court that had left him bored and annoyed and aching to get back to what he considered his real work, he passed an inn where he saw a ring of onlookers standing around outside, peering in anxiously. Spotting a man he knew in the crowd, an apprentice to a printer he sometimes dined with, he asked the man what the commotion was about.

"Lady murdered her husband," the young apprentice said, nodding his head toward the building's front windows.

Hans found a gap in the crowd, bent down to peer in through a square of glass—and his breath caught at what he saw:

Two armed men were questioning a woman who sat at the head of a table, a glass resting before her. A few feet away was a dead man slumped across his plate, still clutching an empty goblet in one hand.

It was an exact rendition of the first new drawing Hans had given Death; the only element missing was Death himself, in the position of the waiter.

Hans stumbled back in shock, carelessly bumping into others who cursed or cautioned him. He barely noticed when the apprentice laid a guiding hand on his arm. "Take care, there, sir, you don't want to hurt anyone..."

"Too late for that," Hans said, before turning to flee.

He staggered back to his studio, his thoughts racing past possibilities and deceptions: *it's a coincidence/Death put the image in my head and I didn't even realize it/perhaps I've gained some fortune-teller's ability...*

But only one explanation made sense: *Death copied my drawing.*

When he reached his studio, he bolted the door and raced to the box of drawings. He tore open the decorated lid, reached to the bottom of the stack of drawings to pluck out the first.

A woman—no, *that* woman, who he'd just seen—poisoning a man. In that room. Even the glasses matched perfectly.

He slammed the drawing down, his motion causing some of the others to flutter aside. There was a woman being raped while Death kept her hands tied; there, a field of soldiers blown apart by some explosive, while Death stood apart, one arm still upraised from the deadly missile he'd just hurled.

Hans leafed frantically through the drawings, realization growing like a cancer within him.

He hadn't created entertainment for Death; Death had never intended to accept these works as art to restore his own flagging spirit.

No, this was an instructional guide.

These were signposts pointing to the future. Hans Holbein the Younger had assembled a manual of coming murders. Death had lied to him when he'd told him he had no control over who he took and how; He *was* the final authority. He *was* God.

Hans collapsed onto a work bench, his hands tearing at

his beard, at his expensive collar. *What have I done? Is it too late to undo it?*

The drawings hadn't gone to the engraver yet, and these were the only copies. He could simply burn them now, destroy them. Death had already seen them, true, had committed them to memory; but perhaps a memory as well-used as His was faulty, wouldn't retain details.

Hans stayed up throughout the night, turning over options and possibilities. By morning he knew there was only one course of action. But first...

There was one final drawing to be made.

❂ ❂ ❂

Death returned a few nights later. Hans was waiting for Him.

"What have you got for me this week, friend?"

Hans passed him the last drawing he'd made. Death looked at it, perplexed. "What is this?"

"You lied to me. You've lied to me from the start. There is no authority over You, and I was a fool to ever believe there was. There is only You."

Death stood silently before Hans. After a few seconds he glanced aside—and noticed the wooden box full of drawings was missing. "Where are the others?"

"Gone. I burned the entire box."

The skull head twisted back and Death trembled, the first real display of emotion Hans had ever seen from Him. "You *destroyed* them all?"

Hans held his ground. "Yes."

"You know what this will mean for you?"

"I do."

"Look under your arm."

Hans could already feel the skin there swelling, as heat began to course through him. "There's no need."

"You're a fool."

Smiling, Hans answered, "Not anymore."

With that, Death vanished.

❂ ❂ ❂

Hans died two days later.

It was several more days before they found him; by then the blood had dried, but the smell hadn't abated. The messenger from the royal court and the neighbors who had battered down the door pulled back, nauseated. The young printer's apprentice had stopped by to visit Hans and was there as the others were turning away.

"What's that he's got in his hands?"

The apprentice took a deep breath and stepped forward; he wanted to know what could have been so important to the great Hans Holbein that it was what he'd clung to as life had left him.

"Be mindful of the plague, lad," the messenger said. But the apprentice thought art was more important than death, so he reached down to wrest the drawing from Hans's stiff fingers.

The sheet of parchment had been splattered heavily by Hans's blood, as he'd coughed up his life, but the apprentice could just make out the image: It showed a man who looked very much like Hans Holbein in a room that was undoubtedly this studio, dying of plague, his face blackened, (real) blood staining his bedclothes...but the man was smiling, at peace. Above the man's head was an hourglass, the upper compartment empty; from the side, a bony hand reached for the glass, but no more of Death was visible, a strange exclusion. At the bottom of the drawing was a Latin inscription; the apprentice had some familiarity with the language, and thought the words read, "Now I join Ambrosius."

He wondered who Ambrosius was.

"That's plague blood on that sheet, boy," muttered the neighbor. "Throw it on the fire."

The apprentice considered, realized they were probably right. Who knew exactly how death passed from one man to another? Better not to take that chance.

He placed the drawing gently on the cold logs in the hearth, whispered goodbye to Hans Holbein, and left that chamber of death behind forever.

A Girl's Life

Fishing with Father.

The sea was vast, impenetrable, its surface rolling dark gray hills. White mist connected directly to water, no land to be seen in any direction. Their boat felt impossibly small. The motor's fumes combined with the rocking motion to make her nauseous.

But none of that mattered now, because something was tugging at Ammie's line. She began reeling, and it was so hard. How big was this fish? She cranked the line, her small girl muscles straining, her right hand going round and round, the distinctive buzzing sound of the reel louder than either the boat's engine or the sea. She wondered where Father was; what if she couldn't keep cranking? What if her arms gave out before the fish did?

She saw something coming up, something pale flashing just beneath the translucent top of the ocean, and she felt a wave of relief...but as she kept reeling, she saw the catch was pink and not fish-shaped. When Ammie realized what was on the end of her line, relief turned to terror.

It was a severed human hand.

She gave the line a tug, and the thing flipped up onto the deck of the boat. Where was Father? What was she supposed to do? She looked down at the hand and saw the deck of the boat was awash in blood. She felt sick, and she—

Ammie woke up.

For a moment she really thought she might be sick; but

after a few seconds she was able to shake off the dream's queasiness.

She'd had the dream off and on for years, with slight variations. Sometimes she never actually saw the thing on the end of the line, but she *knew*. Sometimes it was a head, or a foot. But there were constants, too: The gray water. The first sight of pale skin flashing through the water. The grind on her muscles. Her missing father.

Ammie debated trying to go back to sleep, but her tablet showed that it was almost six, the sun already painting the sky. She pushed aside her window blinds to glance out; unlike her dream, today would be clear and hot, the water of Innsmouth Harbour clear and quiet. A mile beyond the shore, she could just make out the tiny black line that marked the top of Devil Reef.

The semester had ended last week, Ammie had graduated elementary school, and now she had six weeks to herself. Her best friend Martin was off on a trip with his family, or she would have hung out with him, watching movies and going down to the convenience store for ice cream. She decided she wanted to go to the library today. It was on the other side of town, along Federal Street, which meant a two-mile walk, but Ammie didn't mind. She liked walking through Innsmouth; she liked looking at the old Victorian houses, and the old people who lived in them. Sometimes she saw them, the aged ones, with their skin like crumpled paper and their glasses and canes, and they saw her. They never smiled or waved; some of them gazed at her sadly.

Ammie had once asked her mother about the town's senior citizens. "Why are there so few couples? I always see just one old man or woman around the houses, but never both."

"Old people die, honey," her mom had told her. "It's rare to find an elderly couple anywhere."

But Ammie spent a lot of time on the computer, talking to friends she hadn't met in faraway places she'd never been to, and she saw lots of old couples. Sometimes they posed with grandchildren; they looked happy.

She also saw lots of people her age who knew what their parents did for a living. Martin's father drove a truck; his mother taught kindergarten. Ammie knew only that her mother didn't work. She had no idea what her father did. He was gone for days or weeks; he said he was fishing. He brought home fresh salmon and crab as if to prove that. He talked about adventures wrangling big ones, or spotting a shark, or a whale that bumped the boat.

But they had a big two-story house in a small town. Ammie knew their house was huge compared to a lot of houses around the country; most of the houses in Innsmouth were big. She'd never seen a house for sale in Innsmouth, but she knew they must be valuable, worth more than a single fisherman with a thirty-foot cabin cruiser could make.

Her father had never actually told her that he made his living as a fisherman; it was simply all he ever talked about, on the rare occasions when he was home. She'd asked her mother what he did for a living; Mother had told her that Father's family had money, so he didn't have to work.

Ammie wondered why he was gone so long, if he didn't have to work.

"Maybe he's a spy," Martin had told her once, when they were playing video games at his house. "That's why he can't talk about it."

Ammie tried to imagine her father as James Bond or Jason Bourne, a fast-thinking man of action.

She couldn't. She couldn't, in fact, imagine him as *any-thing*.

She'd been fishing with him, at least. He'd taken her out several times a year for as long as she could remember. He'd almost been like a normal father, then, showing her how to bait her hook, helping her lower her line, teaching her how to watch for the giveaway snap that meant a fish was on. When she'd reeled her fish in, she'd tried not to watch as he'd hauled it up with the cruel gaff, then clubbed it senseless and tossed it into the catch box while fish blood and sea water swirled around her tiny sneakers. Later, he'd clean the fish, swiftly scraping off scales and tossing aside glistening pink innards.

It wasn't until she'd posted photos of herself with Father and dead fish to her circle of unmet friends that she'd realized most children hadn't grown up surrounded by blood. "Gross," one had posted. "Why aren't you hurling?" asked another.

She didn't know. It had never occurred to her that other kids thought all fish naturally looked like Mrs. Paul's Fish-Sticks. They hadn't been raised to accept that death and blood were part of their life.

Sometimes they asked about Innsmouth: "Is that place as weird as they say?" Ammie had heard some of the rumors, old stories about things that had happened in the town long ago, but she thought things she saw in New York or Los Angeles were much weirder.

Ammie checked her tablet for email, and then left her bedroom at just after 6:30. Father had been gone for three days, and Mother would probably be up in another hour. She went into her own bathroom, having decided to shower quickly and leave the house on her library expedition before Mother could come up with chores for her instead.

She pulled her pajama bottoms down—and stared at the red spots that dotted the crotch.

Red spots?

Mother had taken her aside a few months ago and given her "The Talk," about the differences between boys and girls, and how babies were made, and how she would soon bleed for five days a month. "Menstruation," it was called. Or "having a period."

Was that happening to her now? She searched her body for other signs, remembering the dream. She'd never been nauseous from it before; she was still unsettled now. And the blood around her feet...

She felt something warm and looked down. A trickle of

red appeared on the inside of one thigh.

"Mom!"

Ammie ran out of the bathroom, no longer caring whether Mother kept her home with housework or not. She opened the door of the master bedroom and saw the form of her sleeping mother beneath the covers.

"Mom!"

Her mother stirred and looked at her, bleary-eyed but concerned. "What's the matter, Ammie, what's—?"

Ammie thrust her stained pajamas out. "Is that...am I...?"

Mother squinted at the pink flannel, and she turned ashen. She stared until Ammie asked, "Am I okay, Mom?"

"Oh, yes, honey, it's just your first period. Let's get you cleaned up."

Mother led her into the bathroom and showed her how to use sanitary napkins. At some point Ammie realized her mother was crying. "What's wrong?"

"I just..." Mother hugged her. "You're so grown up now."

They held each other a long time; there was something fierce in Mother's embrace, as if she feared Ammie would vanish should she release her.

But she did release her, and Ammie didn't vanish. Instead they spent the day together, chatting and cleaning and shopping and eating.

Almost like normal people.

✿ ✿ ✿

Father came home a week later. As usual, he arrived smelling of brine and fish, carrying a bulging plastic trash bag. "Good catch," he announced, smiling.

Mother gave him a polite kiss and then whispered something to him. He turned to Ammie, his smile gone. "Well, then," he said. Nothing more.

He had the same look she'd seen on the faces of some of the older people when she walked by.

❍ ❍ ❍

Early that evening, while Mother prepared fresh fish fillets for dinner, Father came to see Ammie on the couch as she played a game on her tablet. "How'd you like to go out with me tomorrow?"

"You mean fishing?"

"Sure. We'll have to leave early, though, so I'll get you up about five."

She didn't want to go. She had a stack of new books from the library, she had new music she'd downloaded, and Martin was bored on his vacation (visiting family in Ohio) and spent most of his day texting Ammie. Today he'd sent her a picture of himself in his swimsuit. Ammie thought he looked cute.

"You should probably try to get to bed early tonight," Father said, before walking away. She couldn't argue with him. She wanted to scream, to tell him, *I'm almost an adult now, and I don't like fishing, and it scares me, so why can't I just stay home?* But she didn't. She knew she never would.

❍ ❍ ❍

She was already awake when Father knocked on her door at five a.m. sharp. "Ammie?"

"I'll be right down."

She got up, dressed, brushed her teeth. Her mother was waiting for her in the kitchen; that was strange, because usually Mother didn't bother to get up when Father dragged Ammie out of bed for their fishing trips.

Mother handed her a cup of hot chocolate (Ammie's favorite) and a bag. "I made you lunch for...later."

Ammie sipped the hot chocolate, but was looking at her parents. They were glaring at each other in a way Ammie had never seen before: Mother almost furious, Father warning.

Finally Mother blurted out, "Do you—?"

Father cut her off. "You know we talked about this."

That was all they said. Mother gave Ammie a silent hug before leaving the kitchen. Father led the way out the front door. "Let's go."

Ammie had never quite understood why these fishing trips had to start so early. Father had claimed that it had something to do with the tides, but Ammie couldn't comprehend what or why. The hot chocolate had worked some magic to perk her up, but she was still moving slowly, not fully awake. Father, however, moved with energetic determination, even more than usual.

They piled into Father's pickup, Ammie bundled in a heavy jacket. Father pulled out of the driveway and headed for the wharf, only a few miles away. As they drove through the early morning, the horizon just beginning to turn a blue so deep it almost hurt to look at, Ammie saw that the old people, all the ones in the Victorian gingerbread houses she passed on her walks, were out on their porches or front sidewalks.

What on earth are they doing...?

As they drove through town, Ammie realized: they were all watching *her*. At first she thought it was just an illusion, that it was still too dark to see where their eyes were really turned, but after a few blocks she knew. Their faces were tilting in her direction as the truck passed; she could almost feel their eyes on her, measuring.

Father drove in silence until they reached the wharf. By then Ammie was glad to be away from the houses and the elderly stares.

The Atlantic Ocean was turning gold where the sun was cresting it, and Ammie was pleased to know that at least the day would be spent beneath blue sky and sunshine, not the colorless mist of her nightmares. They made their way around the wharf until they reached Father's boat, the *Nereid*. There were other fishermen going out early, but Ammie felt separate from them, isolated. Of course she was the only girl she saw, but even beyond that...only one man nodded to her father, and then gave Ammie a look of frank appraisal that made her blood freeze. She was relieved when the *Nereid* was untied, the motor started, and they were picking up speed as they headed away from shore.

For a while Ammie sat by the side of the boat, losing herself in the sight of the white froth their passage kicked up. The shore grew smaller behind them as they veered away from other boats. Father steered carefully around Devil Reef as Ammie eyed its uneven dark gray surface uneasily. She'd heard stories about people dying on the reef, that the bottom of the ocean fell away to unmeasurable depths just past the reef. She was always glad when they'd left it behind.

Unfortunately, the bright weather didn't hold. Ammie looked up and saw a bank of mist ahead of them, to the east. Father drove the boat into it, and soon the sun was hidden and the world was white and gray.

Like the dream.

Father slowed the boat's speed down, checking a fish-finder scope mounted next to the wheel. They drove for a few more moments, slower, slower, until finally he cut the engine altogether. They drifted, the only sound the slap of water on the sides of the *Nereid*.

"You ready to fish?" Father was already getting a pole for her.

Ammie peered down into the water. "What are we fishing for today?"

Father didn't look up from the hook and lead weight he was tying to her line. "Something special." He finished and handed her the rod. He went to his big red tackle box, opened it to retrieve an object. "Even the bait is special."

He showed her what he held: it was a tiny box, about the size of one that might contain a ring. It was made of burnished metal, with some sort of swirling symbol carved onto the top. "Is that gold?"

Father nodded and then opened the lid. What Ammie

saw inside made her gasp.

The box held a small semi-translucent grayish blob, about the size of a marble. Within the organic jelly, Ammie thought she saw something moving, no bigger than an ant. "What is it?"

"I told you: it's special bait."

Father continued to hold the box out, and Ammie realized he expected something of her. She looked up at him, uncertainly.

"You have to bait the hook yourself."

"Oh." She started to reach for the quivering ball, but hesitated before she touched it. Father nodded, and she picked it up. It felt oddly warm in her fingers, vibrating slightly. She held it in her right hand, running her left fingers down the length of her line until she found the hook. She lifted the hook gingerly, afraid it would kill whatever the little egg-like mass held.

"Go on," Father urged her.

She swallowed, lifted the hook, ran it through the center of the blob. It seated firmly on the hook, but continued to tremble slightly. Father smiled, pleased.

"Good job. Now get it into the water, quick."

Ammie moved the tip of her rod out over the water, released the catch on the reel, and held her thumb on the line as it unspooled. "How far?"

"About a hundred feet."

The line continued to unwind, sinking, as Ammie watched the depth meter mounted on the reel. She wondered how close they were to Devil Reef, how deep the ocean really was here. Finally the meter reached 100, Ammie gave it a wind back to stop the release, and then waited.

The boat rocked gently, and she was aware of the presence of her father behind her. She asked, "Aren't you going to fish, too?"

"In a bit. But I want you to get the first one today."

She waited, keeping a thumb on the line, feeling for

telltale jerks. She tried not to imagine what might be at the bottom of the ocean, tangled in the weeds and rocks: Bodies, battered by water and predators, torn apart, mere pieces to be hooked and pulled up...

The mist around the boat thickened, cutting out more light. The water darkened as well, going from gray to almost obsidian, polished black that rolled slightly more, hitting the sides of the cruiser with wet smacks.

Ammie asked, "Is there a storm coming?"

"Just keep your attention on your line." The force of her father's tone shocked her. He sounded almost threatening, and Ammie wished she was anywhere but here, on this boat, with him, with this line—

The line jerked.

"That's it," Father said. "Pull it up!"

Ammie started reeling. At first it seemed easier than she'd expected—easier than in the dream—but it went on, and her muscles began to feel the weight of whatever was on the line. She cranked, knew she was sweating even in the chill mist, her arms starting to ache. She paused for a second, and her father's voice was right behind her, close enough that she felt the warmth of his breath on her ear. "Don't stop, Ammie; it's almost here."

She breathed in and continued to reel up line. At last she thought she saw something in the water, flashing just below the surface. She felt relief that it wasn't something pink and gray and human, but it wasn't fish, either. She saw the silver of the lead weight, but just below it, where there should have been the shimmer of scales, was nothing.

Her father was leaning over the side of the boat now, not with the gaff hook but with a net. "Pull it up...just a little more..."

She thought her arms would surely explode, but she gave one last crank, leaning back, and then something was in Father's net. He lifted it and opened the catch box at the rear of the boat and lowered the net in, then withdrew it, now empty.

Ammie kept the line taut as Father moved quickly to grab a long pair of needle-nosed pliers from his tackle box, which he used to remove the hook from her catch. He took the rod from her, and she fell back, exhausted, as he secured it in one of the holders attached to the sides of the boat. Je nodded at the catch box. "Go see what you got."

Ammie rose and walked over to look down.

The catch box had been filled with about a foot of sea water, and something floated in there now, a black mass plainly visible against the white plastic sides. It was about the size of a large tumor, covered with tentacles, dozens of them, jet black and each finished with a long, barbed hook. Even though Ammie couldn't make out an eye, she had the sense that the thing was watching her. She felt this morning's cup of chocolate churning inside her, she smelled the engine fumes, felt the sanitary napkin in her underpants, and thought she might be sick. Instead she sank to her knees by the catch box, staring at the glistening black thing.

"What is it?"

"Do you trust me, Ammie?"

She wanted to turn and look at her father then, but she had the terrible thought that if she did, the creature in the box might leap up at her, attach itself to her. She saw that it was using its barbed arms to pull itself along the bottom of the box, and she wondered if it would eventually pull itself up and out—

"Ammie?"

"Yes."

"Yes, you trust me?"

She didn't. She wasn't sure she ever had, but she did what she thought her mother had always done, what she thought maybe all women had done: she lied. "Yes, I trust you."

"I want you to put your hand in the water."

Ammie looked down again, saw the clawed tentacles, the way the thing seemed to be trying to draw itself toward her. "Won't it hurt me?"

"It'll hurt for a second. But after that..."

Maybe this was some sort of test, and she was supposed to say no. For the first time, she would say no to her father, and he would nod approvingly. Or she would reach her hand forward, and he would stop her just in time, and then turn the boat around to take them home.

Because she wanted to go home, she pulled back the sleeve of her jacket and started to reach toward the black thing.

Father didn't stop her. In fact, she saw determination, even anticipation, on his face. Her hand inched closer to the waiting monstrosity, and still he didn't call out or rush forward. He wasn't going to; she was about to snatch her hand back when pain penetrated her fingers. She stared, dread flooding her, at the mass clamped around her hand, which was engulfed to the wrist. Tentacles throbbed and writhed, and she saw drops of blood—*her* blood—spray into the catch box. She screamed, shook her hand, but still it clung to her. She tripped and fell back, landing hard against the side of the boat. Her father was calling her name and saying something, but she didn't care what, she only cared about getting the thing off her, ending the pain—

And then it was done. The creature fell from her hand to the deck, dead. The pain vanished, leaving her to stare at her hand, at the dozens of pinpricks that oozed crimson, and she watched as the drops fell in slow-motion around her feet...wait, were those *her* feet? Those clumsy parts bound in rubber and canvas, laced with strings? And that bleeding mass at the end of her arm—how could that be her hand?

Her head spun, and she instinctively reached out for the side of the boat. She had a flash of panic—*I've been poisoned!*—before her consciousness somehow detached itself and floated, calm. She was disconnected...or truly connected for the first time. She saw the water around the boat not as a lightless seething danger, but as a comforting blanket, something a mother would wrap an infant in.

"Ammonite."

She heard her name—her *real* name, not that ridiculous short version—and she understood it at last: An ancient sea creature, beautiful and strong and protected, thought to be extinct...but it was not. She stood, trying to grasp it all. One thing rose above the rest: she wanted to be in the water.

"Take off your clothes," her father said.

She did. They were no longer necessary; she was happy to be rid of them. She was happier still when she leapt from the side of the boat and the sea received her like a lost lover. She swam down, her new sight adjusting as she dove lower and lower, her strokes sure and powerful. As the light from overhead dimmed, she saw more of her kind—the older ones, the ones who had spent their time on land (just as she would) and had finally returned to the sea, leaving behind the mammals, the ones they bred with who would never change.

She swam toward the black mass that was called Devil Reef, down and down along its length, until she saw the ruined temples. She understood that their gods (*her* gods) had died, and they were a failing race. They diluted their blood by mixing it with the land-dwellers; soon, their descendents would no longer be able to return to the sea. She wondered if she were the last of her father's family who would know this change.

But the grieving could wait. She swam past one that looked familiar and asked how long they could stay. "For weeks, if you want to," Father answered.

"Yes," she said, and wondered how far she could go.

Trigger Fate

Rosita's heart hammers as she crouches beneath the study table. She flinches at a new round of *pop-pop-pop-pop* sounds, followed by screams and thick groans, closer this time.

The shooter is coming her way.

She looks around anxiously, realizes the table is little or no defense; all the gunman needs to do is bend over slightly. Maybe he won't. Maybe he's already killed whomever he came to get. Or maybe he'll go the other way, leave the library, head for the classrooms. Maybe he'll run out of bullets. Be shot first. Shoot himself. *Anything.*

She looks up at the sound of sobbing. Two tables away, a blonde girl kneels below her own table, uttering choked cries. Rosita wishes she could reach her arm out like a comic book character to stifle the girl's sounds. If the shooter hears and looks down to see the blonde, he'll see Rosita, too, and the boy who's huddled under his table on the other side of her.

She doesn't dare call out, but she stares at the flaxen-haired girl, mentally urging her to stop, or look up. Finally she does glance in Rosita's direction. Their eyes lock. When Rosita is sure she has the girl's attention, she raises a finger to her lips and then points in the direction of the unseen shooter. For a few seconds, the girl's eyes widen, as if Rosita has just conveyed the most startling message of all time; then she gulps back the last sob, nods slightly, and goes quiet.

Rosita has no time to be relieved, though; she hears

three more shots, this time just on the other side of the history stacks, less than thirty feet away. A male voice grunts. A *thud* sounds as something big hits the floor.

Footsteps are nearing.

Plans race through Rosita's head: *Run / crab-walk out of here / use something to trip him if he walks past / throw the laptop at him / confront him and talk him down / plead, beg...*

...but somehow she knows none of those things will work. She's heard others run or beg; the shooter—whoever he is—gunned them down, without words, without any sound but *pop pop pop.*

Rosita imagines what she'll do when this is over, how she'll call Mama and tell her she's fine, and Mama will cry with relief. Newspapers will interview her, she'll tell them that she forgives the gunman and has no plans to drop out of college, that her major in law is more important to her now than ever before, that she wants to work to prevent more tragedies like this—

Boots step into view.

Rosita's thoughts shatter as she watches the heavy boots, two tables past the blonde girl. They move slowly, too slowly. The blonde girl has her hands clamped over her mouth and her eyes shut, she's curled into a knot of terror. Rosita tries to make herself as flat as possible, reasoning that if he shoots the blonde girl, the bullets might pass over her if she's narrow, thin...

The boots stop.

They turn slightly.

Rosita hopes he can't hear her heart.

A head comes into view. A young man's face, so young that his beard doesn't look full; it seems soft and patchy, acne still scars one cheek. His expression is dispassionate as his dead eyes scan the area under the tables.

He lowers a rifle barrel.

He pulls the trigger.

Pop pop pop pop pop

Pain explodes Rosita's consciousness, like two supernovas burning inside her, one in her shoulder, one in her thigh. She grits her teeth and focuses on keeping the scream in, but the pain o god the pain is—

Gone.

With the release from pain comes a startling clarity. Rosita knows she's been shot. Twice. But she's also alive. She's on her stomach and finds that she can move her right arm, but not her left; she feels her right leg, but not the left. She turns her head left, sees the blood pooling around her.

Her blood.

I'm in shock.

Rosita turns away, the biggest movement she can make. She focuses instead on the gunman, hears his footsteps receding. He's moving on past her. She looks at the blonde, sees the girl is also face down, limbs sprawled, in an expanding red circle. The blonde, closer to the shooter—closer to his gun—took the brunt. She's dead.

But Rosita isn't. If she could call for help...but she left her phone on top of the table, just three feet above her.

And the gunman is still in the library.

Even if she can summon the strength to reach the phone, she'll have to wait.

She's not wearing a belt or shoes that tie, anything she could use as a tourniquet. She can't raise herself to remove her shirt, which could staunch the bleeding in one place. She has to hope this will end soon and she'll be found. Maybe it's like a movie, where being shot in an arm or leg means you don't die. You live, you come back as long as you don't panic, don't do anything to make the shooter come back and put a bullet into your head or chest. Think of other things.

Other things...

❂ ❂ ❂

Elizabeth peers at herself in the bathroom mirror, gives a weary grin, holds up two fingers in a victory salute.

"Are you *ever* going to stop preening, woman?" Tony calls from the bedroom.

She smiles, raises her voice to answer, "I think I've earned it."

Elizabeth returns her gaze to the mirror, noticing fresh lines beneath her eyes. The campaign has definitely aged her. She still thinks she looks surprisingly good for 45, but she can no longer pass for thirtysomething. She remembers something that Mama once told her: for many women life really began in their forties. While that's not strictly true in Elizabeth's case, she's achieved her career dream in this decade. A Congresswoman, elected by the people to the U.S. House of Representatives. She already has great plans, a platform of good works. She wants to make the people in her district safer. richer, healthier, better educated, happier. She wants to speak out against things that are oppressive and unfair. She wants to avoid corruption.

She's reaching for the bathroom light when something catches her eye: movement, glimpsed in the mirror. Hackles rising, she turns, but there's nothing behind her, just the familiar green tile and matching towels of the master bath. She looks back into the mirror, is surprised to find herself shivering; the bathroom feels ten degrees cooler than a moment ago. She hesitates, waiting, feeling slightly foolish.

Just then the house's central heat kicks on, and Elizabeth stifles a small laugh. *See? Nothing to it; just a cold night. Everything's fine; your handsome husband's waiting for you, your children are asleep down the hall, and all is as it should be.*

After turning off the light, she fumbles through the darkness until she finds her bed. Tony's arm is waiting to go around her, pull her close as she snuggles beneath the covers. He kisses the top of her head and says, pride evident in his voice, "I think Congresswoman Sosa has a damned nice ring to it."

"It's not a sure thing yet..."

"Oh, come on, it wasn't even close. At this point it wouldn't matter if all the provisional ballots go to him. *You won*."

Feeling warm and drowsy, Elizabeth admits out loud what she already inwardly knows. "You're right; I like 'Congresswoman Sosa'."

"Attagirl."

It's been a long day, with victory speeches given, hands shaken, donors thanked; now it's late, *very* late, and Elizabeth drifts off. But just before sleep takes her, something prickles at her consciousness again: a presence, one uneasy and fearful.

Please, let me have just this one night, Elizabeth thinks at whatever is in the house with her.

She doesn't think *it* has heard.

۵ ۵ ۵

A door closes. Rosita listens.

Pop pop pop, this time from the hallway outside the library.

The shooter has left this room.

She thinks about reaching for the cell phone, but is afraid to move; will that increase her bleeding? Can she even move at all? She's not sure.

No, she needs help. Are there other survivors in here? She draws in a breath, calls out, "Is anyone around? I need help..."

She hears scurrying, turns to her left, looks past the blood to see the boy who was two tables away crawling to her. It's difficult because he's got a cell phone raised, he's talking as he moves forward. "Hello, 911? We need help, we've been shot, a lot of people have been shot..."

Rosita listens as he gives more details. He ends the call as he reaches her, he sets the phone aside. "They're sending help, we just need to hang on..." As he looks down at her, his brow furrows. "You've been shot."

The boy has a bloody scrape across one cheek; he's a

good-looking kid, with flawless black skin, but she knows he'll be scarred for life now. "So have you."

He wipes blood from his face. "It's nothing, just grazed me. But you..." He bends over her, assessing. "Looks like you got hit twice."

The boy is already pulling off his shirt, balling it up to press against her shoulder. "My name's Jaivon Mason. What's yours?"

"Rosita Morales. That's a pretty name, Jaivon."

He smiles, keeps the pressure on her shoulder, but looks down at her leg. "Rosita, we need to do something about your leg. I'm going to take off my belt and use it as a tourniquet, okay? By the way, I'm Pre-med."

"And I'm lucky."

Rosita doesn't feel it as he cinches the belt tight around her leg; she doesn't feel anything there.

They both look up when a male voice from somewhere nearby groans loudly. The groan is followed by a raspy call. "Can somebody help me? I can't move, I..."

Jaivon looks down at Rosita, says, "Look, you're gonna be okay, but I want you to stay awake, you got it?"

She nods. He offers her a last look of concern before crawling out from under the table. "I'll be back," he says. Rosita doesn't want him to go, but she understands that he's too valuable for her to hold on to, and he's gone.

Rosita feels cold. She wishes she had a blanket. Or that Jaivon would come back, or that she had someone else to talk to. Or her cell phone—damn it, she should have asked him to get her cell phone before he left. She'd call Mama, tell her how much she loves her, listen to her mother's voice a last time—

No, don't go there.

She wants to live. She wants to see her mother, and her sisters again. Her mother has always been so proud of her, the eldest daughter, the first one to go to college. Rosita's mother didn't finish sixth grade before her family fled El Salvador for the U.S., and the look on her face whenever she tells strangers about her daughter who's attending college on a scholarship, who's going to become an attorney someday...

Rosita feels herself fading. She shakes her head, determined to stay conscious, to live, to continue to give her mother something to be proud of. If she doesn't make it, she can't imagine what it will do to her family.

She determines to fight.

❍ ❍ ❍

Elizabeth awakens with a jolt. She's disoriented, her heart hammers, at first she doesn't know where she is or what's awakened her. She forces herself to think:

This is my bedroom. It's still dark, so I haven't been asleep long. Did I hear something...?

Beside her, Tony snores softly. The only other sound is the gentle thrum of the heating.

She remembers a dream she was having when she awoke: she's lying on the floor of a large room—a library—and she's surrounded by her own blood. She has a terrible premonition of danger, disaster, but she can't move. From somewhere nearby, she hears rapid gunfire and screams from many voices.

Elizabeth shakes her head as if the motion will somehow loosen the dream and release it, force it out of her head forever. She's puzzling over the dream when she looks into a corner of the bedroom, over near the mirrored doors of the closet, and her breath catches.

There's something there, a figure, darker than the surrounding darkness. It's almost impossible to see, but it's there. A shadow, small, feminine in size and shape.

Elizabeth almost calls out to it, but her voice catches in her throat, strangled by fear. She can only wait, paralyzed, trying to watch something she can't really see.

Why is this happening, she thinks, why today, of all days?

She rouses herself enough to whisper to her husband.

"Tony...Antonio..."

He doesn't wake.

She gives up, turns her attention fully on the shadow presence. The more she studies it, the more she senses something pathetic about it, something tragic...

Something familiar.

She finally says, softly, "Hello?"

There's no response; the shadow doesn't answer or move, but neither does it vanish.

Elizabeth waits.

⊙ ⊙ ⊙

Rosita's eyes are half-closed when Jaivon returns. "Hey... come on, stay with me..."

She opens them, sees the handsome young man with the bloodied face smile in relief. "Good. I just heard sirens pull up outside. It shouldn't be long now."

"Can you..." Rosita tries to speak, can at first muster only a cracked whisper. She clears her throat and tries again. "Can you get my cell phone...from overhead..."

"Sure."

He reaches up, comes back with the phone, puts it in her good hand. She punches the button that calls Mama, praying that Mama is near her phone, that whatever cleaning job she's working, she's got her purse nearby—

As the call is connecting, she hears a large BOOM; the floor beneath her vibrates. "What was that?" she asks Jaivon.

"I don't know—"

Then Rosita's not listening anymore as her mother picks up the call. "Rosita, my baby, madre di dios, we see on the TV what is happening, are you okay—?"

Rosita struggles to make her voice sound as normal as possible. "Mama, there's a man with a gun who went crazy here. I've been shot—"

Her mother's cry interrupts her. She tries to raise her voice. "I need you to listen: I've been shot, but there are people trying to help me. I just wanted to say that I love you very much—"

She breaks off at a fresh round of gunfire outside, this time from multiple sources. Next: voices in the hallway outside the library, a lot of voices.

"I think they got him," Jaivon says, straining to hear.

But now all Rosita hears is her mother crying. "I love you, Mama," she says again, as the phone slips from her hand.

❂ ❂ ❂

Elizabeth peels back the covers and swings her legs out of the bed. She rises in the dark, drawn to the shadow in the corner. As she moves to it, slowly, cautiously, she is struck by a sudden sensation of unreality, as if her world has tilted off its axis and spun down into someplace else. Her head screams, *Something is very wrong—don't do this*, and for a second she stops. She starts to reach back for the lamp at the side of her bed, but her fingers close on empty air, and she realizes she doesn't know if there really *is* a lamp there. She can't recall specific details about her own house. Where is the children's room? What color are the walls? What does the neighborhood look like?

As her life runs through her fingers like the most precious sand, she reaches out to hold on to certain memories: Her college graduation, as her mother sat in the audience, silently crying in joy. The day she made junior partner at the law firm, the party they threw for her. When she opened the women's shelter and saw the looks on the faces of battered wives clutching the hands of children with bruised cheeks.

Above all, though, was during the campaign for the House of Representatives seat, when the eighteen-year-old Latina college student approached her, shyly extending a hand and telling Elizabeth what an inspiration she was. That eighteen-year-old had reminded her so much of herself at that age, and that moment had touched her on a profound level.

The shadow in the corner of her bedroom somehow reminds her of that girl. Same size and shape, something else, something she can't define...

"Do I know you?" Elizabeth knows how ridiculous the question is even as she asks it; she's talking to a shadow.

When there's no answer, she becomes angry. "Either talk to me or get out of my house!"

The ghost—if that's what it is—doesn't respond. Elizabeth doesn't know how to threaten it, or what it could want. Is it here for her children? For...for...

She can't remember the names of her own children, who are both sleeping soundly down the hall.

"What's happening?"

She turns to her husband, her beautiful, successful husband, her...Tommy, was it? No, that doesn't seem right...

Panic is replacing everything else. Elizabeth takes another step toward the blackness and says, "Please, for the love of God, *help me*."

The shadow moves now. It steps forward, takes on more form and light, and Elizabeth sees a young girl—*the* young girl, the one who held her in such high regard...but no, this girl is covered in blood, her dark-skinned face paler than it should ever be. "I'm sorry," the apparition whispers, sounding as if it speaks from a distant cosmos.

❂ ❂ ❂

"I'm sorry," Rosita whispers.

Jaivon clutches her hand. He's saying something to her, but she can no longer hear.

She was only shot in the arm and leg. She should have been able to survive this. This isn't fair. But one of the bullets hit something major, and she's lost too much blood. She can't fight any longer.

❂ ❂ ❂

Elizabeth clenches her fist and shouts at the spectral girl. "No, NO, you can't take this! NO!"

The girl embraces her, the girl whose name is Elizabeth Rosita Morales, who might someday have married a handsome man named Antonio Sosa. In that instant Elizabeth vanishes, everything she might have been gone, the ghost of a future cut short. Rosita embraces cold nothingness now, unable to hang onto the dream any longer, the dream that has kept her alive.

She wishes she'd had time to think of names for her children.

Larue's Dime Museum

Live on Stage The Human Squid

The first thing that caught Julia's eye in the old photo was the banner strung across the rear wall of a small stage. It took her a few seconds to realize that the tall man standing in front of the banner had appendages that looked like tentacles pushing up around the sides of his 1940s-style shirt and double-breasted jacket.

There were more banners, all sporting whimsical lettering in a curving style long obsolete.

Mr. Inside-Out Appearing Daily

Next to the man with tentacles was a smaller performer whose skin glistened darkly, highlighting the whites of his eyes and his bared teeth. Although the glossy photograph was in black and white, Julia guessed the dark color was a deep crimson red...like blood.

See Conundra World's Greatest Contortionist

The woman to the far right of the stage stood with her back to the audience, hands on her hips, and her head, smiling, sitting between her shoulder blades facing the camera.

Larue's Dime Museum

Between Conundra and Mr. Inside-Out stood a small, dapper African American man, grinning proudly, one arm around the contortionist. The stage the quartet stood on was raised perhaps three feet, lit by overhead bare bulbs dangling at the end of wires, surrounded by banners proclaiming their unusual attributes.

Julia felt one brief stab of guilt at being so fascinated by the image. It was no longer politically correct to gawk at... what had they called them back them?

Human oddities?

Sideshow attractions?

Freaks?

But she couldn't deny that the photo exerted a pull on her. It wasn't just the performers, nor even the quaint banners and the cheap stage, but also the composition and lighting of the photo. It was brilliant, bringing the subjects to life with rare skill. She turned the 8"x10" over, saw a name written on the back: *Greta*. No last name, not enough to go on. Was that the photographer, the woman in the photo, or someone who had previously owned the photo?

She set the photo down on an old scuffed teak end table with inlaid glass and thumbed through the rest of the photos and clippings in the handwoven basket. One more gem emerged: another large still obviously by the same photographer, showing the box office/entrance to "Larue's Dime Museum." Inside a glass-and-wood cubicle papered with notices ("Dr. Mostel's World Famous Flea Circus!"), a bored clerk who couldn't have been more than twenty didn't even muster a hint of a smile.

Once again, Julia was taken by the photographer's obvious gifts. She felt as if she knew that clerk, as if they'd often gone out for coffee, chatted about boys and college classes. Even though the photos dated back probably seven decades, Julia had *seen* this young woman's expression in the faces of baristas and social media junkies.

Julia picked up the two photos and turned to find the store's checkout counter. She hadn't really expected to buy anything when she'd come into Round Again Antiques; she'd only wanted to visit the new business in the neighborhood (even though they'd been open for two months now). She found the rest of the store unremarkable, a typical collection of termite-ridden cast-off furniture, American primitive art and hip reproduction tin signs, but she at least wanted to know more about these photos.

She spotted a thirtysomething with purple hair behind a wood-paneled desk and approached. "Excuse me," she said, holding the two stills out, "but I was wondering if you could tell me anything about these?"

The clerk examined the photos. "Oh, those! Yes, believe it or not, we're pretty sure that place used to be *this* place. We found those in an old file cabinet in the back when we took over this spot, and a maintenance guy who's worked here forever said he remembered Larue's. He thinks it closed sometime in the '60s."

"Do you know the person whose name is written on the back?"

Shaking her head, the clerk answered, "Sorry, I don't. If you want those, I'll let them go for five each."

As the clerk rung up the purchase, she glanced at the photos again and laughed. "Wow, look at the guy with the tentacles. You don't think those could be real, do you?"

Julia shrugged.

That was the first time Julia saw the man with the tentacles.

◐ ◐ ◐

Julia's shift at Java Jane's started every morning at 5 a.m., preparing the shop for a 6 a.m. opening and the soon-after influx of downtown's government workers and bankers heading into their offices and cubicles. Julia didn't mind the time; in fact, she enjoyed the commute, driving through

L.A.'s quiet pre-dawn streets, a world of shadowed door-ways and sodium lights that reminded her of the film noir movies she loved.

She felt more comfortable in the black-and-white world of men in wide hats and black, wet pavement than she did in her own time. She'd been born and raised into a Southern California that gave success to the beautiful and the ambitious, and she was neither. When she'd seen the two photos in that basket at Round Again Antiques, what she'd immediately felt was a sense of *belonging*.

She'd googled Larue's Dime Museum, but there wasn't much to find. She learned that dime museums had once been popular attractions across the country, offering "low-brow" audiences a mix of displays, freak shows, magicians, and even music. They'd largely died out by the mid-twentieth-century, undoubtedly replaced by a combination of changing morality, rising real estate values, and ubiquitous television.

Larue's had started in 1888 as a series of tents on the outskirts of downtown. A year later, Walter Larue moved his displays into a building at Eighth and Temple. The museum had apparently been popular clear into the '50s, long after the Larues had died and sold it to "Slick" Charlie Johnson (who Julia guessed was the well-dressed man onstage with the performers). Slick Charlie had converted most of it into a game arcade by 1960, but it passed away with the rest of old L.A.'s glamor in the following decade, about the same time that once-elegant Bunker Hill had seen the last of its old Victorian mansions vanish. There was no mention in any of the articles on Larue's of a "Greta."

Downtown L.A.—or DTLA, as some promoters insisted on referring to it—was now one part faceless bureaucracy in shining towers, one part trendy artists' lofts, and one part Skid Row, where thousands of the discarded slept in cardboard boxes and rat-chewed blankets. Julia passed them all on her way into work. She felt sorry for the junkies, the handicapped, the vets, the unlucky, but at the same time she was thankful that Java Jane's was many blocks removed from the alleys and crumbling warehouses that formed the bulk of the homeless encampments. Java Jane's covered her monthly parking fees, in a structure across the street, so she didn't have to walk far to reach the shop.

This morning, she parked and hurried to the nearest crosswalk; she'd slept badly, had finally dozed off and then overslept, so she was a few minutes late. She didn't see any sign of her usual work partner Gabriel, though, so she decided to wait for the light to change rather than risk (as she often did) dodging across the wide street illegally.

As she stood on the corner, she noticed a man standing in the doorway of the office building next to Java Jane's. The man was backlit by a single overhead light in the entryway, so it was difficult to make out details, but he seemed to be wearing a long coat. A trench coat, in fact, like the ones in her old movies. His head was bare, but something about his neck—was he wearing a bulky scarf? Did he have something draped around his shoulders?

As she stared, he stepped forward into the dull overhead light of a sodium lamp, and Julia saw what wound around his neck: tentacles. Or at least they were tentacle-like, long fleshy appendages about as thick as two of her fingers. They were moving slightly, as if caught in a breeze, except they all moved independently of each other. There seemed to be six, or—no, eight.

He was the man in the photo. The Human Squid.

No, Julia thought, her heart picking up speed, *that's not possible. He'd be a hundred years old. This man isn't even bent.*

His head swiveled slightly, gazing up and down the street, and then his eyes fixed on her.

Julia's pounding heart froze. She locked eyes with him—*The Human Squid*—as a rush of emotions coursed through her. Fear, yes, and dread, of what might happen next...what if he stepped into the street, came toward her? She imagined him pulling her roughly into an embrace, those writhing lengths of flesh against her neck, her face—

Her paralysis broke when the rumbling of a bus sounded. It crossed between them, an early morning Metro already packed with riders, cutting off her view of the man. The bus slowed, only for a second, surely not long enough to let anyone off or on, but when it moved on down the street the man was gone. Julia let out a shaky breath and gulped in air, her eyes still on the bus as it headed into the heart of the city. Where would he go? How could he take public transportation? Had those really been tentacles, or had she been deceived by light and shadow, like any sucker who ever bought a ticket for the sideshow and soon realized the mermaid was nothing but a mummified dolphin?

When her heart slowed again, the bus gone from view, she walked across the street and entered Java Jane's, almost relieved to be back among the mundane concerns of obligation.

☉ ☉ ☉

When Julia returned home that afternoon, she tried to look up more information about Larue's Dime Museum, but her phone had stopped functioning. She'd recently replaced the battery and knew it was fully charged, so the only other alternative was to take it in for repairs. Irritated, she tried to turn on her laptop, but it also failed.

What are the chances?

Instead, she pulled out the two photographs, examining them closely for clues. There was the Human Squid, gawky and angular except for the mass around his neck.

Julia was certain it was the same man she'd seen in the pre-dawn morning.

Had she misinterpreted the age of the photos? Could they have been recent, perhaps even staged? A play, a piece of performance art, a Halloween attraction?

No, she was sure they were authentic and decades old.

They possessed the startling, harsh quality that cameras (and their flash bulbs) from the '40s had. The prices on the ticket booth ("Only 50¢!") were obviously obsolete.

In the photo, the Human Squid looked thirty years old. That would mean the man she'd seen earlier would have been a century.

Julia didn't sleep much that night.

0 0 0

She awoke at her usual time of four a.m. As always, she showered, dressed, had a piece of fruit as she stood before her second-floor living room window, looking out on Wilcox Avenue.

Julia was about to leave when two figures ambling along the sidewalk caught her attention. They were on her side of the street, moving toward her apartment building.

One was tall, with something massed around his neck.

The other man, smaller, wore a chauffeur's cap, a dark jacket, light shirt, and chinos. The two seemed to be chatting, leaning toward each other as they walked.

When they reached Julia's building, they stopped.

She pulled back from the window, but not away. Moving to the side, she peeked around the vertical blinds.

They'd stopped beneath a street light that painted them in yellowish hues. The tall man had a circle of narrow, fleshy appendages around his neck. The other had dark red skin above his white shirt. After a few seconds, Julia realized it wasn't a shirt at all but bandages, wound horizontally around his torso. His wrists and fingers were similarly bound.

They didn't look up toward her. The one in the bandages was patting the pockets of his jacket. He found what he wanted, pulled out a package of cigarettes, shook one out, returned the rest to the pocket, and lit up. He sucked the smoke in, tilting his head up.

His face gleamed, as if moist. It was a deep crimson color.

The Inside-Out Man.

When he exhaled, his companion coughed in disapproval. The tentacles around his neck rose to wave the smoke away. The Inside-Out Man laughed and blew out more smoke.

He waved the cigarette in Julia's direction. Then both the Inside-Out Man and the Human Squid turned and looked up.

Julia had to stifle a scream. She stumbled back, certain they'd seen her, nearly overwhelmed by panic. She started to move toward her phone, thinking to call the police, *anyone*, but remembered the phone didn't work. Should she rush to a neighbor's, ask for help? She realized that she didn't know any of her neighbors, only the manager, who was rarely around. And what would she say? That two human oddities from eighty years ago were looking up at her as they smoked in the street?

She waited for several minutes, willing her pulse to slow. At last she crept, slowly, back to the window and risked a look out.

The crimson man was just stubbing out the cigarette with a foot. He and his friend turned and walked away down the street, nonchalant, as if they were completely at home in a world where they shouldn't exist.

Before heading down to the parking garage, Julia walked to the front of the building, where the two men had just been standing. If she'd needed proof that what she'd just seen hadn't been a dream or hallucination, there was the lingering scent of tobacco in the air. She looked down and saw something on the sidewalk. She knelt to see what it was, and only the short, tan end showed it to be a cigarette butt, flattened into the concrete—and covered in blood. Julia poked it with a finger and immediately regretted the act; the blood was warm and sticky. She wiped her finger tip on her pants leg, and, resisting an urge to rush back to her apartment, lock the door, and spend the next hour scrubbing her hands, she headed for her car. When she pulled out onto the street she looked for them, but they were gone.

She knew she'd see them again.

◐ ◐ ◐

That afternoon she drove to the phone store, located in a strip mall, where she'd bought her phone.

Every space in the strip mall was vacant. It looked new, as if it had just been renovated. There was a liquor store next to the mall that Julia remembered going into for a bottle of water. She went in, picked out a cheap bottle of wine, and asked the clerk when the phone store had moved out.

"I don't know anything about a phone store," he said in a thick middle eastern accent.

Julia didn't pursue it. The only person who ever called her, aside from robot salesmen, was her mother, who wasted the time complaining about her life or Julia's. Julia decided she could live without that for a few more days.

◐ ◐ ◐

She spent that evening with the wine, gazing at the photos. The photographer's skill at capturing the scenes captivated her, caused her to fall into the world of Larue's Dime Museum all over again. It was a world she felt comfortable and happy in.

By the end of the evening she'd decided (albeit drunkenly) that the photographer was the key. But how could she find out more? Was it "Greta"?

In college, Julia had been on exactly two dates (neither had led to a second). One had been with a young man named Ivan who had been obsessed with photography. He'd taken her to an exhibit at the Mulholland Museum that she'd found thoroughly boring, but which he found so fascinating that Julia began to suspect there might be something wrong with him.

The next day was her day off. By 11 a.m. she was waiting in an office at the Mulholland Museum, a chic modern structure located in the hills above Westwood, to speak to the Museum's Associate Director of Collections.

Catherine Deane turned out to be an affable forty-something whose natural elegance was so unattainable to Julia that she couldn't even feel envious. Catherine (and Julia knew instinctively that no one *ever* called this woman "Kate" or "Kathy") met her in the museum's lobby and led her to an office cluttered with bookcases and photos spread out across a long work table.

"I understand you have some interesting material," she said, after they were seated.

Julia handed her a manila folder with the photos. "I hope so."

Catherine opened the envelope, withdrew the photos, eyed them critically for a few seconds, turned them over— and gaped. "Oh my God," she said, softly.

"What?"

"I'm sure these are Greta Hoffman's work."

"I'm sorry, I don't know her."

Catherine rose, scanned her bookcases briefly, and plucked out a hefty coffee table book she handed to Julia. The book was labeled *Greta Hoffman: 1943-1956*. The cover showed a photo of old downtown L.A., when the theaters were vital and hadn't yet become flophouses or abandoned curiosities, when men wore fedoras and women stylish dresses. The image centered on a little girl, eating a chocolate ice cream cone, her chin and cheeks smeared, while her mother stood over her, looking down with a mixture of disapproval and amusement; behind and around them was Broadway Avenue, packed with pedestrians and old cars, the whole scene bursting with life.

Even though the subject matter was completely different, Julia recognized the similarity to her photos immediately. The slightly off-kilter framing, the contrast between the little girl's pale face and the chocolate, the excitement and glamor of the city...

Julia flipped through the book, seeing page after page of extraordinary shots, many of L.A. in the '40s and '50s, but nothing else showing Larue's. As she scanned the book, Catherine moved up behind her. "Greta Hoffman is one of photography's great unsung heroes, or I guess we should say unsung *heroines*. We don't really know much about her: she was born in Germany, left when Hitler rose to power, and found her way to New York, where she got work as a nanny. She'd only been there for a few months when the couple she was working for relocated to Los Angeles. She came with them and ended up spending the rest of her life here. When she died in 1962, they cleared out her apartment and found thousands of photos; it turned out that Greta, who never married, had a secret passion for photography. The photos were boxed and stuck away for fifty years, but found in an attic a few years ago and brought to us. Now Greta's a *cause célèbre* more than half a century after her death."

Julia flipped the book to the back. On the rear dust jacket flap was a grainy photo of a plain-looking woman dressed in a severe black dress and matching hat. The photo was captioned *Greta Hoffman in 1952*.

Catherine leaned over her desk, picked up Julia's photos almost tenderly, and examined them again. "I know Greta's work very well and I've never seen these before. Where did you find them?"

"I bought them in an antique store downtown. They said they'd found them in a box when they took over the space."

Squinting at the photos, Catherine shook her head. "Extraordinary. Greta almost never even showed her photos to anyone, let alone gave them away." Looking up at Julia, she added, "I don't suppose you'd be interested in selling these...? I'll make you an offer right now, if you're interested. Five thousand."

Julia blurted out in surprise, "Five *thousand*?"

"That's for each photograph, of course." When Julia didn't answer, Catherine added, "I'll be frank with you: you could probably get more if you go to auction—a *lot* more. But I would love to have these as part of our collection, and I can write you a check right now."

Julia sat back, trying to wrap her thoughts around what she'd just been offered. Ten thousand dollars? More if she went elsewhere? Why? Did other people experience the same thing she did when she looked at the photos, that sense of being drawn into another world?

She didn't want to live without that.

Reaching for the photos, Julia said, "Can I think about it?"

Catherine nodded, but not without a hint of resignation. "Of course."

Julia left with a business card, an astonishing offer, the photographer's name, and a renewed sense of the power of Greta Hoffman's art.

❂ ❂ ❂

When she got home, she idly turned on the television, but none of her favorite channels were working. Only a few of the local channels came in, showing images blurred with lines of static. She'd have to remember to call her cable company from work tomorrow.

❂ ❂ ❂

The next day at Java Jane's, she asked her co-worker Gabriel if she could borrow his phone. He gave her an odd look before passing her the handset from an old black dial phone mounted to the wall. Its presence didn't surprise her; it gave her only a moment of panic before she accepted it as the real, natural order of things.

Looking up from the phone, she glanced out the shop's front window and saw a woman waiting on the sidewalk, her back to the store. Something about her was familiar.

Julia stepped from behind the front counter, curious. She ignored Gabriel when he asked, "Where you going?"

She stopped just past the counter. The woman was moving—or at least her head was, turning to look back into the store...and *turning*...

Her head turned all the way until it was aligned between her shoulders. She was blandly pretty, like a forgotten film ingénue. She saw Julia, smiled, and winked.

Julia stumbled back. As she turned, clumsy from shock, to move behind the counter, she barreled into her co-worker, who reached out to steady her. "Whoa, you okay?"

She looked up at Gabriel, a dark-skinned young man with a face that betrayed a losing battle with acne, and saw that her co-worker was now completely covered with tattoos. Every square inch, including his throat and the back of his hands, demanded attention with swirling, colorful designs. As she staggered back, he asked, "What's wrong with you?"

She fled the store, using the back door to avoid Conundra, the World's Greatest Contortionist.

○ ○ ○

On her drive home, she sensed that something was missing. Looking around the landscape of downtown Los Angeles, she finally pinpointed it:

The new skyscrapers—the bank buildings, all gleaming metal and glass—were gone. City Hall's iconic spire now loomed above everything. She saw nothing but old-model cars, men and women in out-of-style suits and dresses. She drove past the longstanding Clifton's Cafeteria, but it was Polynesian-themed.

She pulled up to a stoplight at the intersection of Seventh and Figueroa. The light was a strange design, with a sign that read "STOP." As it moved from red to green, the sign slid down while one reading "GO" slid up. When a car behind Julia honked, she hit the gas too sharply and her car lurched forward, slamming her back into the seat. She nearly rear-ended a 1943 Packard in front of her before braking, throwing her forward.

A few seconds later the car's engine died.

Julia coasted to the side of the street, pulling into a red zone. She tried turning the key three times while hitting the gas, but the car didn't even grind or click. It was simply incapable of functioning, like her phone or television.

She sat in the driver seat, gripping the wheel tightly while anxiety held her in a strangling grip.

What's going on? Am I crazy? What do I do now?

Looking around, she saw that the car had stopped almost in front of the Pantry, a restaurant she'd eaten in many times. The historic eatery was the one thing in the street completely recognizable, a rock standing against the river of time. Julia went to it, a desperate traveler seeking an oasis.

Inside, she was seated and handed a menu. The items listed were what she was used to—but they were offered at a fraction of the price.

When the waiter returned, Julia ordered coffee. Maybe it would help her sort things out, decide on a plan.

The coffee arrived, strong, black, reassuring. Julia wrapped both hands around the sturdy cup and stared down into the contents, as if she'd find an answer there.

"Excuse me..." A feminine voice with a slight accent interrupted. She looked up.

A woman with black coat and hat stood over her, holding an old-fashioned, bulky camera, the kind with a fat glass lens and no LCD screen on the back. She spoke again, gesturing with the camera. "...would you mind if I took your picture?"

Julia set the coffee down and said, "You're Greta Hoffman."

The woman blinked in surprise. "I'm sorry, have we met?"

"No, but...I'm a fan of your work."

Greta frowned. "My work? How do you know my work?"

"I own two of your photos. In fact, someone just offered me a lot of money for them."

Emotions flickered across Greta's features—skepticism, hope, pleasure—and after a second she motioned at a chair across from Julia. "May I sit here?"

Julia nodded. Greta took the chair, placing the old-fashioned camera to one side of the table. Up close, without the confines of a blurry photograph, Julia saw that she'd been wrong to judge Greta Hoffman as plain-looking; her eyes in particular were extraordinary, creased lightly with humor and worry, the pupils ringed with rich hazel irises.

Greta cleared her throat, trying to speak, and Julia wondered if the other woman shared her astonishment at this meeting. "What is your name?"

"Julia—Julia Chandler." Julia almost extended a hand, but something told her not to, that Greta would frown on physical contact with someone she'd just met. "Your photographs are very special to me," Julia said, barely looking up. "They take me places."

"As all art should."

Now Julia did look up, and Greta was smiling at her. It was a smile of shared understanding, of secrets exchanged. Julia was about to say something when the waiter returned. "Can I get you something?"

Julia looked up, and couldn't stifle a gasp when she saw the waiter was tall, with a ring of tentacles surrounding his neck, poking out from over his waiter's apron. She must have gone pale because he asked, concerned, "Hey, doll, you okay?"

When Julia couldn't answer, Greta said, "Give us a minute."

"Sure thing." The waiter moved off.

Greta said, "That's Stanley. He's a nice man, works hard at two jobs."

Her voice barely a whisper, Julia said, "The other is at a museum."

"Yes, Larue's. Have you seen him perform there? He's very gifted."

Julia looked up, surprised. "Gifted?"

"Yes. He's an extraordinary pianist. They call him 'The Human Squid' because of how he can seemingly reach eight octaves at once."

"But I thought..." Julia glanced over at the waiter, now leaning over the grill to retrieve plates of food. "...I thought..."

"They called him that because of what grows from his neck?" Greta's face twisted slightly in disapproval.

"Yes."

Greta hesitated before picking up her camera. "Miss Chandler, do you know why I wanted to take your picture?"

"No."

"Because you seem out of place. It's not just your clothes, although they are strange, or your hair, but...*you*. I think maybe you are still trying to find your place in the world, yes?"

Julia nodded, uncomfortable, as if she'd been caught doing something illicit. "I don't know why I'm here, but I think...I think it has something to do with your photos."

"Did you know," Greta said, pausing to smile up at Stanley as he set a steaming cup before her, "that some tribes of primitive people believe that cameras capture the soul?"

Julia glanced up as two people sat down in the booth behind Greta. The man was wrapped in bandages, the exposed skin of his face glistening red. The woman was slender, pretty but forgettable, until she yawned, stretched, and rotated one arm all the way back until it was behind her head. They laughed together over some small joke, grinned at Stanley when he approached to take their order. Julia envied their ease with each other, their camaraderie; she wanted to be with them, in their world.

Greta asked, "May I take your picture?"

"Yes," Julia said, composing herself.

Greta raised the camera's viewfinder to her eye.

❂ ❂ ❂

LIVE ON STAGE THE HUMAN BLANK

The first thing that caught Stanley's eye in the old photo was the banner strung across the rear wall of a small stage. It took him a few seconds to realize that the woman standing in front of the banner had absolutely nothing special whatsoever to offer. He pitied her dull, symmetrical form, her unmarred skin, her unmemorable features.

Stanley's tentacles writhed in irritation; it was warm in the antiques store, and he was getting uncomfortable. But something about the photograph drew him in, caused him to examine it with more care—

There. He had it: the girl's face, while neither beautiful nor ugly, nevertheless possessed one special quality that struck him the more he looked at it.

He'd never before seen someone so completely at peace, so centered in their surroundings.

I'd like to meet you someday, he thought, as he took the photo to the small shop's front counter.

∞

∞

(For Diane Arbus and Vivian Maier)

Night Terrors

The person I love more than anyone in the world screamed in her sleep one night. Soon, it spread.

⊙ ⊙ ⊙

The panic of waking up, heart hammering, disoriented, sleep shattered, the scream still echoing through the bedroom...that was how it started, at least for me.

It had been Kylandra. It wasn't a long scream, and it was finished by the time I was sitting up, trying to see in the dark bedroom. "Kyla...?" I whispered.

She didn't respond. I listened, heard her breathing. Measured. Calm. Like nothing had happened.

I fell back into my pillow, willing my heart to slow down, and then turning to look at the glowing red numbers of the clock on my nightstand. *3:24.* The middle of the night, that time when neighborhoods are at their darkest and most silent, when even the insects have gone quiet.

What the fuck did she dream about?

I lay awake in the bed beside her, too unsettled to join Kylandra in that place that had terrified her.

Sleep did arrive at some point toward dawn, but left me only an hour before we had to start preparing to face the day. Kyla got out of bed first, was riffling through her closet as I raised one heavy eyelid to peer at her. "'Morning," she said, clutching her day's clothing on her way to the bathroom. "How'd you sleep?"

When I didn't answer—too stunned—she paused in concern. "Hey, everything okay?"

"How did *you* sleep?"

She looked at me, puzzled. "Like a baby. Why?"

"Because you screamed."

"What do you mean? While I was asleep?" When I nodded, she said, "You're kidding."

"I'm not." I struggled to sit up, still half-dead from the interrupted rest. "About three. It scared the shit out of me."

Her gorgeous face creased in perplexity. "That's really weird. I don't remember anything. Sorry..."

She moved off to shower. I knew I should get up, too, that we both had jobs waiting, that delaying would guarantee even worse commuter traffic, but I wanted to think for another minute, to understand. Nothing like this had happened before, at least not in the three months that Kylandra and I had been together. We'd fallen so hard and so fast, taken the next big step of living together so impulsively, that we were still in the discovery phase. Kylandra found out that I had a secret passion for cozy mysteries and that I was a control freak when it came to washing dishes; I learned that Kylandra had a brother she hadn't spoken to in ten years and a habit of leaving her shoes all around the house. Two years ago, after she'd broken a wrist in a car accident, she'd gotten briefly addicted to post-surgery opioids, but she'd kicked the habit. She heard about how my father hadn't spoken to me since I'd come out to him. The last thing he said to me was a promise to "vote all those libtards out of office." I heard about the wealthy woman who'd come into Kyla's shop for a latte one day and had told her that it was "wonderful to see a woman of color doing so well with a small business."

But...was there something else, something Kylandra hadn't told me, that troubled her enough to make her scream in the night?

"Kyla...?" I asked, having pulled myself out of bed to lounge just outside the bathroom.

She opened the door. "Yeah?"

For a second, as I looked at her standing there in her

long T-shirt, her legs shining darkly, her hair uncombed and cascading in wild ebony waves, I just wanted to drink the sight of her in, to love her natural grace, even while it made me feel like a clumsy beast, with my short fingers and wide hips. Then I remembered why I'd followed her to the bathroom, and asked, "You don't have any history of stuff like night terrors, do you?"

She frowned, but reached out for me and I let her pull me in. "Oh, baby," she said into my hair, "this really got to you, didn't it?" Pushing away, she looked me in the eyes, said, "No, I really don't. I've never heard anyone say anything like that about me, and I'm sure it'll never happen again, okay?"

That was good enough for me.

❂ ❂ ❂

But it did happen again, a week later. This time the scream was longer, moving from guttural wail to shriek.

We'd had a tense day. We hadn't argued, exactly, but I'd told Kylandra about Jeff, who worked in a cubicle on the other side of my office and was a climate change denier (he chalked up our abnormal storms and temperatures to "nature's cycles"). Kyla thought I should go to HR, or at least confront the idiot. Kyla's passions were one of the reasons I loved her, but I didn't see what HR could do or what difference telling him off would make.

"He needs to hear that he's wrong," Kyla said.

"But me telling him that isn't going to make him change his mind."

Kyla shrugged, looked away; I knew she was disappointed. We barely talked the rest of the night.

The scream came later, at 5:23, just before dawn. I was sitting up and staring as she trailed off. When it was done, she sighed; her breathing fell into sleep's rhythm again. I didn't even try to go back to sleep; instead I got up, checked the whole house, found doors locked and windows unbroken. After that, I made coffee, perused arguments and inane comments on social media.

Kylandra found me that way, seated at my desk in the corner of the living room playing at the computer, when she came out in the morning. "What are you doing out here?" she asked, heading for the kitchen.

"I couldn't sleep. You screamed again."

She paused in the kitchen doorway, turned to look at me, irritated, as if she didn't believe me. "Shannon, are you sure you weren't just dreaming?"

I laughed, a bitter bark. "This one was long. You were still screaming when I woke up. I listened until it stopped, and you just went back to sleep."

She stared at me for a few seconds longer, until I felt my own annoyance rear up. "I'm not making this up," I told her.

"I didn't say you were. I just...I don't know." She turned and vanished into the kitchen.

At work, I spent my lunch break googling a phrase I'd heard tossed around but didn't really understand:

Night terrors.

They were a disorder of deep sleep, more common in children. In adults, they could indicate anything from medication issues to stress in a relationship.

God...was she screaming about me? Had I made this happen?

Something else came up in my search: a social media influencer was living with someone who'd recently developed night terrors. I shivered with recognition as I read about waking up to a scream in the middle of the night, and then finding out that her partner not only didn't remember, but doubted. The post talked about her partner's history of night terrors as a child, though.

Kylandra didn't even have that, or so she'd said.

I wondered how much I really knew about her. She'd *told* she'd never suffered from night terrors before...but what if she had and didn't remember, or didn't even know?

What if she'd had them before as an adult and was too embarrassed to admit it? What else didn't I know about her? How much can we ever really know about another person?

۞ ۞ ۞

The next one came two nights later. I don't want to say I was used to it—I still jerked awake, heart trying to break free of its cage—but I got a few hours of sleep after. I didn't even tell her about it.

That afternoon at work, I noticed that my friend Patti, who worked in Accounting at what Kyla called "the big faceless firm," looked exhausted. "You okay?" I asked, as we both poured coffee in the employee break room.

She sipped and then shrugged; she looked haggard, gray places beneath her blue eyes. "It's Hank." Her husband. "This'll sound really weird, but...he's been screaming at night in his sleep."

I froze, my own cup paused on my bottom lip.

She went on: "Scares me to death, but he doesn't even remember it in the morning. In fact, he says he feels great."

Lowering the bad instant coffee, I said, "Do you want to hear something weird? Kylandra—my girlfriend—has been doing the same thing."

Patti stared for a second before asking, "The *whole* thing, with the screaming and then not remembering in the morning?"

I nodded.

Patti gulped down the rest of the coffee, tossed the paper cup into the trash, said, "Okay, now I'm freaked out," and left the break room.

"That makes two of us," I muttered to absolutely no one.

۞ ۞ ۞

That night I woke up to a scream, but this time it wasn't from Kylandra. It sounded like it came from the house behind us. I knew the neighbor there was an older lady named Paloma. I got out of bed, pulled on a sweatshirt, wandered out into our backyard.

My little two-bedroom house was in the foothills, so my backyard sat slightly above Paloma's. I stood listening, waiting...and heard a door open. It was her rear sliding door. Even though it was four in the morning and cold, she stepped into the night, wearing nothing but a flimsy nightgown. She was barefoot, her face frozen. I watched as she walked across the yard, her head barely moving.

Sleepwalking. It had been cited as a common accompaniment to night terrors.

Paloma turned in my direction, walking forward, not seeing me, not seeing anything...including the thick wall of rosebushes set against the fence that divided our properties.

She was going to walk right into them.

I called out, "Paloma!"

She paused, inches from the bloodthirsty thorns.

"Go back to bed, Paloma," I said.

Without waking, she turned and walked back into her house, not closing the door behind her.

Shivering, I went back into my own house, downed a shot of tequila to fight the chill, tried not to imagine what might have happened to the seventysomething with skin like tissue if I hadn't been there.

❂ ❂ ❂

When I told Kylandra about the incident with the neighbor, she peered at me for a long time before saying, "Shannon, maybe...I don't know, sleeping pills?"

She didn't believe me.

But she still kissed me that morning before she headed off to run her shop. She even laughed as she stepped out the front door. We'd talked about the morning's news—a new war, with a country we barely knew—but she'd shrugged it off with a tossed aside of, "Boys will be boys."

I'd never seen her so happy.

☺ ☺ ☺

The same couldn't be said for me. I was seriously sleep-deprived, edgy, seeing things at the periphery of my vision that weren't there. Judging from the number of accidents I passed on the way to work, I wasn't alone.

It was hard to focus on something as mundane as a job. Numbers jittered and frayed on the computer screen. At one point I found myself in the supply room, staring at a wall until someone asked, "Did you need something?" I had, but I'd forgotten what.

There were others like me. Patti moved with half-lidded eyes and heavy limbs, like me.

And then there were those who *chirped*, whose steps were light and quick.

"They're screaming at night," Patti muttered to me as we wearily eyed a small clutch of them, chattering together in the break room. "Have you tried to wake one of them up?"

I turned to look at Patti. "No. I read that you aren't supposed to."

"Doesn't matter anyway, because *you can't*. I tried with Hank, but...you can't," she said, watching our co-workers as they left the break room, nearly gleeful.

Why were they enjoying life, and I wasn't? Why couldn't I be the one shrieking at night, never knowing, waking up in the morning apparently purged of whatever troubled me, rested and calm?

"Why?" I whispered, but my friend heard me.

"I keep wondering that, too," Patti said. "I asked Hank that last night, and you know what he said? 'If the world's breaking down, why shouldn't we?'"

☺ ☺ ☺

Kylandra's scream that night was truly terrifying. It left me shaking and shaken, wondering if I'd *ever* be able to sleep again, wondering if I was damned to stagger through my days in a haze of exhaustion.

I got up, dressed. I wanted to leave the house, drive somewhere far away, bury myself in a cave, leave all this behind.

Instead, I went for a walk. Even though it was the middle of the night, chilly and dark out, I wanted to walk, as if I could burn off the effects of my loved one's screams.

The night's coolness at first felt good, renewing, like diving into a shadowed pool. I took long strides, walking fast, anxiously, looking up into a sky only slightly reddened by its layer of smog—

Before I'd gone three houses, I heard screaming.

I remembered that neighbor: his name was Ernesto. He was a middle-aged Filipino man with a wife and two grown children who visited on weekends. He'd once helped me put new windshield wipers on my car when he saw me struggling to figure it out.

Now he was in his bedroom, screaming.

But he wasn't the only one. Screams echoed up and down the street, passing beneath the sodium street lamps like spirits.

A lot of them.

I stopped, my desire to walk instantly drained. Shrieks of terror, bellows, echoing up and down the avenues of my quiet little suburban neighborhood...

Bushes near me rustled. I stood there, paralyzed, watching as Paloma emerged from her roses, covered in bleeding thorn-pricks.

I should have tried to help her, but instead I panicked and fled back to my own house, where I stuffed as much tissue into my ears as I could and cowered under a blanket.

෴ ෴ ෴

I saw Ernesto the next morning; he was watering his drought-resistant yard as I drove past, on my way to another meaningless day in my worthless job. He waved, and I pulled the car over. "Hey, Ernesto..."

He grinned, his entire face lighting up as he stood there spraying water on his aloes. "Hey, hi! How are you?"

"I'm fine," I answered, before asking, "How's everything with you?"

"Never been better! They just laid me off from my job, but it's great, you know? Because I'll be able to really get this yard into shape now." He laughed. Something about it seemed hollow. When he finished, he gazed at me fixedly.

His eyes looked dead.

"Gotta get to work," I said, offering a half-hearted wave as I drove off again.

I glanced in the rearview mirror, saw him waving exaggeratedly as he sprayed water all over his legs.

✪ ✪ ✪

"Wanna hear something funny?" Patti said to me at work during our morning break. "Hank said I screamed in my sleep last night."

She laughed, delighted.

I didn't.

✪ ✪ ✪

I saw the first headline three days later: *Mysterious Sleep Virus Reaches Epidemic Status*

The online article went on to talk about how hospitals and doctors were reporting a massive rise in night terrors. Sales of sleeping pills had gone through the roof, but they were bought by the spouses, partners, roommates of those who'd been hit by the mysterious disease. The screamers, those who manifested night terrors, didn't need any aid; they weren't suffering tiredness or fatigue. In fact, they said they'd never felt so good.

I didn't even read all of the article; I *couldn't*. I'd lost the ability to concentrate on anything longer than a few seconds, a few words.

But that was only the *first* headline; it escalated from there. Soon, it seemed as if those *not* shrieking in their sleep were the odd ones; they were, at least, the ones endangering everyone else.

There were stories from Europe, Asia, South America. It was happening everywhere.

There were studies, theories, suggested treatments. One was about enzymes and hormones. Another suggested a drug normally used as an anti-psychotic.

The only one that made sense to me came from a noted psychologist, a man who had written bestselling self-improvement books. He suggested that the epidemic was a "mass response to the stresses of our failing way of life." Sufferers, he theorized, were *not* suffering during their waking hours because they'd worked it all out in their sleep. Those who weren't affected simply had a different brain chemistry. Or the virus (if that's what it was) worked slower on some than others.

Skeptics called that "pseudoscience"; other doctors said it was "downright irresponsible." Pharmaceutical companies hesitantly agreed and offered up new drugs as solutions.

I thought Patti's husband said it best: *If the world's breaking down, why shouldn't we?*

Meanwhile, I spent every night listening to the woman I loved screaming in her sleep. *Every. Night.*

Kylandra should have been my wife. In another place, another time, we'd have been married by now. Ernesto and our neighbors would've danced with us at our reception, joked with us after about settling down and having kids.

Then again, they were all screaming, too.

I ached to join them. I wanted to be like the rest, hiding the parts of me that worried, the parts that knew that everything was *not* going to be just fine, down in the deep, dark places, where they festered and simmered until they exploded every night. I wanted to be able to walk through a day without hallucinating, without feeling like I bore invisible lead weights.

At work, Patti sauntered by my cubicle, said she was worried about me. Then she spilled her coffee, giggled, nearly skipped back to her desk.

Even Jeff smiled all the time, as he told me about a secret cabal of lizard people controlling politics, or the ring of child molesters operating out of a fast food restaurant near the White House. He laughed, giddy; behind his glasses, his eyes were glassy.

Maybe, I thought, as I sat at home one evening watching Kylandra sing to herself while she folded her laundry, *it's all for the best. After all, she seems so happy.*

But we hadn't really been together in months, not since all this started. Sure, we still talked, watched movies together, ate together...but nothing else.

We never talked about marriage anymore. In fact, we didn't talk about much of anything. I'd ask her about something I'd read in the news, about a new political scandal, a revised report on climate change, a shooting back east.

She'd tell me to lighten up.

I didn't know this woman at all.

❂ ❂ ❂

Things changed for me not long after that.

There was a terrible accident on my drive home from work one day. They tell me I caused it. I don't remember.

I wound up in the hospital with a long recovery time in front of me. They gave me drugs to ease the pain of broken bones. I began to heal.

The first few nights in the hospital, I heard screaming from nearby rooms, but it gradually stopped. It's like the whole world is righting itself at last.

About the Author

Lisa Morton is a screenwriter, author of non-fiction books, and award-winning prose writer whose work was described by the American Library Association's Readers' Advisory Guide to Horror as "consistently dark, unsettling, and frightening." She is the author of four novels and 150 short stories, a six-time winner of the Bram Stoker Award®, and a world-class Halloween expert.

Her most recent releases are *Weird Women: Classic Supernatural Fiction from Groundbreaking Female Writers 1852-1923* (co-edited with Leslie S. Klinger), which received a starred review from Booklist, and *Calling the Spirits: A History of Seances,* which Library Journal has already called "fascinating" and "fun and thorough." Lisa is also a weekly reporter on the popular podcast *Ghost Magnet with Bridget Marquardt,* and has guested on many other radio shows and podcasts, including *Coast to Coast, Midnight in the Desert, Paranormal Perception,* and The *Big Séance.*

Lisa lives in the San Fernando Valley and online at www.lisamorton.com.

Made in the USA
Monee, IL
15 October 2021